# Bawdy Double

# Bawdy Double

Galactic Adventures Book 1

*Scott Michael Decker*

# Titles by the Author

If you like this novel, please post a review on the website where you purchased it, and consider other novels from among these titles by Scott Michael Decker:

**Science Fiction:**
Bawdy Double
Cube Rube
Doorport
Drink the Water
Edifice Abandoned
Glad You're Born
Half-Breed
Inoculated
Legends of Lemuria
Organo-Topia
The Gael Gates
War Child

**Fantasy:**
Fall of the Swords (Series)
Gemstone Wyverns
Sword Scroll Stone

Look for these titles at your favorite book retailer.

*Thanks to the following beta-readers:*
*Anne Potter*
*Michael Clancy*
*Shelley Klemm*

# Chapter 1

The uterpod convulsed wildly, and somewhere, a muted alarm began to ping.

Even from a distance, Fred F4RB8C3 knew the mutaclone was in distress. Not another! he thought. That'll be the fifth this year! Maneuvering his extensile to the uterpod, Fred shoved the catch basket beneath it, and then examined the figure inside the transparent membrane.

Arms and legs akimbo, a fem mutaclone stared back at him, eyes wide with terror. At the sight of her, five thousand copulation positions tried to crowd into his mind at once, his escoriant simumems intruding, nanostimmed into him during his gestation. He pushed aside the memories.

Where'd she come from? Fred wondered, only factory drudges growing in this sector. Mutaclone drudges, like himself. He pulled up her gestation history on his corn. She'd been recently moved from the escoriant sector, where escort variants were grown to order, this perfect-looking specimen flagged as defective.

Doesn't look defective to me, he thought, in spite of her contortions. Even limbs akimbo, she looked perfectly proportioned, her anatomy visible in all its detail.

Fred considered a sedative. Her flailing jostled the mutaclones all around her. The tough uterpod membrane gave at every jab of her limb, the derma designed to contain but not restrict. He had to do something, the uterpod derma too tough, too resilient, and too elastic to escape from the inside.

Fred F4RB8C3 looked both ways. To the right and left, uterpods extended for hundreds of feet, two walls of glistening pods facing each other with just enough room between them for his extensile lift. Above and below, more pods, his sector nearly two hundred yards tall.

Glad no one was near, Fred pulled out his injectile. The needle looked deadly, its fat, menacing barrel ending in a sharp, shiny point.

Her eyes went wide, and she kicked at him violently.

He pulled the injectile back and took the kick on the shoulder. Without backing or force, she couldn't hurt him. He grabbed a handful of derma and stretched it toward him, then put the injectile point to it and tore.

The uterpod retracted as if in pain and peeled away from the mutaclone, dumping her into the catch basket. A spray of amniofluid fell toward the waste sluice a hundred feet below.

She lay there a moment, gasping and glistening. "Thank you," she said breathily, venturing a glance his direction.

"You're welcome," Fred said. He tore his gaze away, desire and embarrassment sending blood rushing into his face. The front of his allsuit tented from the bulge underneath.

The specimen in front of him looked just as delectable and healthy as any he'd seen when he'd worked the escoriant sector. Escort variants sold for thousands of galacti on the open market, sometimes tens of thousands. And this one was fully formed, all her anatomical features visible through the transparent derma as she'd struggled to escape the uterpod. He knew what some of his coworkers did in the escoriant sector when they thought no one was looking. Product-testing, they sometimes joked.

Trying his best to keep his eyes off her, he maneuvered the extensile back toward his workstation. "Let's get you an allsuit. Got a spare over here."

"Nice of you."

He threw her a grin but tried not to glance. And failed.

"Awful young to be doing this kind of work, aren't you?"

"Born here on the asteroid five years ago. I'm Fred Eff Four Are Bee Eight Cee Three," he said, spelling out his clone designation. She sounds far too alert to have just aborted from a uterpod, Fred thought, bewildered. He docked the extensile, silenced the alarm at his workstation, and stepped to the locker. He handed her the allsuit, averting his gaze.

She took the allsuit and began to dress. "I'm—"

He waited until the rustling ceased and looked at her.

Fear and bewilderment rippled across her face. The allsuit couldn't disguise her alluring curves. She stood five-eight and was generously endowed, possessing a figure that would turn the heads of either sex. She had wheat-blond hair cascading straight past her shoulders, sported a V-shaped face that took the breath away, had a small smile that was warm and inviting, and had large, wide-set, intelligent eyes, their color as blue as amethyst.

Eyes that searched inside for a name. "I don't know who I am."

She has a lot of ease and confidence for not knowing who she is, he thought, admiring her composure. "Your designation is KTX552Y, so your name probably starts with Kay. Why don't you know your name?"

"I don't know." She shook her head. "I know I had one, back when I lived on—" She stared at him.

She's not seeing me, he thought. Her confusion was fairly common, even if her awareness wasn't. "—on Tantalus?" he asked. "I don't think so. You were just aborted from a uterpod. You've never lived anywhere."

"But I—"

"You see that chute?" he interrupted, pointing toward the floor. A narrow strip of concave sluice drained amniofluid and other detritus that sloughed off the twelve hundred mutaclones in this sector. "I'm supposed to send you down that chute. All aborted mutaclones go down the chute. You think you've lived 'cause the uterpods infuse pseudo-sensory simumems through nanostim tendrils into your brain.

But it isn't real." Although she does seem remarkably alert, he thought, keeping it to himself.

"And the simumems give the mutaclones a sense of past," she added, "each memory tailored to the environment where they'll be serving. I know because I'm a doctor of—" she stared at him, that bewildered look taking hold of her face again.

"What, rocket science?" He snorted at his own joke. "Look, just have a seat, and when my shift ends, I'll take you over to the escoriant sector. They'll know what to do with you."

"Escoriant? An escort variant? Do I look like an escoriant?"

The equivalent of calling her a whore. She did have the face and body of a goddess and would fetch a steep price at open auction. What was he supposed to say? "Your gestation history tells me that's where you were transferred from."

"Oh, I see." Her ardor deflated, and she glanced around.

"You'll stay put for another hour?"

"Of course," she said matter-of-factly. "Oh, uh, thanks, Fred."

He smiled. "You're welcome. All right if I call you Kate?"

"Sure," she said, giving him a brief smile.

"Pleased to meet you." He gave her a bow and a grin. "Got to clean up," he said, gesturing up toward the uterpod where she'd been hanging. He engaged the extensile, lifting himself back to the now-limp and -empty uterpod, the derma hanging slack.

He maneuvered the extensile in between the full uterpods to get at the placental stem. The collar came away easily, and he inspected the nanostim base for damage. None visible, but just to make sure, he ran a bioscan. Some contusions from the abrupt withdrawal, the nanostim filaments having infiltrated the mutaclone's nervous system. Usually, a struggling mutaclone triggered the uterpod to withdraw the filaments to avoid such damage. When they didn't, placental stems were damaged and had to be replaced. Under the placental stem was the sector wall, ribbed with conduit. Soft slurping accompanied the peristalsis as the conduits pumped nutrients to the uterpods. Other conduits pumped waste out to the recycler. Silvery bundles of nanostim filaments crossed conduits like filigree.

The collar and empty uterpod derma went down the chute, the biomatter recycler reconstituting every bit of waste. Fred pulled back to look over his handiwork. On his corn, he scanned the vitals of the surrounding uterpods. The neighboring mutaclones hadn't been damaged by the aborted mutaclone's struggle, other than some slight bruising.

Most were factory drones, in a variety of shapes and sizes, tailored for specific tasks. The one beside him was a hulking male with six arms sprouting from his back. Two short, squat legs could hold him in place for twenty hours at a stretch. The vestigial penis and scrotum would remain infantile, his gonadotropin output genetically restricted.

Fred maneuvered the extensile away from the wall, checking his corn for any latent vitals out of range. No signs of distress. He breathed a sigh, the number of aborted mutaclones far higher in his sector than normal, especially this late in gestation. Inviability was far more common at the zygote stage, just after fertilization. The gene jockeys bragged in the lunchroom about colony extermination, propagation across cell lines, mutavariant anomalies, and RNA reticular recombinants. Fred didn't need to know all that. They hadn't even trained him in cardio. Either the mutaclone lived or died, and this late in gestation, heroic resuscitation wasn't a priority. A glorified mutaclone sitter in all I am, he thought.

Peering toward his workstation, he didn't see Kate.

Where'd she go? he wondered, sending his extensile that way.

He could just imagine the recriminations, seeing the newsvid headlines: "Escaped escoriant rampages through asteroid mutaclone facility." He'd surely be fired. There'd been talk about him, of course. He was a rarity, one of the few aborted mutaclones working in the sectors, nearly all the other workers having been successfully extruded from their uterpods or having emigrated from Tantalus. Most of his peers who'd lived through their gestation could be sold on open market. Aborted mutaclones might be sold thus, but only as refurbished or reconditioned, and the company barely recouped its costs. It was unusual for workers to intervene and take abortivariants home to rear as their own.

Fred was one such abortivariant. Five years ago, he'd wriggled out of his uterpod prematurely and had fallen toward the chute for recycling. A swift extensile maneuver by Greg, the sector monitor, had stopped his slow, asteroid-gravity fall with the catch basket.

Maneuvering the extensile back to his workstation, Fred leapt to the platform and peered out the door to see which way she'd gone, but to no avail.

No trace.

He sighed, wondering what he'd tell his father, Greg.

\* \* \*

Dr. Sarina Karinova blinked the fatigue from her eyes and looked again at the genalysis.

I hope this is some sort of mistake, she thought. A primary care physician who'd originally specialized in recombinant development and propagation, Sarina knew what she was seeing.

But didn't believe it, even after checking a third time.

The genalysis before her exhibited the allele smoothing common to mutaclone gengineering.

Dr. Karinova didn't want to see what she was seeing. Premier Colima Satsanova had asked her to examine her twenty-eight year old daughter, Tatiana, because she'd recently looked listless and detached. So, as a matter of course, Dr. Karinova had run a full panel of tests, including a genalysis. Which she was looking at now.

The lab must have mixed up the samples, the Doctor thought.

Long stretches of genetic ribbon exhibited the kind of smoothing that mutaclone cells lines had been subjected to rid them of recessive genetic traits. As the human genome had developed, it had incorporated multivariate sequences to encode responses to plagues, diet, disease, climate, and numerous other environmental hazards. All species

6

encoded their survival strategies into their genes. The oldest chromosomes from the loblolly pine on old Earth were seven times longer than the human genome sequence. A species that had survived for three hundred million years, the loblolly pine bore in its labyrinthine genome how it had survived thousands of pestilences, including insects, molds, fungi, bacteria, viruses, and lichens. For each, the loblolly pine had articulated in its genes just what countermeasures the pine had taken to combat these herbicides, encoding those responses to help future generations fight off similar infestations.

Just as the human genome had. In addition, in doing so, the human DNA had incorporated weak recessives whose cumulative expressive potential sometimes manifested in maladaptive syndromes, such as schizophrenia, autism, Down syndrome, or fragile-x. Some conditions were actually incorporated into the mutaclone cell lines, such as hypogonadotropism, resulting in restricted gonad development. Small testes and ovaries helped to increase docility and compliance.

When mutaclone production had started, gengineers had pinpointed genes known to be problematic and had either resected that gene—removed the offending sequence and tied the two ends together—or had replaced that gene with its healthy recombinant. This "smoothing," as it was known generally, had sharply reduced the incidence of abortivariants. With the advent of nanostim neuraplants, which inculcated protective coping factors such as antianxiolysis, the viability and integration rates easily topped ninety-nine percent.

In the final years of her doctoral program, Dr. Sarina Karinova had taken a year's residency at a Genie-All asteroid clone production facility, to see if that field was what she wanted to specialize in. She'd been revolted at their treatment, and had elected to pursue general practitioner. But the yearlong exposure to mutaclone production had given her enough background to say definitively that the genalysis in front of her was a mutaclone genome, not a normavariant.

She glanced at the clock. Eight twenty-five. The lab was certainly closed by now, and she'd have to get them to retest the sample in the morning. I'll send them a trake-mail, she thought. "Trake message to

Natalia Filipova, Statlab Kaspi. Natalia, I've got some anomalous results on the sample I sent you this morning, specimen OLGS562. Can you verify the sample and rerun the genalysis? Thanks much for doing so." She set the delivery for Natalia's arrival at work, not wanting to disturb her at home.

"Log off," she traked to her office computer, and she watched as it closed its feed to her corn. She sighed at how late it was.

Sarina then traked her wife, knowing she was supposed to have left her clinic an hour ago. I'll have to apologize again, she thought to herself, staying over at work far too often.

I'll order her a dozen mutaroses, Sarina thought.

She ordered up a bouquet on her corn, and then tidied her desk. Grabbing her valise, she stepped from her office and headed toward the rear entrance. She was sure to be accosted by waiting patients if she didn't take the back entrance, the clinic a busy place during normal hours. The waiting room was dark and empty now, the doors closing at seventeen hundred.

At the rear entrance, she traked up a hovertaxi, the sky a deep indigo, the two moons of Tantalus hovering full just above the Premier's palace to the east. Sarina's wife, Anya, an astrophysicist at the Royal Ukraine Observatory atop Mount Mithridat, had often smirked at humanity's ingrained inclination to designate the direction the sun rose as east and where it set as west, no matter what world they colonized. But that too was as inculcated into the human psyche as the desire to reproduce. I'll wager we'll someday find an allele where that's articulated, Sarina thought.

The hovertaxi hissed to a stop in front of her, and she stepped inside. "Home," she traked. The taxi biometricked her face to obtain her address. It lifted and swung into traffic, its autonav guiding it surely and swiftly to its destination.

Sarina glanced into the hovertaxi beside hers. People went about their lives in taxis as if they were at home, with little if any regard for what others might see. A gentleman in a psychedelisuit with hair to match belted out a raucous song, if his wild gyrations and wide-open mouth were any indication. The pulsating thump from that direction confirmed her suspicion. A couple on her other side were coupling vigorously, if the shapes beyond the frosted frames were doing what she thought. She was surprised they'd frosted the panes, some passengers not bothering.

A sleek personal hover pulled alongside momentarily. None but the very wealthy owned their own hovers. Her hovertaxi careened away just as she got a glimpse of the face. Premier Colima Satsanova herself, Sarina saw, the hawkish, elegant face recognizable throughout the galaxy, far beyond the boundaries of Ukraine-held constellations along the Norman Arm.

Sarina's hovertaxi zoomed between two towers and circled a third as it homed in on her flat on the thirty-fourth floor of her forty-floor apartment building. She felt privileged to live so near the top, able to afford such steep rents, prices going up exponentially as they neared the penthouses.

A hoverpark extended itself from her balcony and fixed itself to the taxi's side. Sarina stepped onto her balcony as if it weren't four hundred feet above the ground. She couldn't remember the last time she'd used the elevators, when she'd last taken a walk on the street.

The door biometricked her face and slid aside and a gust of wind from behind pushed her in. "Anya? I'm home." She set down her valise and shrugged out of her smock. The clock remonstrated her for not arriving home until 8:45 pm.

Then the silence struck her.

"Anya? Honey?" She peeked into the kitchen.

Multiple things instantly struck her as odd. The bouquet of mutaroses was in the sink, and beside it was a quarter-full vase. The mutarose stems had been partially trimmed, a pair of shears also in the sink. The oven ticked away as though heating or cooling, and inside a casserole bubbled merrily. The apron that Anya always wore in the kitchen, and always hung beside the sink when not in use, was gone.

"Anya?" Sarina called again. She heard that slight edge of panic in her voice. Must be in the sanistall, she thought, turning off the oven as she went past.

The sanistall was empty, its door wide open.

She poked her head into the bedroom. "Anya?"

Silence. Emptiness.

Was she so disgusted with me that she left? Sarina wondered. Her late nights at the clinic were one of the few things they argued about, Anya jealous of any time Sarina spent outside of her presence. If we'd met while I was in residency, Sarina thought, our relationship wouldn't have survived.

She returned to the kitchen, telling herself Anya would return after she'd cooled off.

The oven tick-tick-ticked as it cooled off.

Sarina stepped to the sink to finish cutting the mutaroses. There, beside the faucet, was Anya's wedding ring. Sarina fingered her own ring, identical to Anya's.

Unfinished cutting, casserole still cooking, wedding ring off.

None of those was like Anya at all.

Sarina stepped back from the sink without touching anything, frightened. Then she looked toward the apartment door, the one she hadn't used in months, coming and going almost exclusively by hovertaxi. It stood ajar about an inch.

She gasped, her heart thundering in her chest, cold creeping up her legs, her arms tingling.

"City police," she traked.

At first they refused to send anyone out, and it wasn't until she insisted that they acceded to doing so. Then it took them forever to get there, each moment an eternity, the silence and horror weighing on her. All her efforts to calm herself failed miserably. Visions of her wife Anya in some basement boiler room, bound and blindfolded, wouldn't leave Sarina's mind.

The officer was sympathetic, taking assiduous notes, which appeared on Sarina's corn. He didn't have to share his corneal images with her, and she thought him kind to do so. Seeing the information helped calm her frayed nerves. He took note of the mutaroses, the casserole, the wedding ring, the missing apron, the door ajar, imaging everything. He also bioscanned the front door and hallway just outside. And of course he asked her about her relationship with Anya.

He handed her his comcard when he was done. "Call me anytime if you think of anything else, and if anything changes, of course."

"Of course." She saw it had both a desk contact and a personal contact. "What now?" she gave him her own comcard.

"Well, we wait." The officer grimaced. "If she doesn't go to work tomorrow, then there's cause to worry. Right now, we don't know. I agree, all this seems out of character, especially for an astrophysicist, but people do things out of character from time to time. What people rarely do is miss work or fail to trake-mail to say they won't be in. It'd be useless for me to encourage you to relax and try to get some sleep, because you're probably not going to. But relax and try to get some sleep, anyway."

She managed a small smile. "Thank you, officer." She watched him leave. As the police hover pulled away from her balcony, she stepped to the sink. The mutaroses went into the vase and the casserole into the thermafreeze. Sarina couldn't even think about eating.

Her wife's absence gnawed at her.

She picked up the ring and slid it onto her pinky, Anya's ring one size smaller than hers. The two rings glittered beside each other, as they had on the day Sarina and Anya had married, five years ago.

The Capital of Tantalus, Kiev, sat on a high plateau above rough seas, the planet four-fifths water. Out on a promontory above roiling breakers, Sarina and Anya had exchanged vows, and the Orthodox Priestess had declared them wife and wife before the sight of God. Why they'd elected to have a religious wedding was something of a conundrum. Neither was particularly religious, Sarina having been reared a devout Orthodox Christian but having drifted away from the church in college, and Anya Jewish by extraction but non-practicing throughout her life. As an astrophysicist, however, Anya had always said, "There are mysteries to the universe that defy theory and science, and can only be explained within the cosmology of religion." Perhaps it'd been their immersions into their respective fields of study that had led them to ask God to officiate at their nuptials.

As Sarina looked out the dining room window at the glowing city below, hovers streaming along in dwindling rivers of traffic, she remembered how they had both wept with joy as the Priestess had declared them married in the sight of God, and how their family, friends, and colleagues had told them for months afterward how moving and uplifting the ceremony had been.

She dropped her gaze to the extra ring on her pinky, which immediately blurred, and Sarina began to weep.

\* \* \*

Admiral Zenaida Andropova, Commander of the Ukraine Navy, thrice decorated for valor in combat against those Rusky interlopers but more famous for the pitched battles she's won in the halls of parliament, stood in the living room of her own house, feeling powerless.

Across from her, her son, Captain Fadeyka Andropovich, hung his head at the tirade she'd just delivered.

"What in God's name is it going to take?!" she roared, staring at him balefully.

He'd been such a perfect son, and Zenaida couldn't fathom what might have possessed him these last five years. All through elementary and secondary school, so prim and proper that even his classmates had called him Admiral. The Naval Academy had been a breeze for him, his grades as pristine as his dress had been punctilious. Valedictorian and class president, captain of the football, fencing, and hand-to-hand combat teams, and of course instantly accepted at the Naval Post Graduate School in dual Master's programs of Cryptology and Interstellar Relations.

But he hadn't shown up at the Naval Post Graduate School—not under his own power. During summer break, he'd gone on vacation in the Pleiades, had disconnected his neuralink, and had dropped out of sight.

A day before his first class at Post-Graduate, after two months of silence, nary a word from the boy, she had found him on the beaches of Marseilles, selling his Apollo-like face and Olympian body to vacationing socialites, fornicating with them for money, male and female both, much of his clientele his mother's age or older, the boy twenty-one years old.

Zenaida had physically dragged him from some wealthy boy's bed, naked, and had hauled him to the spaceport and had personally escorted him to his chair in the first class of his first semester at the Post Graduate School.

She hadn't asked him for an explanation and hadn't wanted one. Neither had he offered one.

The first month seemed to go well. Zenaida had returned to Kiev but had kept in touch with his professors, checking daily that he was in class, where he was supposed to be, dressed the way he was supposed to dress. All reports indicated he participated at Post Graduate as he had at the Naval Academy.

And she began to breathe again, relieved that it seemed to be over, that the episode of dissipation was behind him. Fadeyka even managed to secure a berth on the football team, despite having missed pre-semester practice. "He just needed to sow some wild oats," a female underling had consoled her. "Every boy needs a little of that." The Post Graduate Dean had said something similar, he and his wife agreeing to keep a close if unobtrusive eye on him.

Zenaida got to know the Dean's wife well during this time, the Admiral not wanting to bother the Dean himself with her daily trakes. Galina, the Dean's wife, told Zenaida she wasn't the only mother whose student at Post-Graduate wasn't behaving with quite the decorum expected of them. "I'll know if he deviates even the slightest," Galina had said.

So the first time Fadeyka left the Post-Graduate grounds and didn't return in time for lights out, Galina was the one to go and find him.

Stranded in town without the means to get back to campus, shoeless, shirtless, and without a galacti, he'd gambled away everything, all but his on-post dress slacks. Further, he owed thousands of galacti more.

Zenaida instantly commed him enough money to cover his debts and replace his clothes, expressing her frustration with him to Galina. "Ginny, he was selling himself on the beaches of Marseilles to old women and young men!" Zenaida said. "Who knows where he'll end up if he keeps gambling!?"

"We'll find him some other diversions on campus, Zinny," Galina had assured her. "Don't you worry."

And then, across the next two months, not a single report of aberrant behavior. Perhaps Fadeyka has put it behind him, Zenaida thought, and she scaled back her trakes to Galina to once or twice per week, enjoying her conversations with the Dean's wife, her manner urbane and sophisticated, the kind of wife a Post-Graduate Dean would need.

Zenaida had frequently wished for a husband of similar caliber, but none of her paramours seemed to have the social standing or the parlor skills to match someone of her distinction. Fadeyka's father had been significantly older than Zenaida, rear Admiral of the Fifth Fleet. She'd married him on the eve of her graduation, an appointment to battleship command nearly guaranteed her. Fadeyka had been born a year later.

In Ukraine's long-running battle with their hated Rusky neighbors, skirmishes erupted periodically, and in Zenaida's first pitched battle, she had conducted her command flawlessly and had beaten back the Rusky incursion with minimal losses. Shortly afterward, another skirmish had erupted along the Fifth Fleet's segment of the contested border, a skirmish that had soon escalated. Although able to hold its own under her husband's command, the Fifth Fleet had called for reinforcements, and her battleship, the Nikopol, was among them.

On the outskirts of Oleksandrivka, a cloaked destroyer penetrated the Fleet's outer defenses and attacked its flagship, while a full frontal attack on the Fleet was launched.

Zenaida brought the Nikopol around to engage the destroyer just as the first defensive line failed against the frontal attack. Defend the Fleet or defend the flagship? she wondered.

"Reinforced the front line," her husband ordered, and Zenaida brought her guns to bear on the attacking Rusky invaders. While the Nikopol and other ships fended off the attack, the cloaked destroyer pummeled the flagship into oblivion.

And her husband along with it.

For her part in the battle, she claimed her first medal of valor, and accepted another on behalf of her husband, awarded posthumously.

By then, Fadeyka was five, and throughout his father's obsequies, the personal and the public rituals long and elaborate, and throughout the medal award ceremonies, one for her and one for her husband, he stood at attention for hours, his face impassive, the recipient of multiple comments about how much he resembled his father, the marbled Roman face atop the ramrod-straight posture.

Destined for command, they'd all said.

And throughout his upbringing, Zenaida had little time for a personal life, working her way relentlessly up through the naval hierarchy, and when he was on the verge of attending the Naval Academy on his own merits, she was promoted to Admiral, taking command of the entire Ukraine Navy at the phenomenally young age of forty-five.

In four years at the Academy, he'd earned double degrees in cryptology and interstellar relations, captain of the football, fencing, and hand-to-hand combat teams, his physical prowess equivalent to his mental prowess, graduating Summa Cum Laude, class president and valedictorian.

Destined for command, they'd all said.

Perhaps Marseilles was just a phase, Zenaida told herself at the end of his first semester at the Post Graduate School, his grades as perfect as they'd always been, his football team taking the sector championship, his hand-to-hand combat and fencing as superlative as they'd always been, his physical condition seeming to be completely recovered from his summer of dissipation.

On his visit home during break, Fadeyka seemed reticent to her, his responses cursory, his manner unforthcoming. She attributed it to the stress of a new school whose demands far exceeded those of the Naval Academy, Post Graduate lauded for its rigorous courses.

Across the next semester, Zenaida's contact with her son became more sporadic, decreasing to weekly and then fortnightly, with intermittent trake messages in between. Complemented with weekly conversations with her new friend, the Dean's wife Galina, who regularly assured her that Fadeyka was not only excelling in his studies but was dominating the intramural hand-to-hand combat leagues as well, carrying the Post Graduate team toward a galactic championship.

Intermittently, Zenaida began to hear disturbing rumors from colleagues whose parallel correspondence brought them into contact with other enrollees at the Post Graduate School, or who traveled there for weekend seminars. If the rumors were to be believed, the Post Graduate School was developing a reputation for licentious parties and wild, fraternity-style pranksterism. When Zenaida asked, Galina immediately discounted the naysayers as disgruntled maligners jealous of the Post Graduate's academic and athletic reputations.

Then, near the end of the semester, Zenaida's Chief of Cryptology returned from a conference on ciphering and said to her unbidden, "If I were the mother of a student there, I'd instantly yank him or her out of that den of iniquity." And he'd refused to elaborate further.

Despite Galina's and Fadeyka's denials of anything untoward, Zenaida boarded her yacht at the earliest opportunity. En route, before she arrived, the bombshell blew the scandal into galaxy-wide headlines.

The police raided what was purported to be a full casino and brothel, illicit nanomutadrugs of every type available, where the wealthy were lured, their identities stolen, their activities recorded, and their families extorted. Galina and Fadeyka had been caught *in flagrante delicto*, fornicating vigorously with each other at the Dean's on-campus residence. Bank accounts with astronomical balances were confiscated, barrels full of nanomutadrugs were impounded, and several students and administrators were arrested, including the main perpetrators, Galina and Fadeyka.

Zenaida arrived at the spaceport just as her son and newfound friend were being escorted in restraints from the Dean's on-campus residence, and she rushed immediately to bail him out just as the Dean vehemently denounced his wife and proclaimed his disavowal of his wife's activities from the stoop of his off-campus mansion.

As heads began to roll with the naval chain of command, Zenaida forced her son into a full-scope rehabilitation program, one with an interstellar reputation for discretion in helping the glitterati overcome their most egregious of vices, claiming that her son was the victim of exploitation by the Dean's wife, and that Galina had attempted to extort money from her by threatening to go public with her son's gambling and carousing.

Zenaida barely escaped having to resign.

She looked across the room at Fadeyka, wondering what to do with him now, after this latest fiasco. "What in God's name is it going to take?!" she roared at him.

* * *

"Karl, get your plucky ass over here! I need 0.5 cc's of HCL stat!" Yulia Glushenko looked across the crime lab, which buzzed with activity, the cases in Kiev nonstop. Six technicians like her worked at evacuhoods that siphoned off noxious gasses. Between the six technicians, there was but one titraclone.

Karl looked up from a culture he was leaning over. He tucked an ampoule—looking like nothing more than a perky female breast—back into his shirt. "Here I come, Yulia!" He lumbered over toward her, barely able to fit between workstations.

She was analyzing tissue samples from a crime scene, and may have isolated a fragment of metal that looked like flakes from a rusty old hatchet. A literal hatchet job on the victim. Yulia shook her head, having seen the perfectly triangular punctures in the skull.

Karl walked over. "HCL, 0.5 cc's," he repeated, as per protocol. The titraclone wore a slotted allsuit, and between slits, soft round breasts were visible, nearly twenty of them covering Karl's chest from chin to navel. Stitched into the fabric beside each slit was the name of the chemical compound in that mammary. Karl reached into the slit labeled HCL and pulled out a breast, leaned into the hood and squeezed. Glowing numbers near the teat crept up to point-five, and he pulled back, wiping the nipple and tucking it back into the slit. "There you go."

"You took god damn forever. Hustle, man, hustle!" She slapped his behind to send him over to her colleague, who was calling for a mil of ammonium nitrate. "Can't get a decent titraclone these days, I swear!"

# Chapter 2

"You found her where?" Fred stared at his father, bewildered. Fred had come home after work to find the escoriant asleep on his bed in their tiny dormicube. He didn't know whether to feel offended that Kate had taken his bunk or relieved she was safe.

"In the insemivats, tinkering with the mutasperm," Greg GSH4534 said. "Listen, Son, you should have reported her missing. She could have really screwed up the mutasperm."

More than likely, any changes would have resulted in inviability, such work the domain of gengineers, but Fred didn't want to argue.

Like Fred, his father Greg was a mutaclone. Unlike Fred, Greg wasn't an abortivariant, having gone full term. Greg had been tailored to operate biochemical synthesis units, and instead of arms, he sprouted nanostim tendrils in the thousands from each shoulder, a kaleidoscope of colors among them, constantly moving and probing his surroundings.

Fred had become accustomed to their constant probing wherever his father was nearby, the display of affection disconcerting to everyone else. The nanostim filaments allowed Greg to diagnose and treat any biologic or mutagenic organism, the carbon microtubules so insubstantial as to penetrate the interstices of cell membranes.

"She did say she's a doctor in something," Fred said.

"But couldn't say what it was, or what her name is. I'm calling her Kate." His filaments organized themselves into rainbows, a sign of joy.

But she's my escoriant, Fred wanted to say. They both knew he wouldn't disagree with his father. "I'll take her over to the escoriant sector tomorrow before work."

"They'll probably do a little product-testing before they recycle her." The filaments fluttered in agitation.

"Maybe," Fred said doubtfully. "It would cost too much to recondition her, wouldn't it? She can be overly assertive." Fred realized he was stating the obvious, Greg having worked the sectors for twenty-plus years.

Grey snorted and shook his head, his filaments fanning out in dismay.

"Weird, isn't it?"

"What's that?" Question-mark curlicues formed at the shoulders.

"Insists she's a doctor and has real memories, but can't remember her name. I mean, I didn't know my name either when I clawed my way out of that uterpod, but at least I knew I was a mutaclone. She thinks she's real."

"We all think we're real."

True, Fred thought. Simumems of life on Tantalus were nanostimmed into mutaclones during gestation, most of the mutaclones from this Genie-All factory intended for the Tantalus market. Five years ago, just out of the uterpod, Fred had had the simumems of a thirty-year-old gigolo, the wherewithal of a twenty-three year old stripling, and the testosterone-fueled giddiness of a fifteen-year old adolescent.

Learning hadn't been an issue, however, the company providing didactistims to its employees. At first, their security systems had stymied his access, but he'd decrypted the files in moments. Operating on similar principles as nanostims, didactistims inserted their nanocarbon filaments into the brain and stimulated learning on the topic of the person's choice.

"Kate seems to know far more than a mutaclone should," Fred said.

Greg nodded, filaments waving. "I'll fix us dinner while you figure out our sleeping arrangements."

Fred nodded and looked around their dormicube. Already too small for the two of them, it would be cramped with three, and the addition of a female would challenge their privacy all around. The unitized partitions helped, but they'd still have to avert their gazes as others came out of the sanistall.

"Kate?" He woke her gently so he could move panels.

Her eyes snapped open, and she gave him a gentle smile. "Sorry I didn't stay put. I couldn't help exploring. And after I found the insemivats, I lost all sense of time."

Fred waved it away. "Help me rearrange the room so we can sleep in comfort tonight. I'm glad Father found you, and not one of the other sector geeks. That would have been a disaster."

"They're going to recycle me, aren't they?"

He met her gaze and was instantly floating aloft on her beauty.

He knew in that moment he couldn't allow it, no matter what the consequences. It wasn't just her beauty. She had an equanimity he found disconcerting, a disquieting sense of purpose so elemental as to be a fundamental force. He saw the evanescence of her soul, that spark of spirit which sang for mercy and salvation, the point of light inside her waiting like a singularity to explode into the universe, as though inside her incubated the dawning of time itself.

He knew he looked at her in the way Greg had once looked at him.

Then his escoriant simumems intruded with five thousand copulation positions. An erection quickly followed. Grimacing, he pushed aside the memories. "They might try to recycle you, but I won't let them."

"How can you stop them? They own this rock—and nearly all the other asteroids in the Tantalus constellation."

How'd she know that? he wondered. He mulled it over while they rearranged the room. When they were done, he noticed she didn't have a condicoon—a conditioning cocoon. Low-gravity environments leached minerals from bone, and condicoons stimulated their reabsorption, each night infusing their skeletal systems with nanostim tendrils.

"I'm going over to Wreck to get you a condicoon." Requisition was where you went whenever you wrecked something.

"I'm coming with you."

Fred heard a hint of desperation in her voice. "You'll be safe here."

"I'm coming with you."

The certainty in her voice told him not to object. He stepped into the corridor and saw a trio of sector monitors coming toward them from the Wreck room, where people went to destroy things in a leisurely fashion.

"Hey, Fred, doing a little product-testing?" Troy said, his twenty-finger hands spread out over his own outsize mammaries.

"When you're done, can I have a turn?" Mike asked, his octopus arms squishing on the piping-ribbed walls.

His boyfriend Stan jabbed him in the ribs with a hammer-sized finger. "Hey, you don't like women, remember?"

Wreck was near the commissary, where goods imported from Tantalus tempted nobody, the prices exorbitant, the company markup at least two hundred percent. Interstellar law required the company to provide conditioning cocoons on the assumption that employees would eventually be returning to full-gravity environments.

Jane at the Wreck desk looked Kate up and down. "Where'd you come from, Sister?"

Fred could see Kate bristle like a brush. "The condicoon, please?" he said, stepping between them.

"Hey, I got to look her over, get her dims, all right, Fred? Not like I'm making comparisons. Back in a spiff." She turned, revealing the extra pair of arms growing from her back.

"That bitch!" Kate hissed.

"Uh, don't rattle her, all right? I broke up with her last month." Jane had been looking to settle down, a good ten years his senior.

"Oh." Kate almost smiled, a mischievous gleam in her eye.

Jane returned with a tightly-wrapped bundle. "This should fit you, Kate." She pushed Fred out of the way and handed it to Kate directly. "He's a nice man," she added with a wink. "Good choice."

Fred felt his face flush, and Kate giggled. "Thanks, Jane. You're not so bad yourself."

He couldn't understand why the two women were laughing so hard. Shaking his head, he turned and left, somehow thinking they were ridiculing him.

She caught up to him, the bundle under an arm.

"What was that all about?" he asked.

"You wouldn't understand."

Fred threw her a glance, understanding one thing about her. Social cues of that depth were beyond a mutaclone. Nanostim neuroprogramming wasn't sophisticated enough to ingrain cues that nuanced, current mutaclone development protocols not that advanced. A Wreck room confab with a gene jockey had alerted Fred to ways of detecting mutaclones. Subtle expressions and social expectations were notoriously difficult to program into mutaclones, and could only be acquired by spending years among normavariants.

"Not the kind of behavior you'd expect from an abortivariant," Kate said.

He grunted, vaguely remembering his father saying similar. About him.

Back at their dormicube, Fred dug into the mush Greg'd made, hungrier than he thought. He pushed away his empty plate and belched. "Good stuff, Dad. Thanks."

Kate leapt to her feet to clean up.

Fred exchanged a glance with Greg. Escoriants weren't nanostimmed to take on domestic duties, recreational procreation being the usual focus of their development.

The kitchenette sparkled when she was finished. "I'm in the sanistall. Get me a clean allsuit, would you, Fred?" And she'd stepped out of her allsuit before he could turn away.

He whirled, his face fiery. His escoriant simumems flooded his mind, gonadotropins flooded his system, and desire flooded his crotch. He wished she'd warn him when she was going to disrobe.

The sanistall was a slot in the wall, barely wide enough for a person to stand upright. When she was done, he held out the allsuit, his head turned the other direction.

"Thank you."

Greg was already in his condicoon, the white fluffy material wrapping all but the oval where his face peeked out, the bunk under him empty.

"I'm sleeping across the room?" Kate asked, the new condicoon bundle at the foot.

Fred nodded, setting a clean allsuit outside the sanistall. "My turn." He twirled his finger at her.

She dutifully turned away.

He disrobed and hurled the dirty one at the chute. All hydrocarbons were recycled. He didn't care to think what they were recycled into. When he finished in the sanistall, he poked his head out.

She was already in her condicoon. "I'll close my eyes, I promise," she said, her face scrunched in exaggeration.

"Roll away toward the wall," he told her.

She did so, and he stepped from the sanistall to don his allsuit.

Crawling into the condicoon on the bunk below Greg, he sealed himself inside. As it sent its tentacles deep into his tissues, Fred wondered what he was going to do with Kate. What do I tell them when they demand I turn her over? he wondered, staring at the darkened underside of the bunk above him.

His father's soft snore drifted down to him, and he could tell by the soft breathing from across the room that Kate was deep asleep too.

His worries swirling through his head didn't stop him from drifting off, and visions of a verdant world filled his dreams, a world where lush vegetation cascaded down terraced hillsides, boab trees sprawled everywhere, their branches draped with vines, and the gentle rains of warm tropical days washed away his troubles.

A dream he'd had many times, a dream that had been planted in his mind during his uterpod gestation, a simumem of the planet Tantalus.

\* \* \*

Her pump heels tap, tap, tapped the plascrete as she walked up the broad avenue between apartment buildings, the chill night wind slicing through the thin, jacquard jacket, funneled up the avenue by the multistory buildings on either side.

Dr. Sarina Karinova felt none of it.

She hadn't been able to relax or sleep, and finally she'd given up and had decided to walk back to her office, hoping to distract herself. She'd left a note for Anya in the faint hope her wife had departed in mid-task in a fit of pique, in spite of its being so out of character it wasn't worth considering. But it was a straw she could grasp at.

Odd, she thought as the plascrete slipped past her, how faint hopes loom large, far out of proportion to their statistical probability, particularly when the alternatives are so gallingly unthinkable.

She'd considered comming her family on Tbilisi or her in-laws on Petrograd, but both sides were so distant that at most they'd only provide emotional support.

This was one of the few circumstances she wished they'd purchased a mutaclone. Anya hadn't balked for a moment at taking on household management, even though a saniclone would have been an inexpensive convenience. Sarina had eschewed their use since her stint on the Genie-All asteroid, the conditions behind their manufacturing objectionable. Anya, out of respect for her preference, had taken on the laundry, meals, shopping, and housecleaning.

But if we'd had one, Sarina thought, the saniclone could tell me what happened.

Striding along the darkened street toward her office, chin tucked to her chest against the chill, Sarina noticed how few hovers zipped past above her, the hour late. Far down the boulevard was a cluster of emergency vehicles, their bright, flashy lights difficult to ignore. Not too far from my office, she thought, gauging the distance.

Her practice fronted one of the major boulevards in the Capital, but it had been her membership in the Society for the Humane Treatment of Mutaclones that had brought her to the attention of the Premier's Chief of Staff, Feodor Luzhkov. At one of their forums, Sarina had piped up and had asked what was being done to insure mutaclones received adequate medical care, and the speaker had asked her to introduce herself. After the forum, Luzhkov had approached and asked if she might examine a family friend for him. His comcard, she'd seen immediately, had the Tantalus government emblem.

The next day, he'd come to her office alone after business hours. "May we use the back entrance for this appointment?" he'd asked.

"Sounds as if some discretion might be required," she'd replied.

Luzhkov had smiled. "Indeed. A doctor understands discretion."

She'd made a guess. "Why me, and not the palace physician?"

"Discretion, as you noted." Again that smile. "And what might be a good day and time?"

She'd set an appointment, making it the last one of the day and giving herself a clear half hour before then.

As she'd begun to enter it in the appointment book, he'd stopped her. "No records, please."

She'd blinked at him. "Very well. But I'll need to send out labs and genalysis samples."

"May I make a suggestion?" he'd asked. "Let's use a mutaclone designation, a part of your philanthropy."

And she'd agreed it was apropos cover. So nowhere did the name of the Premier's daughter appear, only the contrived designation, OLGS562.

How ironic, she thought, striding purposively toward her office, that we'd chance upon such a contrivance and that her genalysis somehow got mixed up with a mutaclone's at the lab.

The emergency vehicles appeared to be very near her office, she saw. Her ground-floor suite had been less expensive due to its being on the ground floor, the most desirable and most visible premises being higher up. Some of her patients noted the inconvenience of having to walk into her building. You could take a hover directly to most places and avoid the effort of actually walking.

Firehouses snaked across a sidewalk soaked in water. She passed the first fire truck and saw, to her horror, that it wasn't beside her office. It *was* her office. Demolished.

Tattered frames stared eyelessly at her, fragments of glasteel giving the windows a toothy edge. Burn licks scored the upper sills, a thin reed of the smoke still seeping from the doorway. The door sat agape at a forlorn, awkward angle, its glasma busted out.

Sarina stared, her mouth agape.

"Move along, miss," said one firefighter, glasma crunching under his feet.

"That's my office." Her voice came from someone else. It couldn't have been her who was speaking. She didn't have the faculties to believe what she was seeing.

"Please, step back over here."

Her body obeyed a command that her mind wouldn't process.

All of it, gone.

She'd barely paid off the examination equipment, and now she'd have to relocate while...

"Captain Gennady Ovinko, ma'am."

"Doctor Karinova," she said woodenly, "Sarina Karinova." The emptied window frames stared at her from over the Captain's shoulders.

"Looks like some sort of explosion, Doctor. Any explosives inside?"

"No, Captain. Just the usual items in an outpatient medical practice. No oxygen tanks, no anesthetic. You can check the inventory, inspected two months ago by the Department of Health. Oh, and my insurance carrier has as full inventory. Here's their contact info." She traked her insurance information to Captain Ovinko.

"Sorry, Doctor. Checked it already. Record's unavailable for some reason. Do you have an inventory in your office records?"

"Of course, Captain. Here, let me send that to you." She brought up her office files on her corn—or tried to. A blinking red warning flashed in her cornea: "Records unavailable." She told him what she found.

"That's odd," he said. "What a coincidence."

It *was* odd. Her office records—including patient files—were stored remotely on a secure skyserver with multiple redundancies, guaranteed immediate restoration if the archive should fail. It wasn't only good practice, it was required for patient health records. Further, the encryption was unbreakable, impossible to penetrate without passwords.

She tried to access her patient records on her corn.

"Records unavailable" flashed in red.

"But you're sure nothing was explosive?" the Captain asked her.

"I'm sure." She couldn't understand why her office records couldn't be accessed. She put in a trake to the records management firm.

"Well, looks like you'll have to practice medicine somewhere else for a time," Captain Ovinko said. "Here's the Fire Marshall's contact info. They'll be investigating. Sorry about your loss, Doctor. You might as well go home, nothing you can do here now."

She nodded numbly, barely seeing him, the eyeless windows holding her gaze, like the sockets of some corpse.

Sarina left only because they told her to. She didn't know where to go. Home was empty of the person who mattered to her most, and now, she had no other place to escape to, her office a wreck. So she walked, not seeing, adrift, unmoored.

An autocom appeared on her corn from the records management company. "Account deleted at account holder's request, yesterday at 8:30 pm."

She halted, uncomprehending. But—but—

There must be some mistake, she thought, eight-thirty having been about the time she'd logged off to go home. She pulled up her trake-mail message to the lab. Eight twenty-seven, she saw. She remembered her regret arriving at home at eight forty-five.

I couldn't have deleted my files, not even accidentally, Sarina thought, since I wasn't logged on.

Anya, my office, my patient files.

All of it far too coincidental to be a coincidence. Sarina whirled, scanning the street and sky on all sides, as though someone pursued her right now.

"Feodor Luzhkov," she traked, tagging her com as urgent. She looked toward the palace. She didn't know whether he'd answer at this time of night, nearly one am. And if he doesn't answer? she wondered. What then?

"Luzhkov here."

Relief flooded through her. "Is this com secure?" She'd marked her message private but was sure he had access to far greater encryption than she did.

"It is now. Yes, Doctor, how may I assist you?" Luzhkov's image on her corn looked prim and neat, as though he hadn't been asleep.

"Apologies if I woke you, Mr. Luzhkov, but I need your help." She almost burst into tears. "My office has been bombed, my patient files destroyed, and my wife is missing. I think she's been kidnapped." There, she'd said it, her worst fear, and a sob escaped her.

"I'll have a hover there in one minute, Doctor. A black crown vick. I'll stay on com with you until you're safely inside. You think it's related to the examination?"

The genalysis. Chromosomal smoothing. She knew it, and didn't know how she knew it. "I think so."

A black hover descended to street level and pulled alongside her. It looked so nondescript that it stuck out like a nebula on a night sky.

"That's your hover, Doctor. Climb aboard."

She collapsed onto the seat as the door slid shut behind her, and his neuralink disconnected.

Dr. Sarina Karinova stared out the window as the hover banked toward the palace, her life chewed to pieces, disbelief threatening to swallow her whole.

\* \* \*

Looking across the room at Fadeyka, Admiral Zenaida Andropovich wondered what she could do anymore. *What the hell is a mother supposed to do?* she wondered.

First the beach on Marseilles and then the Post Graduate Program. And now *this!*

Fadeyka's treatment at the glitterati recovery program had been intermittently interrupted by court appearances, and he'd seemed appropriately remorseful at having destroyed his own career and at having very nearly destroyed his mother's.

Destined for command, they no longer said.

The treatment program included multiple components, including psychodynamic therapy, reparative family interventions, nanoneural reprogramming, and in-vitro condicoon immersions. Rumors rife on the neuranet hinted that the program's methods had been adapted from the unconscionable practices invented at that infamous Rusky gulag, Magadan, rumors that Zenaida dismissed as outlandish.

The court sentenced the Dean's wife, Galina, to twenty-five years at Brygidki, and Fadeyka to court-ordered treatment, finding him culpable only of youthful dalliances. Further penalties for drug possession were suspended pending his completion of the program he was already in.

Zenaida kept close tabs on Fadeyka whilst he participated in the six-month program, visiting occasionally and comming frequently. She became acquainted with the program director, a neuropsychoanalyst with a stellar interstellar reputation. Dr. Innokenti Pablov was as gentle with her as he was stern with his patients. Any deviation from his exacting schedule of treatment was received with scathing rebukes and threats of expulsion.

She and Dr. Pablov of an age, Zenaida thought the galaxy of him, and they began to spend hours in neuranet conversation, connected on coke, corn, and trake, becoming completely immersed through their neuraplants in a way that reminded Zenaida of her dear lost husband, the Rear Admiral of the Fifth Fleet.

Then, at the five-and-a-half month mark of Fadeyka's recovery, Dr. Pablov invited Zenaida to a weekend family retreat at the glitterati recovery center for a reparative family intervention with Fadeyka that Dr. Pablov volunteered to facilitate.

Zenaida arrived the night before and was met at the spaceport by Dr. Pablov, looking even more handsome than his neuranet avatar portrayed him. How she ended up in his embrace, and then in his bed, she couldn't have said, and all she remembered of the night was how fulfilled she'd felt.

The next afternoon as Dr. Pablov escorted her through the facility toward Fadeyka's room, Zenaida soared with his every gesture and word, her long-dormant libido now in full flagrant bloom, her face flush and her loins awash.

And then they arrived at Fadeyka's door.

Two young men lay on the floor of his room, locked in a grotesque, monkey-puzzle tangle of limbs, stark naked, their members in each other's mouth, the other residents crouched in a circle around them and taking bets as to which could resist having an orgasm the longest.

Belatedly, Zenaida recognized one of the young men on the floor as her son.

She was transported back to the first time she'd discovered Fadeyka in some scion's bed on the planet Marseilles, and as she had then, she hauled him sans clothing from the treatment program to the spaceport and threw him into her yacht, berating him ruthlessly the whole way.

She ignored Dr. Pavlov's trakes throughout the trip home, learning from his trake-mails that the other young man locked with her son in the two-backed, monkey-puzzle embrace had been the top counselor at the recovery program, whom Dr. Pablov had instantly fired.

Despite his pleas, she never returned his trakes.

Once back on Tantalus, while Zenaida tried to figure out what to do next, Fadeyka continued his dissipation, knowing somehow never to bring it into her house and consequently disappearing for days at a time. She'd thought she'd have to give up on him then.

Not long afterward, an officer appeared at her door, warrant in hand, glasma cuffs out and ready. A condition of Fadeyka's sentence was his completing the treatment program, which he'd made a complete wreck of.

At his sentencing, Fadeyka was given a two-year term at the Zamkova Correctional Colony on Ternivka, a day's journey from Tantalus. Relieved, Zenaida hoped the former monastery might osmalize into him some of its asceticism simply through his being there. Unlike the full-fledged prison at Brygidki, infamous for its barbaric conditions and routine executions—some of them extrajudicial—the Zamkova Colony was a country club in comparison, the facilities decentralized, park-like plazas in the center of each unit, a low guard-to-inmate ratio, a serene setting on the mostly Mediterranean-climate planet.

Zenaida visited him once per month, no more than the rules allowed, not asking for any special privileges, staying aloof from the colony administration (her last two episodes having soured her on such relationships), and offering Fadeyka very little support during his incarceration. After she rebuffed his first two requests for money, he stopped asking, but when he asked for a modicum of supplies, such as an extra allsuit or another pair of shoes, she was happy to oblige.

What Zenaida did notice, three or four months in, was how the guards began to treat him during their visits. They became increasingly deferential, calling him "Captain Andropovich," and snapping to attention whenever he approached, holding doors, pulling back chairs, and even bowing.

"It's just respect, Mother," Fadeyka told her when she pointed it out. "Nothing more than the son of an Admiral deserves."

Skeptical, she kept a sharp eye out for anything untoward, and in these observations, did notice among the guards a curious ennui, their passive demeanors incongruous to the kind of attentive discipline she'd expect in such an environment.

"It's just a low-key place, is all," Fadeyka said nonchalantly. "Used to be a monastery, long ago."

Then Zenaida began to notice a similar lassitude in some of the prisoners visiting with their families in the booths beside hers.

At the same time, she became aware of increasing requests for the interdiction of clone-smuggling ships at the Ukraine borders, the military sometimes assisting the domestic authorities when problems became so severe they threatened to overwhelm civilian law enforcement. Mutaclone smuggling had become big business, the government having stringent regulations on the proportion of mutaclones to citizens within its borders. Further, each mutaclone was registered and required to have a Galactic Positioning System locator in their neuraplants to monitor their locations at all times. In spite of these stringent regulations, several thousand mutaclones with deactivated GPS locators had been apprehended inside the border, smuggled in with forged registrations. Given that much of the Ukraine's interstellar borders consisted of open space, the Navy was frequently called upon to assist in patrolling that border, especially during peacetime.

One such batch of mutaclones was intercepted by a cruiser on random patrol, unaccompanied by a civilian interdiction ship, and a vid of their capture and apprehension was circulated through the naval command structure and finally made its way to her desk. When Zenaida viewed the vid, it struck her as oddly familiar, groups of mutaclones shuffling morosely from point to point, their gazes vacant, their faces blank.

It wasn't until she went to visit Fadeyka again that she put the pieces together. The prisoners and guards moped about morosely, their gazes vacant, their faces blank—just like the mutaclones.

Shaken, she'd said nothing to Fadeyka, but as she'd left the visiting center on her way to her yacht, she'd conferred with another family who'd been visiting.

"You know, I'd noticed that, too. They all seem so depressed!"

Back in her office, she asked for an analysis of the fleet's participation in the mutaclone smuggling interdiction. The smugglers' vessels were frequently too small and too fast for the ponderous naval ships to intercept, and often all they could do was track these vessels.

What alarmed Zenaida was the concentration of sightings near the border adjacent to Ternivka, site of the Zamkova Correctional Colony. Further, her analysis indicated an increase on sightings about three months into Fadeyka's incarceration there.

Zenaida needed no more evidence than that. Fadeyka is at it again! she thought. She tipped off the border patrol through its director, the head of the Immigrations and Customs Enforcement, and sent a trake-mail to the Penitentiary Service Director, and then offered to send in the Fourth Fleet to blockade the planet.

Instead, the Penitentiary Service investigated, infiltrating the Correctional Colony by sending in investigators disguised as convicts.

They were courteous enough to arrest her son during her next visit. Zenaida made sure that her wooden stare told him exactly who had alerted the authorities to his operation.

The headlines were lurid, the depth of his corrosive influence extending all the way to the warden, whom Fadeyka had co-opted. Nearly all the prison guards had been kidnapped and mutaclones put in their places. Further, mutaclones had been substituted for about half the prisoners, who'd been freed and were now working for Fadeyka in his far-flung mutaclone smuggling enterprise.

This time, the evidence of his masterminding such an extensive criminal operation was overwhelming. Zenaida expected nothing less than a life sentence at the harshest, most dreaded gulag in the Ukraine: Brygidki.

Zenaida was right about the location, but wrong about the length. He got only two years. Further, he was placed in high security, where the most incorrigible prisoners were kept in twenty-four hour isolation.

She visited only once.

She stared at him through six inches of reinforced glascrete, Fadeyka held in chains twenty feet back on his side of the impermeable barrier. His eyes were dull and defeated, his shoulders slumped, his complexion wan and pale. He was a ghost of the boy she'd loved.

Finally, Zenaida thought, he'll come around.

This period was the worst of her. Listless and sedentary at home, Zenaida was perfunctory at work, but her heart was no longer in it. The Admiralty was a ship without a captain, cruising along on its momentum, but now absent any guidance, its rudder fixed and its course straight, but traveling blindly for all that.

Now, after this latest fiasco, she didn't know any longer. Maybe he was completely incorrigible. "What the hell am I supposed to do now?!" Zenaida screamed at him.

* * *

Ivan the shovelclone gestured with one pan hand at the pulp on the sidewalk. "This one?"

"See any other dead mutaclones around here, idiot?" The sanicrew lead glanced up the side of the building and looked over at the pulp's erstwhile owner. "What floor do you live on?"

The older man standing a few feet away in a bathrobe also glanced up. "Fifteenth."

"Name?"

"Why do you need to know my name?"

"Look, Popushka, every mutaclone is registered to somebody, and each has to be tracked. Bureaucracy, all right?"

The man shrugged. "Yiktor Balanchuk."

"Mutaclone?"

"Mira."

"Mira what, Sir?"

"Oh, uh, you mean her designation?"

"Yes, Sir."

"Let me check." He stared at the mutaclone pulp on the sidewalk for a moment, his iris twinkling as he consulted his corn. "Mira M775RKK."

The sanicrew lead noticed that the mutaclone was naked from the waist down. He looked at Balanchuk in his bathrobe and then at the half-clothed mutaclone. "Helluva way to keep your wife from finding out you were fucking the maid."

"That doesn't have to go into the report, does it?"

"What report? There's no report, just a record that this saniclone has termed. Thanks for your help, Mr. Balanchuk. All right, Ivan, scoop her up."

Ivan the shovelclone took one two-foot wide panhand and placed it at one end of the corpse. He then placed his other panhand like a stop at the other, then scooped up the bloody pulp in one swift motion.

The sanicrew lead opened the back of his County hover, a utility model with a bin in back for just such detritus. In went the pulverized meat. He and Ivan then sprayed off the sidewalk, but only because this was an upper-class neighborhood, the apartments here easily thrice what he could afford. If it had been a poorer neighborhood, he wouldn't have bothered.

The sanicrew lead turned to seal the back panel and found Balanchuk staring at what was left of his saniclone. "Get a male mutaclone next time," he said. "Less tempting."

He closed the back and looked up at the high-rise apartments around him.

Expecting another mutaclone to splatter the sidewalk from above.

# Chapter 3

Violent pounding roused Fred from sleep. "Company security! Open up!" More pounding.

Fred crawled from the condicoon and dragged himself toward the door, thumbing the sleep from his eyes.

Outside stood two uniformed secuguards, behind them a corpreaucrat, judging by the herringbone skirt and jacquard jacket.

"We're here for the mutaclone you should have recycled yesterday," said one uniform.

Fred looked over his shoulder toward her bunk.

They lunged, forcing their way inside and hurling him backward.

"What'd you do with her?!"

Her bunk was empty, the conditioning cocoon neatly tied in a bundle.

"What's this about?" Greg said, just extracting himself from his condicoon.

"You know very well, Gee Ess Aitch Four Five Three Four," the corpreaucrat said. "Harboring a recycle is punishable with termination." She turned to Fred. "Where's she at, Eff Four Are Bee Eight Cee Three?" She pronounced each syllable with exacting certainty.

Fred hadn't heard anyone use his designation in a long time. He was livid she hadn't used his name, the denigration on her part deliberate. "How should I know, Eff You Cee Kay In The Ass!?" A distant part of his mind marveled at the utility of a phrase at least three thousand years old. He wondered how he'd even known it.

Stars exploded in his left eye, the truncheon spinning his head around. Of its own free will, his left fist rabbit-punched the guard twice, his right foot found the other's crotch, and his right hand grabbed the corpreaucrat by the throat.

The two guards writhed on the floor, and the corpreaucrat gurgled.

"Fred, no!" Greg said.

The muscles of his right arm bulging, Fred stared into the terrified eyes of the fem exec.

"She's just a corpreaucrat."

He let go, and she dropped to her knees, gasping for breath. Then, again without a thought, he cold-cocked both the guards and did the same for her, his motions fluid, certain, precise. All three went limp.

Fred stared at his hands, disbelieving.

Greg gaped at him, open-mouthed. "How'd you do that?"

Fred raised his gaze to his father, shaking his head, convinced he looked just as terrified as the corpreaucrat had.

"Not sure when they made that recycle rule," Greg said. "Either way, you're mulch if you don't leave. Here." He turned and loosened a panel beside the door with his filaments. Behind it was a handcomp. "Been saving this for a rainy day."

Fred knew what he meant, but only had a vague idea what rain was. He took the handheld computer cube from Greg.

"Controls an emergency shuttle near the execusuites on the corp side of the asteroid. You're on your own getting there, but try the servi-tubes." The service tubes gave maintenance staff access to all areas of the asteroid factory. Servitubes went everywhere. "Hurry! Go! If I can find Kate, I'll bring her." Then Greg frowned. "One more thing before you go."

"Yeah, Dad?"

"I love you, Son."

Fred hugged him, blinking away his tears.

Greg pushed him away. "Now me."

Fred swung before he thought about it, the punch calculated and launched before he had any inkling that he was assaulting his own father.

Greg crumpled, and Fred eased him to the floor.

He didn't understand why the corridor was blurry, why the hatch to the servitudes wouldn't come into focus. He opened it by feel and slipped inside, his body lithe and spry as though he'd been trained in stealth. He closed the hatch above him and wriggled his way into the servitube.

He palmed the handcomp, which came alight. A map appeared on his corn, the green lines servitubes, the blue ones corridors. Along the corridors moved red dots, purple dots, and yellow dots. The red dots were security, the purple dots were execs (all of them normavariants), and the yellow dots were mutaclones like himself. Chaos was erupting in the corridors. The large, yellow dot was him, Fred F4RB8C3.

Mutaclone abortivariant F4RB8C3 has now gone rogue, the corn alert would read, klaxons blaring, strobe lights flashing.

"Cloak," he traked, and his large, yellow dot disappeared. How did I know I could cloak myself? Fred wondered if he could secuchannel Kate and find out where she was. But that could only work if she weren't cloaked.

If the secuguards are coming to find her, he thought, then they can't locate her signal either.

Trust, he thought. If the emergency shuttle is the only way off this rock besides the regular supply vessels every two weeks, Fred thought, then that's where she'll go too.

All functioning mutaclones were being pulled from their condicoons, from their sector posts, and from the Wreck rooms to help with the search.

His body a machine, he took the service tubes as a worm might work its way through an underground burrow: hand, foot, exert, hand, foot, exert, hand, foot, exert. His eyes and senses tuned, coke and corn feeding him info, Fred was a burrowing machine. He was halfway across the asteroid when the first squad of mutaclones was sent into the servitubes.

Had they traced his route from his thermal signature? He felt his trunk and legs go cold, as if his metabolism were responding to his thoughts. His hands were hot and his face was aflame, trying to compensate. His core temperature began to rise.

On his corn, he located coolant and detoured into an air duct. His metabolism stabilizing, Fred waited a moment, sweat soaking his allsuit. He was cold in moments. His trail would be too. A heating duct would be equally baffling, he realized.

Moving again, his pace fast, Fred looked ahead on his corn.

Red dots were moving into the servitubes ahead, blocking access to the execusuites.

They knew what he was after. Had they caught Greg and forced the info from him? Fred didn't think so, seeing Greg's dot among his pursuers behind him.

I need a decoy or a diversion, Fred thought. The emergency shuttle was to the left of the execusuites, the main tarmac to the right. A storage yard full of cannibalized quadcarts sat to the far end of the tarmac, forlorn skeletons eviscerated for parts.

Even a rogue quadcart resurrecting itself might draw off a few secuguards, he thought.

The storage yard erupted, an extensible hurling quadcart parts left and right. The extensible ripped itself from its base and stomped toward the execusuites.

Did I do that? Fred wondered, darting forward as secuguards scrambled in response. Fred traked the shuttle to start its prelaunch sequence. The shuttle computer balked, asking for an access code. Cryptology awareness flooded through Fred's mind, supplying him with the likely sequence. Where'd that come from? he wondered. He decoded the encryption in an instant.

Without time to question, he saw an opening where the secuguards had spread themselves thin. Fred slithered around a corner, did a reverse vault off a handrail, and brought his foot crashing into a secuguard's jaw. The man went limp, and Fred dropped from the ceiling to the floor in front of the shuttle hatch.

As it slid aside, the shuttle warming up, Kate loped around the corner and dove at him, tackling him into the shuttle. "Launch, blast it!"

And Fred traked, "Launch!"

The hatch slid closed, and a red glow lit it from behind, the metal absorbing a laser blast. A rumble shook the shuttle, and it shot into space.

\* \* \*

Dr. Sarina Karinova's conversation with Tatiana Satsanova, the Premier's daughter, had taken place three days ago.

Sarina had greeted the patient in the now-empty waiting room at her clinic, having dismissed her receptionist. "Pleased to meet you, Dr. Satsanova."

Like her, Tatiana Satsanova was a medical doctor, but unlike her, the young woman had pursued gengineering as her specialty.

"Mutual, Dr. Karinova. By the way, call me Tatya."

"Certainly, Tatya. Pleased. Sari for me."

"You come highly recommended, Doctor. Feo speaks well of you. I might not be here without his gentle suasion."

"If I may, I'd like to start with a physical examination. Come this way." She led the younger woman into the exam room. "I've set out a fresh gown for you. I'll wait outside while you change."

Dr. Karinova stepped into the corridor and reviewed the file that Feodor Luzhkov had given her.

Tatiana stood five-eight and was generously endowed, possessing a figure that turned both men's and women's heads. She had wheat-blond hair cascading straight past her shoulders, sported a V-shaped face that took the breath away, had large, wide-set, intelligent eyes as blue as amethyst, and had a small smile that was warm and inviting.

Twenty-eight year old female, no known medical conditions other than occasional calcium leeching, broken arm at age eight from a fall off a swing, menses onset at age twelve, sexually active at fifteen, now married three years, no children, two off-world tours on asteroid clone manufacturing facilities each for a year, returned to Tantalus after the second tour due to excessive bone loss, a syndrome that the conditioning cocoons hadn't been able to compensate for, now head of prototype gengineering for Genie-All, responsible for designing and articulating mutaclone models to spec for production.

"Ready?" Sarina knocked on the door.

"Yes, Doctor."

She stepped into the room and started through the basics. "Mr. Luzhkov referred you?"

"Well, not exactly," Tatiana said. "My mother, God bless her, has been insisting for weeks that I be examined, and I'd have continued putting her off if Feo hadn't encouraged me to see you. My mother, the Premier, rules all of Ukraine from the base of the Norman Arm to halfway out its middle, but she hasn't been given the memo that that doesn't include me."

"Tell me about yourself," Sarina said, continuing with the exam, interjecting with occasional prompts. She listened as the young woman described herself in a voice she noted as rather devoid of inflection, as though she described events in someone else's life.

"And what of your future?" Sarina asked, concluding her physical exam. "Kids planned? Vacations? Ambitions?"

The younger woman closed her robe. "I suppose I'll want children someday, but for now I'm content piecing mutaclones together for production and sale. Last year, Karl and I went to the galactic core for a little sightseeing, and it was spectacular. We're going to the Baltics in Cassiopeia next year, but I'm not keen on travel, as you might imagine, since my recovery from the bone loss takes about as long afterwards."

Again, delivered with that monotone of describing someone else's life. "Your bone loss places you at risk of early-onset osteoporosis. It could be reduced somewhat with vigorous daily weight-bearing exercise. Most passenger vessels have such facilities aboard."

"That's what I've been told, but I can't seem to find the motivation. I just want to relax when I'm on vacation. Silly, I know."

"How is your motivation?"

"Fine. I do what needs to be done."

"And your enjoyment of day-to-day activities?"

"Fine. I do what I do and then I get to the next task."

"And how have you been sleeping?"

Tatya shrugged. "I sleep just fine. Karl swears I never sleep, especially recently, but he's a man. He expects hand-and-foot service, even from me in this day and age when we've got a mutaclone practically in each room."

"And how is your libido?"

"I keep Karl quite happy," Tatya said.

"I'm not asking about his libido."

"I have orgasms. Is that what you wanted to know?"

"Not quite. Libido certainly encompasses that, but I'm asking about your desire for sex. If may seem a bit of a personal question, but I'm your doctor, and it's important."

"Yes, I desire sex, perhaps not as often as he likes, but he's a man, after all." She didn't giggle, her monotone speech and manner evincing little or no insight.

"And how about your energy level?"

"Adequate. Always going. That's how I've been since I can remember. High maintenance, Feo calls me."

"Mr. Luzhkov calls you that?"

"Like a father to me. Before he became Chief of Staff, he was Mother's household supervisor, kept me from running around with a snotty nose."

"And how about your anxiety?"

"I don't have anxiety. Doesn't occur to me to worry."

"And your appetite?"

"I eat, I drink. Karl tells me I eat like a bird, always insisting I eat more. It's not as though I starve myself or never go near a condicoon for weeks at a time. No, not at all, in fact, I'm rather punctilious about using the condicoon every night, which annoys Karl terribly, since he has to get it off to have sex with me."

"And what about the future?"

"Oh, I've got one, quite bright for that matter, or at least that's what everyone tells me. But I don't want to go into politics, which Mother has tamed quite to her liking. Everyone always asks me that, but why would I do that to myself, parade and pander shamelessly to donors? I might as well be an escoriant without the sex. No, I'd rather not go into politics."

"What about your dreams?"

"I never remember my dreams. Karl swears that's odd, but I don't think it is. He says I used to, but now I don't have them. Is that the reason I don't remember them, do you suppose? That I don't have them? Is it abnormal not to have dreams?"

Sarina hesitated, finding Tatya's manner difficult to penetrate. She sounds so diffident about everything. "I'd have to refer you to a psychologist for that, as I'm no expert on such subjects. The question I was asking was somewhat different from the one you answered. What I meant was, 'What's the one thing deep inside that you really, really want from life?' "

Tatya smiled. "To do what I'm doing, I suppose. That must sound a little fatuous, but I've no illusions about who I am. I like where I'm at and what I'm doing, and there isn't really much I want to change in the galaxy. It is as it should be."

"So, Tatya, your mother encouraged you to see a doctor, and Feodor was concerned enough to find me and to encourage you to see me. Why do you suppose they were concerned?"

"Professional busybodies, both of them. Feo at least is sweet about it. Gentle man, don't you think?"

Sarina nodded. "You mentioned your husband's opinions a few times. Doesn't it seem he might also be concerned? Anyone at work mention similar concerns?"

Tatya shrugged. "They're colleagues. They look at me odd, sometimes, but I don't place any particular importance on it. I've gotten strange, desirous glances from people all my life, as though I might somehow have absorbed some of the authority that Mother's wielded these last twenty years. But it's opened doors that might otherwise have been closed to me, so I suppose there's a benefit."

Sarina nodded, realizing the young woman had avoided the question about her husband. A primary care physician, Dr. Karinova knew she didn't have the expertise to penetrate the thick shell that encased the younger woman. "I'll need to get a tissue sample and a blood sample. Oh, and your history mentioned a broken wrist at age eight. I'd like to order some imaging, just to make sure everything's all right. Since you've had issues in the past with bone loss, I'd like to get a full geno neuro chemo, ferret out any sequela from the bone loss, if there is any. And finally, I'd like to recommend that you see a psychiatrist."

"See a psychiatrist? That's a laugh." Tatya didn't laugh. In fact, her tone hadn't changed.

Sarina had expected some defensiveness, but Tatiana evinced none whatsoever in her manner. Token resistance in her words, but that was the extent. As though the suggestion had struck the impenetrable armor and had bounced harmlessly off. "Given your initial reluctance to see me, I sensed you'd probably decline the suggestion, but it's clear based on the interview that I need to make the referral, if only out of due diligence."

"Why, what's wrong?"

And Tatya's asking the question as if the last half-hour hadn't transpired was itself clear evidence that further psychiatric work up was merited. If she weren't so monotone! Sarina thought. "Here's the psychiatrist I'd recommend, a superlative clinician with the bedside manner—" She changed her mind in midsentence— "somewhat like Feo. Doctor Floyd Benjamin." What she had wanted to say was that the psychiatrist was a lot like the Premier herself, Tatya's mother. "I'd like to get a release and include his results, if indeed you consent to seeing him. Is there anyone you'd like to have access to your medical information? Your mother, Feodor, your husband?"

"Just Feo, please." Then she hesitated. "But just that I came to the appointment."

"Appointment verification only."

"Is that it?" Tatya asked. "I thought for certain you'd put me in a condicoon and run the full geno neuro chemo yourself."

"I'm a general practitioner, not a specialist. Yes, that's it. I'll be in my office next door when you're finished dressing."

Stepping from the exam room, Sarina queued up the forms on her corn and trake-mailed them to Tatya for signature. After the signed releases came back over her neuralink, she put in orders for the labs, the imaging, and the geno neuro chemo.

Tatiana emerged from the exam room, looking slightly disheveled.

"Thank you, Tatya, it was a pleasure. The one thing Feo forgot to mention was how delightful you are."

"Thank you. You're very kind, Sari. Here's my comcard in case you're in need of a mutaclone. I can get you a discount."

"Nice of you to offer, Tatya. This way, please. I'll show you out."

Sarina had returned to her desk, wondering what had just walked out of her office. No evidence of pathology, but enough in the way of anomalies that she'd found the interview disturbing.

At her desk, she reviewed sections of the vid, just to insure it'd recorded successfully. Generally, she didn't get a full video and audio of her examinations, but given the circumstances—she didn't often examine a Premier's daughter—Sarina had thought it prudent to record the examination.

She'd even recorded the young woman disrobing, Sarina realized. That segment began playing, and she didn't know why she let it run.

Tatya's body was as perfectly proportioned as her face.

Her heart hammering in her ears, her face flushed with heat, and her loins soaked in high arousal, Sarina shut off the vid, surprised at herself. During the exam, she'd imposed her usual clinical detachment. Seeing the vid afterward had caught her with her guard down. I'm a happily married woman! she told herself. I'll have to erase that segment later, she thought, the images unnecessary for her examination.

Dr. Karinova tagged the file as confidential and secured it with two forms of encryption. Even the receptionist wouldn't be able to access the vid.

Securing the premises, she traked her wife to let her know she was on her way home.

And when Sarina arrived, she escorted her wife to the bedroom for a rousing episode of marital relations.

Doing her best to put from her mind the disturbing examination she'd just conducted.

* * *

Four and a half years after that first episode on the beaches of Marseilles, when Admiral Zenaida Andropova had hauled her son by the ear from the arms of the wealthy scion to his first class at the Post Graduate Naval School, Fadeyka Andropovich was released from Brygidki into her custody, the conditions of his parole requiring him to live at home and remain free and clear of illegal activity for the next five years. Even a simple infraction such as a hover ticket would land him back at Brygidki for the remainder of his parole.

Having Fadeyka home was such a relief for Zenaida that when he enrolled in college, she was overjoyed. His two years in solitary seemed to have finally inculcated in him the knowledge that he was required to abide by the law.

Brilliant by any standard, Fadeyka delved into Cryptology the way he had when he was younger. Interstellar diplomacy was longer of interest, his multiple convictions closing nearly all the doors in that arena.

About three months into his first semester, he began staying out all night. "There's nothing illegal about *that*, Mother!" he complained when she told him to stop.

"If it continues, you can live elsewhere."

When the behavior was recounted to his parole officer, Fadeyka was reminded in no uncertain terms that he was required to live with his mother, the Admiral, or go back to prison.

"Twenty-two hundred, or live someplace else," she demanded.

To her surprise, he complied.

Finally, she thought, some cooperation!

She did notice an increase in the number of "friends" who were dropping by, but none of them appeared after twenty-two hundred and none of them stayed later than that.

Then the school chancellor called, just after the semester was over. "Forgive me, Admiral, but it appears your son decrypted the security protocols on our grading database, and he's been changing grades for money."

Now, Fadeyka Andropovich sat in her living room, his head hanging, Zenaida having delivered what she hoped was her final tirade, ready to make sure the doorknob hit him squarely in his misbehaving behind as she kicked that same behind out the door to the curb, knowing she was condemning him to the remainder of his parole in solitary at Brygidki.

"What in God's name is it going to take?!" she repeated, convinced there was nothing more she could do for him.

"You're right, Mother. I'm beyond redemption." Fadeyka shook his head, his gaze on the floor. "I guess I've got some genetic predisposition to criminal behavior."

Zenaida caught herself before she blurted the first thing that came to mind.

"So, it's my entire fault, eh?" she'd been tempted to say. As much futility as she'd encountered with him, he might have even deserved the rebuke.

But what if there's merit to what he's saying? she asked herself. I *was* swept rather easily off my feet by Dr. Innokenti Pablov. Perhaps there *is* some genetic vulnerability to licentious behavior. One that he's inherited. "I want you to submit to a genalysis."

His head spun toward her so fast she was afraid he'd hurt his neck. "I'm not a very good candidate for reparative theragenesis. Twenty-seven is far too late for that kind of intervention."

"At least do the genalysis, Fedey. What can it hurt?"

He sighed and re-hung his head. "If you really think it'll help, Mother."

"I do. At least we'll know, Son."

"I suppose."

"And I think I know a doctor, too." The clinic in Kiev that'd been bombed, Zenaida was thinking, the doctor now in protective custody. "Let's see if she's available to examine you."

Zenaida was relieved when Fadeyka didn't object.

* * *

The thin, almost boyish mine supervisor whipped her arm at a rock face. "Yuri, that one, but reinforce the ceiling first." Olena Doroshenko was fetching. Thin as a rail and nearly absent a single female curve, but pretty. The breather hid most of her features.

And she ran the most efficient mining crew on Zasyadko, pulling five tons of ore daily with just three mutaminers.

Yuri stood seven feet tall, and his biceps at their slimmest easily exceeded Olena's thickest point in circumference. He was a mass of raw sinew and brute force muscle. Around his neck was a remocollar, which monitored his movements; although bred for docility, hypogonadism spiked into their genomes, these beasts occasionally turned on their masters. A remote in Olena's hand would disable all three mutaminers in an instant.

But Olena never had to worry about that.

They worshipped her.

Reared personally by her, fed only by her, cared for and coddled and spoiled by her, these mutaminers jumped to do her bidding and never once questioned what she asked.

Her jealous colleagues, unable to match her output, spread nasty rumors that she slept with them too, but their hormonal profiles lacked the slight amount of gonadotropin and oxytocin needed for an erection, their penises practically vestigial.

Yuri stomped to the wall she'd indicated, lifted an I-beam to the ceiling, and held it there while his crèche-brother Yufi sank a post at one end and his crèche-sister Yuli sank a post at the other end. Then Yuri lifted a pick-axe whose blade was as long as Olena was tall.

The point sank halfway in on the first swing, and it took both Yuri and Yufi to dislodge it. The rock face crumbled under the assault, all three mutaminers loading shovelfuls of rock ten times Olena's weight.

They'd exceeded their quota of ore before lunch, and now as day drew nigh, Olena saw they'd double it. She smiled, pleased with their work. She decided they could knock off ten minutes early, thinking to get them showered and back to their dorm before the crush of mutaminers coming off shift turned the locker room into a seething pit of sweaty, wet mutaminer flesh.

Yuli being a female wasn't a hindrance. She showered and slept and worked beside her crèche-brothers in blissful sibling harmony, their physiques so bulging with muscle that Olena doubted they could have sex even if they had the gonadotropins needed for arousal.

She herded them through the locker room, their bodies so transmogrified beyond anything resembling humanity that their nudity was nothing more than acres of bare skin. The sexual dimorphism between the crèche siblings was so slight that Olena sometimes got them confused from a distance. From the back she couldn't tell them apart.

"All done? To the mess hall," Olena ordered. "Awesome work today, people. Extra rations all around."

Yuli, Yuri, and Yufi grunted gutturally, grinning like ghouls, their stump-like legs barely keeping pace with Olena as she led them toward the cafeteria, the short, thick stumps spliced into their genomes, better for the huge weights they bore, helping to reduce their mobility in the event of a rampage.

Olena had never had a mutaminer go rogue on her.

She herded them to a table in the corner and went to fetch a feed bin. It weighed more than she did, the antigravs helping her wheel it over to them.

Yuri reached into the bin.

She rapped his knuckles. "Oh, no, you don't!" She always insisted on feeding them the first bite of every meal. "For that, you're last. You know better, Yuri. That's not like you." She scooped a handful of lukewarm mush and fed it to Yuli, who took her whole hand into her toothless maw. Her lips and tongue tickled Olena's hand like prehensile phalanges as they sucked every bit of mush off her fingers. She then fed Yufi a handful, Yuri whining plaintively, drool dripping down to his massive chest in buckets.

A large glop of saliva dropped onto the remocollar's control nodule. Olena thought nothing of it, the remocollars impervious to just about anything. Yuri stared longingly at the mush as she fed Yuli another handful.

The control nodule fizzled. Yuri screeched, pawed at his neck, and ripped it away. A thin trail of smoke traced its arc across the room. Then he lunged toward the feedbin, pinning Olena. His massive upper body flopped onto the table, Olena under him, his weight popping her skull like an egg.

# Chapter 4

"Evade!" Fred yelled as Kate's tackle slammed him against a bulkhead.

The ship careened away from the asteroid on a preprogrammed course, slewing wildly at his command, throwing them across the corridor.

"Grab hold!" he shouted, just grasping a handhold as the ship slewed the other way, but Kate looked helplessly at him as the corridor wall slammed into her.

He braced himself between the corridor walls with brute strength and grabbed the fabric of her allsuit as the ship pirouetted.

Her hands flailed for holds, Fred holding her suspended with one hand while his other three limbs kept him stabilized between corridor walls, absorbing horrific changes in momentum with his immense strength.

The ship slewed, slamming her weight into his, and she wrapped him with her arms and legs. Somehow, he held their combined weight steady as the ship bucked and heaved through a series of evasive maneuvers.

"Cancel evasion and set course for Tantalus," Fred ordered when he felt enough time has passed.

The heaving stopped.

"Let's get buckled in," he said and towed her into the cockpit. Kate was on the edge of tears, he saw. Strapped in, he saw she was just buckling her harness. "You in?"

She checked her harness. "In," she said with a sharp intake of breath. "Execute course," he traked the ship. "Rearview vid."

On the display, the clone factory asteroid dwindled quiescently behind them, no sign of pursuit.

"Why aren't they chasing us?" Kate asked. And then she gasped.

"I don't know," he said, the acceleration pressing him into the seat. Then the lights flickered and died.

"External override," Kate said, wincing.

"No wonder they aren't pursuing us." He pulled up the ship controls on his corn.

A flashing "Encrypted" danced on his cornea and a password prompt appeared. "The control interface is encrypted," he told her.

"So we're fish in a barrel." Kate looked distressed, sweat beading on her forehead.

Fred knew what fish were but hadn't heard of a barrel. "Not yet," he said, analyzing the signal to his corn. Forty-eight quad-state bit-driven code spiked down his eyes. No simple algorithm.

"What are you doing?" Again, she gasped.

"Quad-state algorithms in a forty-eight bit code have vulnerabilities at their third-power logarithmic junction points."

"Huh?"

"They can be cracked." He fed it the first character of the forty-eight possible, analyzing the code as it self-modded to check the character.

"A shuttle just launched from the asteroid!" Kate said, her voice a harsh whisper. "Hurry!"

The ripples in the self-mods gave him the first character, and he fed it the next guess. The second bounced through the code, its permutations pointing to the right character.

"Stay put, and you won't be harmed," blasted across their vidscreen, the remove override giving their pursuers an open com channel.

On Fred's com was a warning. "Three password errors will require an administrative reset." Fred wouldn't get another opportunity to be wrong.

"Quick! They're nearly alongside!"

On screen, the open maw of the shuttle's cargo hold threatened to engulf them.

From the first two characters, Fred extrapolated. The "Ge" had to be the company name. He entered "Genie-All," and the craft came to life.

"Evade!" Fred said, and their ship rocketed out, clipping the lip of the closing cargo bay door.

The ship alerted them to a damaged starboard sensor array but otherwise seemed undamaged as it gyrated through a series of loops and zigzags, its evasion pattern randomly generated.

"Kill evasion, resume course to Tantalus, full speed."

Without weapons, the shuttle could only follow, and their ship, an execuyacht designed for speed and agility, would easily outrun the other vehicle.

It tried to hail them, but Fred blocked the signal. Then he turned to Kate. "Are you all right? You took a beating back there before I got a hold of you." He jerked his thumb at the corridor behind them.

She gingerly felt her ribs. "I think I broke something. Hurts to breathe."

He checked the increasing distance between them and their pursuers. "Can it wait until we lose them?"

"Sure. Won't they call the patrol?"

Fred shrugged. "Eventually, after they consult with corporate. They won't like admitting that a pair of mutaclones escaped from the factory." He grinned at her.

She grinned back, wincing with each breath.

He didn't like her pallor. "Lean back in your chair," he said. "Nanostim tendril analysis on copilot," he traked to the ship computer.

"Good idea," Kate said. "I'm pretty sure I have a cracked rib." She gasped as she leaned back. "This one is swelling, and I feel a bump." She held her hand below a breast. "I can't even lift my arm."

He saw tendrils from the co-pilot's chaise infuse her, right through the allsuit. An image appeared on screen of her ribcage fracture. The two ends of the bone were completely separated, one end in the thoracic cavity.

"Breathe very slowly," he said.

"Fifth vertebrosternal compound internal fracture," she said. "That'll puncture my lung if it's not repaired."

Sweat popped out on his forehead. He realized she was soaked in sweat. He glanced at the rearward sensors. Their pursuers had turned back. "Ship, medicoon."

A diagram appeared, a schematic of the ship, the medical cocoon highlighted. From its position, it appeared to be housed within the sanistall.

"Medicoon won't work," she gasped. "You'll have to open me up to set the bone. Only way to do it."

"But I don't know how to do any of that."

"I do. I'll guide you. Lay me flat in this chaise." Her face was white with pain, and sweat poured off her.

He stretched out the chair laterally, pushed aside his own so hers would fit. He was glad he didn't have to move her.

"The condichair can anesthetize me and even separate the flesh, but you have to set the bone. I'll link with the condichair. Ready?"

He nodded.

"First, the allsuit."

He ran his finger down her sternum, and the allsuit split along that line. Then he made similar lines out to her shoulder from her neck, and from her solar plexus to her side. He peeled back the fabric. Beneath the breast, livid bruising purpled a hand-sized patch of skin. He noted the perfectly-formed breast and again five thousand copulation positions crowded into his mind.

"Now underneath. It all has to be sanitized."

Pushing aside the simumems, he ran his finger down her side, and then did the same to the arm to remove the allsuit fabric there. He was grateful that it was a uniseam allsuit, or he'd have had to reposition her to remove her clothing.

More nanostim tendrils extruded from the chair and sank into the flesh up and down her side. A bundle of them bunched up on either side of the broken rib, the lump of bone visible, protruding like an angry knot.

"All right." Kate gasped sharply. "Local anesthetic." She relaxed visibly, her face smoothing. "Put your hands on the chair so they can be sterilized."

He did so, and the tendrils swarmed over his hands briefly.

"On the count of three, the tendrils will open an incision below the rib. You'll need to put your fingers in, grasp the bone on both sides of the break, pull them apart, and fit the ends together. There'll be some blood, but the tendrils will constrict most of the blood vessels. Get a firm grip. The bones will be slippery because of the periosteum. Stand beside the chaise for better leverage. Ready?"

Fred stood beside her, hands poised, his heart in his throat. "Ready."

"Three, two, one."

Tendrils pulsed around the bruising, and a three-inch gap split the skin. Red speckles dotted the pink and purpled flesh. He thrust his two index fingers into the incision, quickly finding the break, and put his thumbs to the bone on the outside to grasp the rib ends.

"Now pull them away from each other and then align them."

He was surprised how easily they spread. They wanted to spring back into place. He aligned their ends. "They're in position."

"Now ease them toward each other."

He brought the two ends together slowly, the tendrils slithering around his fingers like angel hair pasta.

She gasped. "Keep going," she whispered.

He eased them into position.

On screen, the two ends of bone looked aligned.

"You did it."

He withdrew his fingers and dared to breathe.

The tendrils holding the skin apart eased the two flaps together, and more tendrils swarmed the wound site, then withdrew. Blue-black bruising still blotched the area beneath her breast, but the angry lump was gone.

Kate, he saw, had lost consciousness. Her breathing was smooth and regular, and her vitals on screen were green normal. The tendrils continued to slither around the rib, the image on screen showing their rebuilding the bone.

Sleep was what she needed, he knew. Nutrients, calories, and fluids would be supplied by the conditioning chair through the tendrils. The healing would take time and rest, and with a little tendril acceleration, she might be fully healed in a month, not the usual two months.

Her clothing still peeled back, she looked ravishing. Images of their coupling surged into his mind, testosterone surged into his system, and the bulge in his allsuit surged in size.

Fred pushed the images out of his mind and found a blanket to cover her, pleased at the peaceful look on her face.

How does she know all that? he wondered. No clone was ever given a full medical education in uterpod. The didactics might be imparted, but the multilineal contextual decision-making needed for diagnosis and intervention were far beyond current nanostim development.

How did I know all that? he wondered. Back at the dormicube, when the corpreaucrat had come to the door with secuguards looking to reclaim company property, Fred had rendered all three of them unconscious with a few swift blows. Further, he'd intended to knock them unconscious, his awareness providing him the information he needed to kill them as well. Such knowledge might be imparted didactically through in-uterpod nanostim programming but the multilineal contextual decisions could only be absorbed through rigorous training and practice.

When did I ever practice killing? Fred wondered.

When did Kate ever practice medicine?

\* \* \*

The conversation that Dr. Sarina Karinova had with Fadeyka Andropovich was disconcerting for its similarities to a conversation she'd had just a few days before.

Sarina wasn't averse to doing such an interview again, but given her personal circumstances, she was hard pressed to concentrate. The insurance company will pay for the damaged clinic, she reassured herself. The police will catch the perpetrators, and I'll be able to return home, she thought. They'll find Anya soon, Sarina kept telling herself, fingering her wife's ring on her pinky.

She'd agreed to the interview as much for the distraction as the professional interest. And of course they were paying her usual rates plus hazard incentive. The latter had puzzled her. When asked, she'd been told it was retroactive to the interview with the Premier's daughter, Doctor Tatiana Satsanova.

For the interview with Admiral Andropova's son, Sarina had company: Feodor Luzhkov. Initially she'd questioned his presence. "I'm here to observe, Doctor Karinova," he'd said, when asked.

"To insure I'm safe."

Feo had simply smiled.

She'd given strict instructions as to where he would sit and how he would act. He would be introduced as a member of palace security. Despite her every effort to mitigate the presence of a third person, Sarina knew at the onset that his being there was going to skew the interview.

"What is your name, please?" she asked the young man once he was seated.

"You've got my file," Fadeyka said. His marbled Roman face atop the ramrod-straight posture swiveled toward her. "Don't tell me you don't know."

"For the purposes of the recording, Captain Andropovich."

Despite his non-active status and his dishonorable discharge from the navy, he merited being addressed by his last highest rank. The young man's gaze went to the corners of the room, as though he looked for the cameras. Then his eyes alighted on Feodor, though he sat at the edge of the interviewee's range of vision. "Your mutaclone is recording this?"

"What is your name, please?"

"Captain Fadeyka Andropovich, retired," the young man said. "Are we done yet?"

Sarina saw it was going to be a difficult interview. "You're certainly welcome to leave at any time. You consented to this interview, Captain Andropovich. You may withdraw your consent at any time simply by leaving. That is your prerogative. Shall we begin?"

Fadeyka waved a hand half-heartedly.

She didn't need his avid participation and hadn't been expecting it. "Tell me, Captain, what might be the reason for your presence today?"

"I'm here so I don't go to prison."

"Could you elaborate, please?"

He sighed. "The conditions of my parole specify that I live at home with my mother, Admiral Zenaida Andropova. She's about to turn me out of house and home for a few shady business transactions. If I don't live there, the Federal Parole Board will send me back to Brygidki for the remainder of my five-year parole. I think she's grasping at straws by having you examine me, but if it keeps her from booting me out the door, then I'm happy to oblige."

"Your tone of voice indicates the contrary, Captain."

"Really? I can't imagine why. I've been poked and prodded and psycho-fucking-analyzed so much over the past five years that no deep dark corner of my psyche hasn't been illuminated brilliantly and all its corpulent rot vented to some balloon-head like you. Of course, I'm not happy to be here."

"You can call me whatever you like after you leave, Captain, but if you'd like this interview to continue, the sobriquets will cease immediately."

"Yes, Doctor. My apologies."

If he hadn't at least mimicked appropriate contrition, she'd have sent him out the door. "And after all these interventions—among the most advanced available to modern medicine—you've exhibited continued incorrigibility. Why would that be?"

"As I suggested to my mother, perhaps my criminal behavior is genetic, a congenital flaw."

"Inherited? Or the sequela of some teratogen?"

"Eh?"

"You know exactly what I'm asking."

"Of course I do, but your mutaclone over there doesn't."

"So which were you referring to?" She hadn't known she'd be practicing dentistry too.

"I was referring to a genetic flaw, simply as a means to blame my mother for my difficulties. Rather Freudian of me, wouldn't you say? But some other factor might also be at work. Anything to deflect my having to take responsibility."

"Might that be the reason for your continued incorrigibility?"

"It might." He shrugged.

"How is your mood?"

"Fine."

"Describe your inner emotional state right now, Captain."

"I feel mildly anxious, but confident that this interview won't damage me irreparably."

"Save the sarcasm for later, Captain. How about your appetite?"

"I eat, I drink, I shit, I piss."

She shot him a look, about to terminate the interview.

"Sorry. You didn't deserve that."

"Thank you for the apology. Follow it up with action, Captain, or this interview is over. How much interest do you have in food?"

"None whatsoever. Mother complains I eat like a hamster."

"Is it lack of interest, lack of appetite, no enjoyment, or does it taste bad?"

"Lack of interest and no enjoyment."

"You mentioned a little anxiety. Any episodes of severe anxiety?"

"In what way?"

"Chest pains, difficulty breathing, sweating, racing pulse, feeling frantic?"

"Never had any of those ever, as I recall. In fact, I'm somewhat surprised I feel any anxiety at all."

"Why would that be?"

"Nothing bothers me. Never has."

"The prospect of spending—" she consulted her notes on her corn—"four and a half years in solitary at Brygidki doesn't bother you?"

"I guess that's what I'm anxious about. Not my idea of an idyllic afternoon."

"How is your concentration?"

"Never been better."

"And your motivation?"

"I don't want to do anything. I do it because I have to. Mother says do this, and I do it. She says do that, and I do it."

"And how is your sleep?"

"I sleep fine, but my mother swears otherwise. Complains she hears me up at all hours. I go to bed, I sleep, I wake up, I feel rested. What more is there to it?"

"No difficulty falling asleep?"

"None whatsoever. I have a guiltless conscience."

"No difficulty staying asleep?"

"None. No nightmares either."

"My next question, thank you. And how about dreams?"

Fadeyka shook his head, a question in his gaze. "I can't remember the last time I had a dream."

"How many hours you sleep per night?"

"Two to three."

She waited for elaboration. "Seven nights out of seven?"

He nodded.

"Never more than that?"

"Never. Doctor Pablov thought that odd as well, but then he was only interested in milking my mother for her money. Why buy the cow just to get a little milk, eh?"

She ignored the jibe, noting the somewhat tangential direction his thoughts had taken. "And your memory, how is that?"

"Perfect."

She did a quick mental status check, asking about date, time, place, name.

"I'm oriented times four, believe me."

"I have a series of questions regarding unrealistic thoughts. I don't think you're experiencing any of these, but I need to ask. Seeing things other people don't see? Hearing things other people don't hear?"

He shook his head to both, giggling.

"Are people following you? Plotting your downfall? Any cameras in the walls? Microphones in the plants? Chips in your head?"

"Other than the ones actually there, no."

She smiled slightly. "Any special powers? Can you put thoughts into other people's minds? Pick thoughts from their minds?"

He shook his head.

"Are people putting thoughts in yours? Are you being controlled remotely by the Ruskies?"

He shook his head.

"And lastly, did you just arrive from Heaven on a double-decker spaceship?"

"Coach or first-class? Direct flight or stopover in purgatory? No, Doctor, none of that."

"Any thoughts of suicide?"

"No, never."

"Any suicide attempts? Any family history of attempts? Any family history of seeing a psychiatrist, using a psychiatry cocoon, being hospitalized for a psychiatric condition?"

He shook his head.

"Any thoughts about hurting other people?"

He shook his head.

"There are plenty of instances in which you've done so."

He spread his hands, pursed his lips, and scratched his face.

"So you've never had thoughts about hurting someone, you've never planned to do so, and you've never acted in such a way as to injure them?"

"No, absolutely not," Fadeyka stated emphatically. "I merely lightened their bank accounts by supplying them with goods and services under entirely consensual terms."

"And what about the extortion?"

"The pressures building up in their bank accounts were far too great for them to bear. I couldn't conscientiously allow their anguish to continue. They just didn't know they were anguished."

"That's a load of dreck. Would you like to try again?"

"I set out to enrich myself without consideration as to whose money it was or how I did it."

"And now you're telling me what I want to hear."

"All right, all right. I spent my days and nights plotting how I might best exploit all my customer's vulnerabilities and filch every last galacti from them until I'd scoured every resource from their entire estates. I once bilked a parliament member of her penthouse suite with a view of the palace, and then I lived there for a week before I sold it to someone at half its worth. I schemed and contrived to ensnare anyone and everyone I could, and had fun doing it."

"Any thoughts of physical assault?"

"None, except flights of fancy on occasion."

"Of what?"

"Murder, just to see what it felt like. But I've never actually wanted to kill anyone. I've never cared for anything so much that I'd kill someone over it. I just don't care."

And that, more than anything, was the impression that resonated with Dr. Sarina Karinova long after the interview concluded and Captain Fadeyka Andropovich had left.

He just didn't care.

As she reviewed his genetic profile, the same chromosomal smoothing she'd seen in Tatiana Satsanova's genome was immediately apparent. Sarina looked up, hours later, realizing she'd sat there in a fugue, the genalysis results on her corn, without moving, the whole time.

I don't know what I'm looking at, she realized. She knew what she was looking at, but she didn't know what its larger implications were.

A general practitioner with some extra coursework and a year of interning on an asteroid mutaclone factory, Sarina had too little experience to say definitively what she fervently prayed was not the case.

"I have to consult with a colleague," she told Feo, approaching him at his desk outside the Premier's office the next day.

"I'd like to assign an escort, if I may?"

"What kind of escort?"

"One with hand-to-hand combat skills."

She stared at him for a moment. Sarina thought of her wife, of whom nothing had been heard. Oh Anya, she thought, biting her lip, fingering her wife's ring on her pinky. "Expecting trouble?"

"Rather," Feo said dryly. "You'll need protection. Also, I want you to have this." He pulled a box from a desk drawer and pushed it across the polished surface toward her.

A handheld genalyzer, Sarina saw. "Feo?" she asked.

He raised an eyebrow.

"What's going on?"

\* \* \*

The assembliclones stood in an orderly row at the conveyance, their arms whirling in a blur.

Danil Bagdanov kept a close eye on them for any slowing, the pace critical to their production quota. Specifically designed for this work, the assembliclones sprouted six arms from each side, pairs of ribs from the thoracic spine fused into clavicles.

Their backs to him, the six overlapping sets of latissimus, dorsi, and trapezius muscles flexed in rhythmic complexity, each arm completely independent of the others. The uppermost set perched atop the spine possessed the greatest range of motion, but the lowest-most set was closest to the work and tended to move faster, just above waist-height. These assembliclones had arm lengths adapted to their position along the thorax, growing increasingly shorter the closer they were to the lumbar.

Danil sweated just watching them, their fluid motions requiring great dexterity and concentration. Additional neurocerebellar tissue gave their heads a bulge at the base of the neck, making their craniums look smaller, their kinesthetic intelligence unmatched in other mutaclone lines.

Danil was worried they wouldn't be able to keep pace with the increased quotas, corporate having insisted on increasing the conveyor speeds. The first three days had gone past without incident, other than some complaints of joint pain. Danil had given them infusions of anti-inflammatories, adjusting the condicoon settings before retiring them for the night.

Today, the fourth day of the increased quotas, Danil could see that they were beginning to falter. Subtle signs—a glance over the shoulder, a wrinkled brow, an escaped whine—indicated that the pace was too fast.

The sorting—picking out less-than-perfect fruit as it whistled past on the conveyance—wasn't itself difficult, but the pace was taking its toll, each assembliclone expected to cull through five thousand fruits per minute at an error rate of less than one percent.

Rumor filtering down from corporate indicated a new assembliclone was being considered, one with an eye for every limb, six eyes down the side of the face, with independent hand-eye neurophysio interface assemblies. With independent assemblies, Danil reasoned, they could use each hand with fewer decisions being processed at the cortical level.

The fruit itself gengineered to perfection, the imperfection rate was exceedingly low, and most of the fruit that the assembliclones culled had been damaged during picking. After culling, the crated fruit was scanned again for molecular integrity, the error rate reported to Danil and his supervisor. So far today, the error rate had been within acceptable limits, but toward the upper end of that range. His crew could usually keep it below half the acceptable limit.

Seeing those little signs of distress, Danil stepped off his lookout, an elevated platform not unlike a lifeguard tower, and slid down the ladder to the floor. He approached Tami, the eldest of his crew, his most trusted and reliable assembliclone, five years out of the uterpod, her arms awhirl as the conveyance whipped past.

"How you doing, girl?"

She threw him a glance and a grin. "Keeping up, but barely. This pace is killing me, boss."

"Yeah, I can see it. How's the inflammation?"

"Hurts like hell, boss."

Always one to minimize her distress, Tami wouldn't say if it weren't so. Danil considered her age. Twelve hours per day for five years straight was nearly twenty-two thousand hours. Twenty-five was considered the industry optimum. That's when the assembliclones tended to require increasing amounts of care, and when they became more expensive to treat than to replace. Tami still had a good year left, if the pace didn't dislocate one of her twelve shoulders first.

"I'm going to have a thorough arthroanalysis done on your shoulder. You're culling at six thousand per minute right now. I don't like the toll it's taking."

"Thanks, boss." She winked at him, nary a pause in her work.

Back up on his lookout, he traked a request for an arthroanalysis. Next week was the earliest slot, he saw with dismay, the other crews experiencing similar difficulties.

The next morning, at shift change, a com awaited him. All arthroanalysis requests were being denied. The new six-eyed assembliclones were to be phased in as the one-eyed ones began to fail their quotas.

"What are they going to do with all the old assembliclones?" Danil asked his coworker as they ambled toward their workstations.

"What do you think? Recycle 'em. Clone mush pie."

Tami's third left shoulder popped out of place an hour into the shift, and the conveyance screeched to a halt. One arm out of twelve hung limp at her side.

A six-eyed assembliclone was brought over. "Here you go, Danil. I'll take Tami over to the recycler."

"Ronald, I'd like to do that. Can you watch the line while I take her over?"

Ronald looked at him skeptically. "No emo, got it?"

"No emo," Danil said. He led Tami toward the recycler, a huge maw with blades as thick as his arms criss-crossing the aperture. "You've served me well, Tami."

"Boss not like Tami?"

"Of course I like you, always will. It's time, that's all. We all have our time. Yours came sooner than either of us wanted."

"Time for Tami." She hung her head. "Good boss, Danil. Tami grateful." She glanced at the maw with its giant blades.

He saw how she tried to hide her fear. "It'll be quick. Lay down here and close your eyes."

She did as he bade her, her head toward the maw.

Faster that way, Danil knew, having done this for others. He turned on the machine and it clunked away.

Danil didn't understand why his face was wet.

# Chapter 5

"Fred, wake up. We're being hailed."

His eyes snapped open, his first thought: Ukraine patrol.

"Garbage scow Zelazny Six to unidentified craft, are you there, over?"

Fred realized he'd heard the same voice in his dream. "On screen."

A face materialized, the heavy jowl covered with a thick, black beard, the brow and head of hair equally dark and thick. "Captain Kyrylo Voloshyn. Just call me Kiri. We have a thruster solenoid that's acting up. Got a spare aboard?"

Funny he would ask. Just before sitting down and drifting off, Fred had done a full inventory of their vessel. A four-person commuter model, the execuyacht had enough fuel to get them to Tantalus and no further, food enough for two people for two weeks, and about enough room for four people to travel, albeit in fairly cramped conditions. The one stateroom with two bunks required four people to sleep in shifts. One sanistall, a two-seat galley, and a miniscule cargo hold, along with only two chaise seats in the cockpit, made for cramped accommodations all around. Searching the yacht after Kate had fallen asleep, Fred had discovered a small cache of spare parts in the cargo hold, and among the items was a spare thruster solenoid.

How he'd known it on sight, he couldn't have said. "Uh, sure do, Captain Kiri," Fred said. "Adjusting course, permission to come along-side?"

"Ah, bless! Permission granted. Thank you. So inconvenient to have one go out. Replacement must've been defective. And you are?"

We're clearly mutaclones, Fred thought, seeing no reason to hide the fact.

"Frederick and Katherine Hubako, of Tantalus," Kate said.

"Well met, and thank you, Fedey and Katya." Captain Voloshyn tipped his hat, and the screen went black.

Fred traked the autonav to coordinate with the garbage scow autonav.

"How do you feel?" he asked Kate.

She nodded. "Much better. I used the sanistall and had a bite while you slept. You hungry?"

He smiled and nodded, not lacking for calories or nutrients, just lacking the sensation of a full stomach.

"I'll get it," Kate stepped around his chaise, using his shoulder to balance, and slipped into the galley.

He'd seen her wince, but he could tell it was momentary.

She returned with a plate and set it in his lap.

He ate heartily, having skipped breakfast, and she stood beside him, her hand on his shoulder while he did so. He could feel her warmth, and felt warmed by it too. He liked the feel of her hand on his shoulder.

He checked their course as they came alongside the garbage scow, finishing the sandwich. "Thanks," he told her, giving her a brief smile.

He rose to get the solenoid. All ships carried a spare, the part easy to replace but prone to failure. It's the twenty-ninth century, and we can mod our bods to our liking, but we can't manufacture reliable engine parts, he thought, bemused.

At the airlock, waiting for it to cycle, the dark and hairy Captain Voloshyn visible through the portal, Fred wondered where they'd go from here, Tantalus not a viable option.

The door slid aside, Voloshyn struck the solenoid from Fred's hand and shoved a blaster into his face. "Cooperate and you won't get hurt."

Fred saw himself bat the gun away and put two knuckles into the larynx. He knew he could do it. He didn't know how he'd come by that knowledge or training. And he knew it wouldn't help him to wonder. "All right, just don't hurt us. Whatever you want." He began to sweat.

Two crew slipped past them, and behind Fred, Kate gasped. "Frederick, what's happening?"

"Just cooperate, Katya," he said over his shoulder.

"Wise choice, Fedey," Voloshyn said. "This way."

They were herded into the garbage scow, down corridors splashed with telltale signs of past loads, the air thick with miasma and rot.

"What do you want? Ransom?" Fred said over his shoulder, making sure they brought Kate along the same route. He knew what they had to be thinking, and he prayed they had other priorities. Or he'd have to kill them.

"Shut up, Fedey," said a male, whose cough had the gurgle of deep infection.

They were taken to an empty refuse bay, the stench overpowering. Fred didn't see any evidence of previous killings, but then, a hold full of refuse might conceal thousands of bodies. Several thousand metric tons might fit in this bay alone, he estimated.

"That's a comfortable ship you arrived on," Voloshyn said, herding them toward the middle, one of his crew keeping watch from the hatch. "Where'd you come from? Nothing out here except that asteroid. What is it, a Genie-All factory?"

Fred had noted Voloshyn was limping. Old injury or current pain? he wondered. "Listen, we lied. I'm Fred and this is Kate. We're mutaclones. We escaped from that factory. The ship is all we have. But we can work for you. One of your crew is sick. Kate's a doctor. She can—"

"A clone doctor?" Voloshyn laughed. "You look like whores, the both of you. Turn around!"

Kate glanced at him, and Fred shrugged.

Obediently, he turned, thinking, this is it. It's all over. A few brief hours off the asteroid, a few hours of freedom, and now we're dead.

Voloshyn tied his hands behind his back, and then tied his ankles. Doing the same to Kate, he laid them both on the floor, facing away from each other, and tied their wrist and ankle bindings together.

"You'll both fetch a steep price on Marseilles." Finished, Voloshyn stood. "No one's to touch these two on pain of death," he told the guard.

"No sampling the merchandise?"

"The less they fetch, the less you get. The difference comes out of your share." Then he was gone.

The floor against Fred's face was covered with a thick layer of organic muck. The stench clotted his nostrils, and the feel made him nauseous. But I'm alive, he thought, relieved.

He saw Kate was laying on her right side, her wound on the left. There was a wild look to her eyes he didn't like. "Holy mother of God, Fred, what are we going to do?"

He didn't know. The one advantage of having his wrists and ankle bindings tied together was how easily he could reach his ankle bindings. He glanced toward their one guard. "Let me see if I can get my bindings off, and then tell him you have to use the bathroom." From the angle, it didn't appear their guard could see Fred's hands.

"At least we don't have to worry about being intercepted by Ukraine patrols," Kate said. "How are we getting off this scow?"

Fred grinned. "Most scows carry their own tug. Sometimes, scows like this simply jettison their loads into the nearest primary, and they use their tug boats for that."

"But why?"

"Tugs have lot more acceleration and are much more maneuverable. If they get caught in a gravity well, they can get out a lot easier."

"So what do we do, walk right up to Captain Voloshyn and ask, 'Can we borrow your tug for the rest of your life?'"

Fred grinned, relieved to hear the humor. He worked the rope around his ankles. Thankfully, it wasn't shrinkrope, which shrank when pulled. Their guard was yawning, occasionally scratching himself, playing with his blaster, but paying them no mind, glancing their direction once in a great while. The rope chafing him, Fred worked enough slack to get his fingers on the rope, and slowly untied himself. He nodded to Kate.

"Hey, hey you," she said, calling over her shoulder. "I need to pee. Help me to the bathroom, would you?"

"No evacutubes here, bitch. Just wet yourself."

"If I do that, I'll get a rash, and there goes your share. Help me to the corner, at least. Be a gentleman."

"All right, but if you do anything, he gets it." He came over from the hatch warily.

Fred watched him, his ankles and wrists behind him, covered with loose rope.

"I'll untie your ankles, but your wrists got to stay tied." The guard stepped to Kate's side and knelt.

She made a feeble attempt to stand. "Help me up, please."

The guard put one hand under her arm.

Fred leapt, caught the blaster with one hand, the neck with his other, and the groin with his knee. The guard collapsed into the fetid muck, fetal.

While Kate held the gun on him, Fred tied the prisoner, and then ripped a strip from the ankle of his allsuit to gag him. Trussed and tied, the guard wasn't going anywhere. Fred calculated the angle and cold-cocked him. The guard went limp.

"Come on," he said, heading for the hatch.

"You'll have to teach me how to do that," Kate said, following him.

Fred guessed where the tugboat would be moored. How he knew these things, he couldn't say. The corridors were relatively empty, the security cams few and easily avoided.

At the boarding hatch to the tugboat, Fred examined the launch interface. Chances were good the bridge had an override. He'd have to tunnel into the scow's programming, disable the bridge override, kill the alerts, and launch the tug. Once aboard, they could outrun the garbage scow, easy.

And where to from there? Fred wondered. He didn't know.

Fred put his eye to the retinal uplink, decrypted the on-board security system, its encryption basic and easily hacked, and found the bridge override. And just to help distract the crew, Fred thought, let's cause a ship-wide failure in the electrical, environmental, and propulsion systems.

"On three, get aboard the tug," he told her.

"Might be helpful if I learned how to do that, too," she said. "Where'd you learn all those tricks?"

He shrugged, not knowing. "Three, two, one, go!" As he decoupled the tugboat, he let loose the viral subroutine into the ship's programming.

The lights died, and Fred leapt through the hatch and into the tug, the vacuum of space sucking at his allsuit as the two ships separated.

\* \* \*

Dr. Sarina Karinova introduced herself to the man across from her.

"And I'm Doctor Oleksandr Motruk, Senior Researcher here at the Institute of Mutaclone Studies. Please, have a seat."

She settled herself in the small sitting area to one side of his desk, the furniture quaint and comforting. "This is Leon." She gestured vaguely over her shoulder, dismayed by his hulking presence. She'd taken an instant dislike to her "escort" at the moment of introduction, and his tagging along wherever she went was beginning to grate on her. Sarina hadn't been allowed to leave the palace grounds without him.

"You'll forget that we visited," Leon rumbled, smiling at Dr. Motruk through teeth that might have graced a shark's mouth.

"Uh, certainly," Doctor Motruk said, smiling nervously. "What have I done?"

"You haven't done anything, Doctor. I'm here to gather information on how mutaclones develop after they're whelped."

"I'd say you're in the right place. That's what we do here at the Institute—we study and suggest improvements for post-uterpod development. What would you like to know?"

"How long, typically, between parturition and full integration?"

"Depends on the mutaclone, its environment, its pre-parturition nanostim interventions, and its genetic potential. A mutaminer might adapt splendidly within a day to its environs; bred for brute strength, they have relatively small brains, aren't burdened with a thick cortex, don't need to acquire sophisticated social skills, and have a relatively brief and simple nanostim regimen. An escoriant is likely to take years; bred for intimate relations, they have regular-sized brains with a healthy cortex, ultimately will acquire some highly sophisticated social skills, and have an extensive nanostim regimen whose focus is to enhance their kinesthetic intelligence."

Sarina had seen such escoriants at dinner parties and other formal events, standing to the sides of the room, their eyes on their patrons, their inflated bosoms heaving with anticipatory desire, their clothing scant. High levels of gonadotropins seemed to slough off them and infuse the air with pheromones. Sarina didn't attend too many events like that. "In the latter case, where sophisticated social skills have to be acquired, how long does that usually take?"

"Again, it depends, Dr. Karinova, but it can be years before such a specimen is considered at or near its full potential. Perhaps it's best to consider in context, given that mutaclones have a lifetime course of development, like their normavariant counterparts. Yes, we have significant sensitive periods in our earlier years, but we never stop growing."

"For a mutaclone of fair sophistication, what might generally be considered an adequate period of development?"

"Such as an escoriant? Five years to acquire an adequate set of skills, ten years to achieve a significant degree of sophistication."

"Can you give me an example of social sophistication?"

Doctor Motruk shrugged. "How to insult people without their knowing it."

"Ah, yes, charm school basics. Why isn't more done in uterpod with nanostim neuralinguist interventions?" She thought she knew, but wanted to hear his explanation.

"It's simply too difficult to recreate in the virtualab the subtle social interactions that take place in real life. *In situ* is the best learning environment, and we haven't found a way to clone that, yet."

"So, going back to early post-parturition development, what are the major indicators to the casual observer that a mutaclone has just come out of the uterpod?"

Dr. Motruk smiled. "Most people see those indicators right away. Don't you have mutaclones at home?"

"I spent a year interning at a mutaclone factory, Doctor, so my wife and I elect not to use them. We had them when I was a child, but I had concerns other than noting subtleties of behavior."

"The first thing that's apparent is the lack of affect. Their faces are almost absent of animation. Their expressions are stoic and flat, even in the face of duress. The second salient characteristic is their amotivation; they lack nearly all normal motivation, even for simple things, such as food. Oh, they eat, simply out of biological necessity, but there's no discrimination. They eat whatever supplies the required daily caloric and nutritional intake."

"What about sleep, Doctor?"

He waved that away. "They don't, effectively. In fact, we've undertaken a study to try to establish a causal link between the absence of a conscience and the minimal need for sleep. You and I, we encounter numerous social, ideological, and moral dilemmas throughout our day. We encounter them so frequently in fact, that most of us are barely aware of doing so. It's the ocean we swim in, as they say. The more dilemmas we encounter, in general, the more sleep we need to work these conflicts through and reduce our cognitive dissonance. It's no wonder that chronic stress leads to decreased energy and increased sleep. Mutaclones sleep between one to four hours per night, rarely more."

"What about concretion?" she asked.

"You mean their difficulty with abstraction? In fact, you've put your finger on the one factor that's correlated with all the others. No matter how intense the nanostim neuralinguist programming, mutaclones always emerge from the uterpod without the ability to process a concrete concept into its abstract counterpart. A simple test is usually sufficient to draw that out. How are an apple and an orange alike?"

"They're both fruit."

"And do you know what a clone will say? They're both round."

"So they'll think first of the shape rather than the category."

"The concrete before the abstract. Exactly."

"How's concretion related to lack of affect, lack of motivation, lack of appetite, lack of sleep?"

"Concretion and abstraction, keep in mind, are two stages on a continuum, not discrete, mutually-exclusive points. Affect is a function of externalizing an internal emotional state, and its translation moves through a complex set of arrays in the brain known as schemas. We can conceptualize and program the major emotional responses such as fear, happiness, pleasure, sadness, and anger, but the more subtle emotional responses are more difficult to encode and to interpret. Anxiety is easy to dissimulate into disapproval, the two emotions—how they are affected through our expressions and body language—are so similar that only sophisticated processing and abstraction can distinguish one from the other. For people to express such fine distinctions in their faces, in their voices, and in their postures requires not only abstraction, but a set of shared experiences within the cultural subgroup—"

"Simply so the expression is interpreted correctly," she interrupted.

"—Which is why cross-cultural communication is full of numerous pitfalls. Appetite is similar, in that mutaclones haven't had the palette of variety to develop distinctions in palate, if I may be so bold as to pun. We Ukraines love our beluga caviar. To us it is heaven on Tantalus. But those unsophisticated Parisians think we've lost our minds. More for us, I say, but a mutaclone fresh from a uterpod is focused on caloric intake, and doesn't care if it tastes like dog food."

"What about motivation?"

"In a mutaclone, a basal desire to function. A newly-decanted mutaclone barely knows what it's supposed to do. It will stand there and wait for instruction until the universe implodes—or some biological necessity requires something else. Keep in mind that we've typically stripped away its gonads. Nearly all mutaclones have hypogonadism built into their genes. The escoriant is one of the few models in which the gengineers leave the gonaticulating sequences intact or enhance them. So you might see hypersexuality in a nascent escoriant."

"You mentioned conscience in relation to sleep. Why is conscience so central to mutaclone development?"

"The acquisition of conscience, beyond all doubt, is the most difficult developmental milestone for a mutaclone to achieve. There simply isn't a nanostim neuralinguist intervention that replaces a firm, nurturing childhood. In the absence of a mechanism by which a mutaclone can internalize empathy, most mutaclones will attempt to fulfill their needs without regard for the wants and desires of others. And without regard for anyone's well-being except its own.

"Probably the most difficult psychiatric patient to be found," Dr. Motruk continued, "is the one with both mania and antisocial traits. He or she will attempt to meet every need to the wanton disregard of everything—society, the law, or other people. The reason first and foremost that they are difficult to treat is the lack of recognition that anything's wrong."

"In the absence of a mechanism, you said. What are the usual mechanisms?"

"The most important one is an empathic owner."

"One who's not cruel and abusive?"

"Certainly. But even an owner who's neglectful or absent can result in a clone's lacking the basic internal structures needed for empathy toward other living beings."

\* \* \*

"Ah! Zinny, come in! So good to see you. Please, have a seat."

Admiral Zenaida Andropova realized she missed her old friend, she and Premier Colima Satsanova having been close companions at the Academy. Colima had specialized in interstellar relations, while Zenaida had chosen naval command. Both had risen to the acme of their respective specializations.

The Premier chased her assistants from the office and escorted Zenaida to the sitting area. "Truly, Zinny, it's been far too long. Coffee, tea, something stronger? Not to worry, my friend, it's afternoon. A peppermint schnapps between friends isn't illegal! Please, no, it would be my pleasure to serve you. I'll get it."

Cherry-wood cabinets on either side held the memorabilia of a long reign behind their gleaming glasma doors, the office overlooking the palace lawns. In the distance, shielding veiled the city of Kiev. The thick carpet underfoot was so plush a person had to concentrate to keep from stumbling. Leather made from the hides of giant carmelopardalis bovines scented the room, each chair easily worth a year of Zenaida's salary. The desk was carved from a single chunk of Borealis conifer root, the trees so large a single one might supply all the lumber to build Kiev itself.

All these furnishings brought comfort to Zenaida. She did feel flustered by her friend's attentions, the warm, hovering manner just like the Colly of old. It had been a long time since Zenaida had felt this degree of welcome. "Thank you, Colly, you're magnificent. I can't tell you what a relief it is to be greeted this way, after what I've been through. It's been an absolute nightmare."

"Fadeyka, eh? No boy should put his mother through all that. How utterly disrespectful. But my saying his behavior is opprobrious helps you not at all, eh? How difficult for you, to remain supportive these five, terrible years."

Zenaida looked at the floor. "Forgive me, your Excellency, if I've let you down."

"Nonsense, Zinny. Look at me."

Zenaida felt compelled to raise her gaze.

"He let you down, not you me. Understood?"

Her directness gratified Zenaida. "Yes, Colly, thank you, but I should have disowned him long ago. And, and..."

No, not in front of the Premier! I can't!

And in spite of herself, Zenaida began to weep. She'd sworn to herself she wouldn't do this! And found she was helpless not to.

Colima's arms around her, Zenaida allowed herself to be comforted, not quite believing she'd let herself get so overwrought.

"Oh, Zinny, don't you worry. I'm your friend, it's what friends do. No, no, none of that, all right? You'd do the same for me, God forbid you'd have to! Oh, I'll tell you, Zinny, you and your son, me and my daughter, what a pair we make!"

"Your daughter? What's the matter with your daughter?"

"Seems minor, but I tell you, I think something's wrong. She's just not the same as a year ago. A month, two months ago, I noticed she was, well, depressed. You know, no verve or vigor. Listless and lifeless. And dismissive, and not just of me but everyone, even her own husband. I was so concerned I had Feo find her a doctor, but she refused to go! Stubborn girl. I know, she's twenty-eight, a Doctor of Gengineering, a brilliant scientist by all accounts, but to disregard her mother that way. Finally, Feo persuaded her to go. Quite bizarre, the results. Your Fedey, he started that way, didn't he?"

Zenaida grimaced and nodded. "He disappeared two months before Post Graduate, and I found him selling himself on the beaches of Marseilles."

"As bad as all that, eh? My Tatya is certainly pretty enough for that, looks as if she might have been gengineered directly from a goddess, but thank God, I caught her depression before she stooped so low. I'd be horrified if I had to go through a tenth of what that boy's put you through. And now he's been tampering with the grades at that college he's attending? Be done with him, Sister. Long past the time to have escorted him to the curb."

"Well, I think so, too, Colly, but there's one more thing I'd like to do. Have his genome examined."

"Not much can be done to repair his genes, is there? Usually only works before the age of seven, yes?"

"Something to do with plasticity," Zenaida replied. "I know, and it's probably hopeless, but at least I'll know why this happened, eh? And I was thinking, that doctor you had to bring into protective custody—"

"I swear I'll find out who did that, and blast them into the next galaxy. Kidnapping her wife and bombing her clinic like some Rusky mafia leader..."

In the sudden silence, Zenaida brought her gaze around to Colima, who'd frozen, her gaze fixed on the distance. "Colly, what is it?"

The Premier's gaze snapped to her face. "I have an idea, Zinny. Don't you worry. See Feo to get a hold of Doctor Karinova. Have Fedey examined thoroughly. I don't think it's hopeless at all. You've been diligent with him beyond all expectation. You're an exemplary mother, Zinny. I so admire how you've stuck by him all this time."

Zenaida found herself walking along a plushly-carpeted hallway at the Capitol, heading toward Feodor's office without much memory of how she'd got there. The Premier's praise had been fulsome to the point of disconcerting, and Colima had a knack for steering people the direction they needed to go, even if they thought otherwise. Especially if they thought otherwise.

"Feo!" Zenaida greeted him like an old friend, his tenure in Colima Satsanova's service having begun at the Academy, the future Premier's father vastly wealthy and insisting she accept Feo as retainer in spite of her objections.

Feodor Luzhkov was nearly seventy, Colima's and Zenaida's senior by twenty years, his discretion legendary. Attempts to suborn him inevitably backfired, his behavior unimpeachable, his weaknesses nonexistent.

"Doctor Karinova? Certainly. For Fadeyka? As you wish, Admiral," he said, his tone perfunctory.

She wasn't a novice to such conversations. "What is it, Feo?"

He cleared his throat, his eyes flicking to her face for a brief moment. "The Admiral is clearly concerned about her son."

Zenaida raised her eyebrow.

"His behavior has lifted the eyebrows of many influential people."

She pursed her lips.

"Leaving a sour taste in the mouths of many."

Her nostrils flared.

"The consequences so inadequate to the deeds as to leave the aroma of influence."

She was done with the innuendo. "Out with it, Feo."

He glanced around, as if he didn't know they were alone in his office. "The Premier is likely to face calls for impeachment."

"Over Fadeyka?" The blood drained from her face. "I had no idea! No, I can't let that happen. She doesn't deserve—"

"Zinny," Feodor said, patting her hand, "don't you worry. She's faced worse. It's the Rusky adherents in the Crimea who've orchestrated this effort to impeach her. And it's all based on fabrications."

"But if there were a sufficient number of substantiated threads in that fabrication, the parliament may vote to impeach anyway."

Feo shrugged. "And after a vote in parliament, the issue goes to the cabinet ministers, who are nearly all handpicked by Madame Satsanova. So don't trouble yourself on her account, Zinny."

"Even so, Feo. For God's sakes, where have I been? My head isn't just for sticking up my ass! I can't believe it's gone this far. Thank you, Feo." Admiral Zenaida Andropova took her leave, knowing what she had to do, whatever the results of the doctor's examination.

# Chapter 6

"That thing? You want to trade it in? I got a rowboat in back worth more than that!"

Fred was glad Kate dragged him away, the humiliating laugh following him out of the building and echoing in his head long after they left the space vessel dealership.

Fred and Kate stood on the tarmac at Alcheusk, both wondering how to get a hold of another ship. He was convinced the garbage scow would soon report their tug stolen, so they'd come to Alcheusk, renowned for its shady, used-ship dealers, hoping to trade it in for something slightly less conspicuous.

"It was a long shot," Kate said, looking their tugboat up and down.

"Problem is," Fred said, "this thing doesn't look like a tugboat for a garbage scow. It just looks like garbage." Dented, dinged, stained, and crusty, the tug looked ready for the scrap yard.

Kate met his gaze. "That's it! The great garbage dumps of Garlivka! We could sell it there, pick up an old junket that needs some work!"

"And who'd do the work?"

"Well…I'm good at surgery."

He snorted and shook his head. "Come on, let's go. I don't have any better ideas, so we might as well get off this rock."

They boarded, something niggling at Fred. Through the launch sequence and tower coms, Fred couldn't shake the idea that something was awry.

Once they were at escape velocity, the old tug clattering beneath them, Fred turned to her and asked, "How'd you know about Garlivka?" It was a conversation they'd started and stopped multiple times en route to Alcheusk.

Inevitably, one would ask the other, "How'd you know—" And though the other would search his or her memory, neither could summon the context in which he or she had learned about the topic.

Kate shook her head and shrugged, again.

"We'd better stop for fuel, soon," he said, seeing their fuel reserves getting low. His piloting was one such topic. He knew all of Ukraine and its two-thousand plus constellations, and a significant portion of their eastern neighbor's geography as well, but he couldn't have said how he'd acquired the knowledge. "You know, they'll eventually be able to trace us through those illicit fuel-depot hacks."

"Eventually," she said, nodding.

His ability to decrypt the security on just about any type of computerized piece of equipment was another such topic. With that ability, he'd filled their tank at no cost, the fuel-station transaction systems all computerized. Where he'd learned cryptology was a mystery.

After their escape from the garbage scow, they'd discussed the dangers they'd be facing.

"Anyone could decide to rape either one of us," she'd said flat out, articulating his worst fear. He was worried what such a rape would do to her, being so fresh from the uterpod. Himself, he'd be able to deal with it, or thought he might, anyway. At the asteroid factory, the staff had subjected him a variety of abuses, most of the normavariants contemptuous of their manufactured employees. As mutaclones, neither Fred nor Kate had any right to redress. The only time an owner was held accountable for abusing a mutaclone was when the treatment damaged some other normavariant's property.

And for either of them to retaliate—or even defend themselves—was tantamount to defiance. Owners might harm or kill their mutaclones if they so chose, to mutilate, rape, and dismember their property if that were their wish, to dispose of their property in whatever way it suited them, be there purpose or cause in it, or not. Owners could do whatever they wanted, for some imagined slight or none whatsoever, for any reason or no reason at all.

"And after we get another ship? What then, Fred?"

He'd grinned at her mischievously. "We'll pick an asteroid that's uninhabited, settle down, break out our Petrie dishes and test tubes, and bake ourselves a whole batch of our very own mutaclones."

They'd laughed for hours, but the question hung between them unanswered.

One fact Fred was sure of: Kate was unlike any mutaclone he'd ever encountered. He'd never known one with such sharp wit and where-withal right out of the uterpod. Having been a sector monitor for five years, where mutaclones matured in uterpod, he'd seen them being whelped and had guided them gently toward neonatal, too disoriented to know which way to go, and then had returned to his duties. He'd heard that in the neonatal pens, they weren't any more aware for weeks or months after being whelped. But once they could use the sanistall on their own, dress themselves, and feed themselves, they were shipped off to their prospective owners or off to auction.

But even then, Fred had observed, watching armies of newly-whelped mutaclones on the asteroid tarmac being marched aboard transport ships, they still looked stupid. Insensate, lacking any aware-ness of their surroundings, having little or no initiative, their stares dull and flat, their limbs hanging listlessly at their sides, their faces without expression.

Kate had been nothing like that even before the uterpod had spat her onto the lift. He'd watched her struggle inside the uterpod, terror and dismay contorting her features as she'd fought the tough, flexible derma, aware.

The one feature all the newly-whelped mutaclones didn't have. Awareness.

Fred glanced over at her and smiled.

"What?" she asked, looking somewhat embarrassed at his attention.

"I was just thinking how different you are from all the other mu- taclones. Alive even before you were whelped, while none of them exhibits a shred of liveliness until they're months or years out of the uterpod. I like that about you."

She smiled demurely. "Thank you," she said meekly.

"I imagine it must've been the same for Greg, when I was whelped. He said he could tell I was different. I guess I really didn't know what he meant until I met you."

"You're full of surprises," she said. "And I like that about you. He's right, you know. You *are* different."

"How would you know?"

That vacant look, the one she always had when she searched her memory, took a hold of her face again. She shook her head. "I don't know, but I do know."

I don't know, but I do know.

The whole conundrum of their circumstance.

"How do you suppose we find out?" Fred asked.

"I don't know," Kate replied, frowning at him.

\* \* \*

Dr. Sarina Karinova introduced herself and then gestured at her bugsplat. "And this is Leon."

"I'm Doctor Petro Chachula, Chief of Design here at Clones-For-All Industries. We have a clone to help with all your calamities."

She snorted at the company by-line, having heard their commercials a hundred times.

"You'll forget that we visited," Leon said, his smile sending a shiver down Sarina's spine.

"I see you've brought a calamity," Dr. Chachula said. "Not much I can do to fix those teeth."

Sarina sat at his bidding and accepted the small schnapps he offered. One of those acquired tastes that most newly-whelped mutaclones didn't have a palate for.

"How may I assist you, Doctor Karinova?"

"First, how might I obtain a mutaclone built to spec?"

"What are you in the market for? Another hundred thousand of him?" Dr. Chachula hiked a thumb in Leon's direction.

"In general, Doctor, say I wanted to malign my neighbor, and to do that I need a doppelganger of her?"

Dr. Chachula laughed. "I wish it were that easy. If you brought me a still, I wouldn't be able to replicate her. Even a vid wouldn't be sufficient either. What I would need would be a sample of her flesh, a full psychosocial history, and several thousand hours of vid. As precise as gengineering is these days, building a clone from an image or even reverse gengineering is still next to impossible. Once the genome is reverse-gengineered and the mutaclone is grown, then the nanostim neuralinguist interventions begin. And after that, there's no guarantee that your mutaclone will be mistaken for your neighbor."

"Why is that?"

"We humans have such incredible situational dependency that getting a mutaclone to mimic us with any degree of accuracy requires years of nanostim programming with nearly full-time *in-situ* modeling. Hasn't been done to any degree of efficacy and probably never will."

Sarina sighed, relieved he was able to defuse her worst fear before she'd even articulated it. "You're sure?"

"When you come home to your husband disturbed by something at work, he notices, doesn't he?"

"She, but yes," Sarina said.

"She instantly notices that slight change in your manner that you use to communicate something's wrong. Of course, she notices, probably more so being female, men usually not quite as intuitive. It's precisely those subtle changes discernable only to our intimates that are impossible to replicate within any sort of program. To do so, we'd need a camera to record the most private moments of a person's life. And no one's going to consent to that."

"No, no one would consent to that." Sarina chewed on the inside of her cheek.

"But something else is on your mind."

"I'd like the process described anyway, from raw DNA to usable mutaclone. If you wouldn't mind."

"Oh, not at all. I might bore snaggletooth there but he's fast asleep already."

She glanced at Leon, whose open maw invited mischief. She giggled at the thought.

"Now, there's a sublimated hostility that no mutaclone could imitate. Anyway, here at Clone-For-All Industries, we pride ourselves on crafting the finest fleshware possible for every customer's need. We're adamant that our development process be as organic as we can make it. This means tailoring the design to best suit the customer. For example, we have our stock templates: laborer, factory assembler, saniclone, groundster, phalangiform, escoriant, and then all the custom templates. On these basic frames, we can then specialize to the task at hand. A laborer might work well for a mutaminer, building clone, loadaclone, or simply a brute clone, which your friend Leon appears to be. A phalangiform might have multiple extensor hands on each limb, each hand filled with fingers so varied in shape, size, and range that its owner might task it with a variegated set of routines. We've even made models with thousands of nanotendrils on each phalange. A groundster might be customized to the terrain, having long gangly limbs for low gravity, or short, stubby, indefatigable legs for extremely high gravity. A saniclone might be specialized for dusting or scrubbing, one with light feathery phalanges, the other with caustic-proof dermas for durability."

"So you have a number of base models that might be customized to suit?"

"Exactly. And that's ninety percent of our business. The one or two that needs genetic customization is relatively rare."

"Tell me about those one or two clones."

"Here—" Dr. Chachula waved his hand, and an image appeared on Sarina's corn—"we have a titraclone." Multiple mammaries sprouted from a thick, generous torso, each mammary as perfectly formed as a peach. "Each mammary produces and extrudes a chemical compound ready to pipette into a solution. The beauty in this model is the innovative digestive system, designed to assimilate the most noxious of raw chemicals and channel them to the appropriate mammary.

"Now this—" he projected another image—"is the domestic variation, whose teats extrude standard household cleansers, including oven cleaner, the most caustic. Now, you notice they're both female, of course—"

"And quite voluptuous, besides."

"But they do come in male models as well. The number of homemakers requesting them with activated gonaticulating sequences is rather titillating. We've even had a few requests that the ejaculate be—"

"How often do you get requests for build-from-scratch models?" she interrupted, trying to put out of mind the images he'd conjured.

"Not often. Keep in mind that despite the advanced state of mutagenics, we're still in the infancy of discovering exactly what neuropeptide sequence articulates what specific characteristic. Thousands of neuropeptides located amidst several different strands might be responsible for the shape and size of something as simple as a fingernail. Think of it as a brick wall. Each brick provides a piece of the structure, and it's only through their aggregation that we get a brick wall. Each time we change the size of a particular brick, it introduces instability. Every time we build a mutaclone from scratch, we're trying to patch together a wall out of bricks of a million different sizes. Once we put all the bricks together, the chance of our assembling a stable wall is one in several billion.

"In other words, we might aggregate several billion zygotes from a stew of neuropeptide sequences, and we get anywhere from a dozen to a hundred viable mutaclones."

"From several billion?"

Dr. Chachula smiled. "And that's before they're gestated in the uter-pods. It's much easier to work from an existing line of viable pre-propagated clones, splice in the variants we want, and see if the result is viable."

"How many do you make of these pre-propagated variants?"

"That's the ninety percent of sales. There is one other category, made by a wholly independent affiliate of ours."

"Oh? What's that?"

"The straight clone. Someone takes them a tissue sample. They grow a replica. Completely unconscionable in my opinion. But it can be done."

"You're right, completely unconscionable."

\* \* \*

"Doctor Karinova," Feo told her, "I want you to ink this app."

On Sarina's com appeared his traked message, a clip indicating an attachment. She inked the attachment, and looked at him. "Ok, I've incorporated it. What does it do?"

"Emergency evacuation. If you have to leave the city, the planet, or even the constellation, activate the app, and a vehicle will appear within moments. This same app has been inked by the Premier and her cabinet, all the legislators, and all the top administration officials. Perhaps three thousand people on Tantalus have access to it. Your use of it is confidential. No one but me and my security staff will be alerted to its use. Every planet in Ukraine has a small fleet of yachts secreted on spaceports around the planet in case of emergency. Each ship is capable of transporting a person the width of the galaxy without re-fueling."

Sarina looked at Feo. "This is really serious, isn't it?"

"The Premier has asked me to provide you with the highest degree of protection possible. Do you need Leon's crèche-brothers? I can get you three more in moments."

She blanched. "Leon is quite enough, thank you." She looked at the app on her corn, hoping she never needed it.

"I hope you never need the app," Feo said.

"Just what I was thinking." Incorporated into all the other apps, she wondered how she would remember it was there.

"It's connected to your adrenocortex, so if there's any danger, it will flag you on your corn."

"So it'll remind me that it's available. You've thought of everything."

"The Premier really needs your help on this, Doctor Karinova."

Then he'd left.

Moments later, she received a trake from the lab with the imaging results. Sarina had requested the testing to ferret out any sequelae from Tatiana's bone loss.

For a few minutes, she stared at the results, dumbfounded.

There was no evidence that Tatiana had ever broken her wrist, and the analysis indicated an above-normal bone density. No evidence of incipient osteoporosis, at all. As if the condition had been removed from her genome. The results confirmed what she'd been thinking.

I'll have to tell Feo tomorrow, she thought, seeing how late it was already.

Sarina looked around the small suite buried somewhere in the palace, guest quarters for diplomats, she guessed, the suite richly appointed with silk brocade doilies, satin wallpaper, conditioning furniture, intelligent appliances. It had also come with three saniclones, one for cooking, one for cleaning, and one for overall household management. Sarina had dismissed them, of course, preferring to do all the work herself, but no matter how much she admonished them, they always returned when she wasn't there and cleaned the place until it was immaculate.

The other thing Feo had done was to divert her expenses to the administration. Now, when she ordered a hovertaxi, ate a meal in a restaurant, bought a suit, read a newsie, or researched a topic in a journavid, it was charged to the administration, and not to her personally. No amount of protest on her part could get Feo to change that.

"You're in this predicament because I asked you to examine the Premier's daughter. All your expenses will be taken care of until your wife is safe. Even if you want your family and your wife's family to travel here to Tantalus."

She'd let her in-laws know that Anya had been abducted, and she'd commed them every evening. The investigation appeared to have stalled, no leads or clues having turned up in either the kidnapping or the bombing. The police hadn't been told of Dr. Karinova's examination of the Admiral's son, Fadeyka, as thus far it appeared to be immaterial. If as Feo suspected the two scions had been compromised similarly, then the kidnapping and bombing may have been perpetrated by the same miscreant.

Oh, Anya! Sarina thought, dropping into an armchair, exhausted after her long day, feeling her despair rising inside her, hopelessness beginning to seep through Sarina's soul like some insidious cancer, eating away at her hope, its corrosive force chewing through her moral strength. She fingered her wife's ring on her pinky.

I have to eat, she thought, forcing herself from the chair. Its nanotendrils retracted into the fabric with a slurp, their massage keeping muscles toned. Adapted from early spaceflight technology, such musculoskeletal-conditioning fabric was incorporated into nearly all sitting or reclining surfaces, their conditioning similar to that of the condicoon, used almost universally for sleep.

Sarina dragged herself into the kitchen. The thermafreeze was kept full by the saniclones in spite of her admonition not to, and she saw they'd prepared several servings of her favorite meal, varenyky, a dumpling stuffed with potatoes, onions, ground beef, topped with sour cream. Looking among the servings, she saw piroshky, holubtsi, and blintz, each looking as delicious as the varenyky. She cursed the servants at the same time as she blessed them, knowing she didn't have the energy to prepare a meal herself.

Something her wife had always done for her.

Despair and hunger battled for her attention. Sarina heated up the varenyky, ravenous. She belched when she finished, and recalled

Anya's admonishing her for doing so. Sarina wished Anya were here to admonish her now, and Sarina bit back her tears.

\* \* \*

"Don't you feel like a fish in a fishbowl?" Dr. Tatiana Satsanova asked the young man sitting beside her.

She knew his name, of course. She wasn't sure what terrible things she'd done to deserve a seat next to someone with such a sullied reputation, but she decided not to let that bother her and to strike up at least the semblance of a conversation with him.

At such state dinners, she listened politely to the usual drivel, this one not much different from the hundreds she'd attended. During childhood and adolescence, Tatiana had been required to attend them. As an adult, she rarely accepted the invitations. And her mother, the Premier, invited her to a lot of state dinners.

Tatiana wasn't sure why she'd agreed to come to this one. Whatever it was in honor of, Tatya was sure it was important, just as the last one had been, just as the next one would be. A long line of dinners convened for causes so important that they faded into a background of other important causes, themselves a patchwork of important causes amidst a thousand other important causes, all conglomerated into a pastiche of important causes that her mother advocated so vociferously that Tatiana heard only the cacophony, and could never discern which her mother might favor.

During these dreadfully boring events, Tatiana's usual way to cope was to smile and nod, offer a polite word or two to her interlocutor of the moment, to focus on the diner beside her and her husband if he happened to be in attendance. She put her mind in neutral and let her thoughts burble away senselessly, and hoped none of the nonsense in her mind slipped inadvertently from her mouth.

Tatya looked around, diners gravitating toward their chairs along the impossibly-long dining table, extravagant porcelain and glistening crystal graced with gleaming silver and origami silk. Bouquets at intervals lent a touch of color to the glitter and glow, tapers sprouting erectly from their centers. The gold-print name card in front of the folded silk napkin held her maiden and married names in perfect balance, a combination she'd found unwieldy. In spite of her aversion to politics, she'd kept her mother's name, her relation to the Premier of Ukraine having its advantages.

"I always feel like a fish in a fishbowl, Doctor Satsanova," Fadeyka Andropovich replied, grinning mischievously. "And if they're not talking about me, it's because I've neglected to give them something to talk about."

"Oh?" Tatya said, raising an eyebrow. This is the Admiral's son, she reminded herself, who'd established quite the ribald reputation. "Why is that, Captain Andropovich?"

"What good is their attention if it isn't focused on me?"

Tatya tittered uncontrollably, a surge of desire flooding her. What a gadfly he is! She was quite certain her speaking with an incorrigible scandalmonger at an official state dinner would set her mother's soul on edge. Good! Tatiana thought, it's only what she deserves, after pestering me to see a doctor for the last month!

Tatya leaned his way and turned her face toward his. It was then that she noticed the fine classical lines to his marbled face, the perfect coif, the scent of apricot, and the glow of his sweet, blue eyes. She was torn between the lure of desire and the call of propriety. "A pity my husband couldn't attend this evening. A bit of a cough, he says."

"Does he like threesomes?" Fadeyka Andropovich replied. "Or just to watch?"

She wasn't sure whether to be offended, shocked, or titillated. The latter won out, her libido on the rise ever since her conversation with that doctor, the one whose clinic had been bombed. "You'd have to ask him. But the more important question is what *I* like." Her laughter was light and she'd wondered what her husband would think if he'd heard her reply.

Captain Andropovich laughed and lifted his glass to her. "Touché, Madame. A conversation to have in surroundings more amenable, wouldn't you say?"

She'd have done anything to be elsewhere. The thought of being elsewhere with such a handsome specimen as him hardened her nipples and flooded her vagina. "Most certainly, Captain. Are you unaccompanied this evening?" she asked him, seeing that the chair on his other side was already taken. "Given the circumstances, I'd have thought a voluptuous escoriant would've been available."

His gaze dropped to her bodice, her evening dress accenting her ample bust line. "I'd much prefer lively verbal intercourse with someone of your inestimable talents, Doctor. I find such conversation an invigorating prelude to other intimacies. Don't you agree?"

"Absolutely, Captain. Although I must say the exclusive male interest in the latter leaves me somewhat mystified." Her husband had always told her she had a lethal pair, a fact apparent in how avidly men's gazes followed her breasts, as the Captain's gaze followed them now. "Tell me, in your inestimable experience, why is that?"

"There is something else of interest?" His gaze flicked between her face and her breasts.

A rush of heat surged up to her neck. Tatiana threw a glance toward the head of the table, where her mother had just approached.

Like a sentinel, Premier Colima Satsanova just stood there, her presence commanding attention. The kind Tatiana wished she could draw. Not that she didn't want the looks her proud bodice usually got. She rather enjoyed the feel of the Captain's eyes on her breasts. She just wished he'd give some attention to her mind.

The room quieted, and cold replaced the warmth where his gaze had been.

Miffed that her mother had drawn his attention away, Tatiana met gazes with her mother and experienced a slight surge of pleasure when her mother's gaze landed on Captain Fadeyka Andropovich next to her with that slight widening of the eyes that often accompanied recognition.

And alarm.

As the only two unpaired adults at such a function, of course they'd been seated beside each other. What could be more natural? But Tatiana's satisfaction at seeing her mother's discomfort gave her a taste of that delicacy an epicure might find served only with haute cuisine.

The taste of her mother's displeasure. For what was bitter to one palate might be sweet to another.

And Tatiana awoke to the epiphany, as if she'd never attended such a function before.

Nag me to see a doctor! she thought indignantly, slyly placing her hand over the Captain's where her mother could see.

# Chapter 7

"Look, I'm not suggesting you empty the bank accounts of every last lonely widow on Tantalus," Kate was saying. "All I'm saying is we need money. We haven't got a galacti to our name, and unless you want to sell your pleasures to that same lonely widow, I don't know how we're going to earn any."

They badly needed money, and not just a little. Fred winced, thinking this was their first major difference of opinion. After three days aboard the tug they'd purloined from the garbage scow and two unsuccessful attempts to offload it, they were growing desperate. Their rations were beginning to thin, and so were their relations. Fred knew she was right.

The water tank had run dry the first day, and they hadn't discovered until afterward that the battered tug didn't have a recycler. All wastewater was vented to space, and Fred was positive they'd left a trail of ice crystals a kilometer wide containing their DNA. Neither had had a shower since, and they both were becoming somewhat aromatic. Fred was grateful they'd stopped showering, the space so tiny that privacy was impossible. They'd both had to shower practically in front of the other, the sanistall having no door. Neither did the excretory, which had posed additional challenges.

He had found some reprieve in sleep. They couldn't both fit on one stretched-out chaise, so Fred just slept on the floor, telling her she needed the condicoon nanostim for her still-healing rib.

"Every transaction is traceable," Fred said again. "And even if I skim a single galacti from fifteen thousand bank accounts, we've got fifteen thousand transactions leading right back to us."

"Well, why not just one account? It doesn't have to be some poor widow's, either."

Fred sighed, having argued this point already. "We won't know whose it is, is what I'm saying. And it's wrong. It's money that doesn't belong to us."

"I know, I know." Kate sighed and grinned at him. "For a mutaclone, you sure do have some strong principles."

"Thanks." He frowned at her, knowing they'd avoided the topic they really needed to discuss. He wasn't quite sure how to raise the subject, but the question went to the core of what they were doing out here, two escaped mutaclones, both possessing skills neither should have, both having contextual knowledge that current technology had no way of imparting. And what did that mean, exactly? How had they come to exist?

"Where are you from?" he asked suddenly.

"The planet—" Then Kate cursed. "I almost had it!" She sighed and looked at him. "Would you mind if I asked you a personal question?"

Fred smiled at Kate. "You're welcome to ask. I may decline to answer."

She shook her head. "That's what bothers me. You shouldn't have that response. It's too difficult to teach that kind of response to a mutaclone." She sighed. "All right, here goes. I'd like to ask about your libido."

"I've got one, if that's what you're asking."

"Well, yes, but…"

"But there's more you'd like to ask? Guess you'll just have to ask, and see what happens." He guessed she was as uncomfortable asking as he was talking about it. "A somewhat difficult subject."

"Indeed. So, uh, what's your orientation?"

"I prefer a female partner."

"And any attraction to the one currently in your vicinity?"

As though she's asking if I like her, he thought. The back of his knees ached with longing.

"I'm not asking whether you like me in particular, just whether you've experienced normal biological impulses."

"Have I thought about sex? At the rate of about once per minute."

"In other words, at intervals normal for a male."

Fred nodded. "Did you want me to deny it?"

She grinned. "No, but you've given me no indication of that except in an occasional glance and in the tremendous amount of embarrassment you've shown with our utter lack of privacy."

He looked at the tiny space available to them and nodded.

"All escoriants, and all mutaclones without gonaticulating mods, inevitably behave without restraint and entirely according to their biological impulses, especially in the absence of social inhibitions."

"In other words, a male and a female mutaclone, entirely intact genetically, will couple with each other ad infinitum—"

"Presuming they are both hetero."

"—until someone tells them not to, or they grow bored or sated."

"Or some other biological drive like sleep, appetite, thirst, or evacuation commands their immediate attention."

"All right, makes sense," Fred said, knowing she was getting at something.

"But not you, despite your being gonado-intact."

He shrugged. "But I lived among other mutaclones for five years on an asteroid clone factory."

"How much socializing did you do?"

He shrugged again. "How am I supposed to measure that?"

"I don't know. Give me some percentage. As rough as you like."

"Ten to fifteen percent of my time, maybe. They kept us working a lot of the time."

"And yet, even in the face of what's got to be a nearly irresistible urge to copulate, despite a brief amount of socialization, you've not only made not a single advance toward me in the days we've been aboard this ship, you've actually made every effort you could to be respectful, gentle, and reserved."

Fred smiled, having thought she hadn't noticed. "Yes, I have." He didn't tell her he'd spent quite a few hours laying awake on the floor beneath her, wanting so terribly much to hold her, throbbing at the thought of her so close by, so alluring, her figure that of a goddess, her face the subject of a thousand legends, her mind sharp, her wit scathing, her heart pure, if somewhat larcenous. "Why?" he asked.

"I just think you'd have given some indication you were attracted to me."

Fred looked at her, mildly bewildered, sure there was something else she was trying to get at.

"Instead, you've done everything you can to hide your desires."

"Well, I didn't want to make you uncomfortable."

"And you've succeeded admirably. Thank you. You're a gem."

He smiled, warm inside. Five thousand copulation positions surged into his mind.

"And you have these fighting skills you shouldn't have."

The simumems retreated. He nodded, not quite sure why the sudden change in conversation.

"And you somehow know how to decrypt any type of security."

He nodded again, looking at her quizzically.

"And I, my dear," Kate said, "happen to know, beyond all doubt, that the kind of development you've exhibited across these last four days, since we escaped that asteroid, couldn't possibly have taken root in a mutaclone, no matter what the genetic build, nor how extensive the nanoprogramming, how exhaustive the simumems, nor how much nanostimming was applied."

He grinned. "How do you know that?"

She grinned back. "That's exactly my point. I shouldn't. And neither should you. Unless..."

Fred looked at Kate, knowing what she was thinking and not wanting to think it too, because the implications were too far-reaching.

And with that, Kate's face crumpled, and she began to weep.

He held her and wept alongside her, knowing and not wanting to know, not wanting it to be true.

Because it meant that they weren't mutaclones at all.

And if that were true, then something dear and precious and unutterably valuable had been somehow stolen from them both.

Their normavariant lives.

* * *

"Was that wise, Feo?" Dr. Sarina Karinova asked, nodding to the couple midway down the table.

Feodor Luzhkov had invited Sarina to the official state dinner, but not as a guest. The two of them sat in front of a multi-paneled display of vidscreens, each piping a strategically placed cam feed into the situation room. Some cams, like the one Sarina was focused on, were planted in the floral centerpieces, close enough to their subjects to make out the slightest change of expression.

Sarina happened to find the camera right between Doctor Tatiana Satsanova and Captain Fadeyka Andropovich. And she'd just heard their exchange.

The two lone singles in attendance, Tatiana and Fadeyka, were deep in conversation, his gaze going to her proudly-displayed bust line, where the subtle flush of increasing pleasure crept its way up her neck.

"Was what wise?" Feo asked. "Putting those two beside each other? Now that you mention it, probably not. I'll put in a trake to Mrs. Satsanova. They *do* look rather enthralled with each other."

"Rather enthralled? Did you hear what they said? He tacitly propositioned her, and she tacitly accepted. The next thing you know, they'll sneak out into the garden together." Sarina nearly wet herself at the thought of what these two would look like copulating.

Both were admirable physical specimens, turning heads of both sexes respectively. Sarina was unreservedly female-oriented and married ten years, but that didn't cool the warmth in her loins when she'd first caught sight of Fadeyka. And the sight of Tatiana had provoked equal surges of desire and envy, and Sarina ten years married! And committed!

They were both that desirable, these two.

And together, they were the perfect pair.

Sarina sighed at the romance that might have been possible between them, had they met when they were younger. Anything between them now could only result in cataclysmic sex of the kind that toppled empires.

Watching the high and mighty socialize amongst themselves held about five minutes allure for Sarina. It was certainly better to eavesdrop from the safety of a monitoring station than from a seat at the state dinner itself, where one might find oneself the subject of their titter and tattle. The dining room carpet was already saturated with the blood of assassinated reputations. She didn't need hers added to it. Even watching remotely, Sarina soon grew bored.

The belowground monitoring station, or situation room, as it was known to security personnel, occupied a bunker some distance away from the formal dining hall in the Guest Pavilion, where the state dinner was being served. The Guest Pavilion was situated on a hill beside the palace itself, the building separate from the main complex.

"I'm going to step out for a breath of air," Sarina said.

Feo nodded. "Mind if I join you?" He waved someone over. "Alert me if Mrs. Satsanova responds to my trake."

She stepped toward the elevator, and together they rode up. "Are you married?"

He grimaced. "To my job. I tried marriage once and felt I was being unfaithful." He gestured to the ceiling. "To the Premier."

Sarina chuckled as the doors trundled apart. Feo gestured to allow her out the door first. They stepped from the elevator onto the walk.

Here, near the perimeter of the palace grounds, the soaring towers of central Kiev but a few hundred yards away, the city lights encroached on everything. A low buzz and slight fuzz alerted her to the shields, the city towers somehow surreal and removed from the sprawling palace compound. The shimmer of shielding distorted their view of the sky, nearby buildings far too tempting to snipers to leave the palace unshielded. Here at the manicured garden perimeter, a peace pervaded the place, just far enough removed from the machinations of government and the bustle of the Capitol.

"How are you holding up?"

She let her worry show, twisting her wife's wedding ring on her pinky, Anya gone six days now. "It wouldn't be so bad if I knew something."

Some nights she'd lain awake, staring at the ceiling, seething with rage at the barbaric Huns who'd dared to abduct her wife, and other nights, she'd wept for hours in despair, praying to a God she'd long ago lost faith in. Somehow, she awoke each morning with the thought that today was the day they'd find something, that a clue or tip or piece of evidence would turn up, and they'd investigate it, trace its source, and somehow discover where the kidnappers were keeping Anya captive, and they'd track her down, and with an assault team leading the way, they'd break into whatever basement or warehouse or boiler room, cut apart the kidnappers with lasers, free her wife, and the two of them would be rejoined on the spot and fall into each other's arms, weeping with relief.

And Sarina would weep as she imagined it, and remain on the verge of tears through much of the day as she awaited word. As evening drew nigh, and the chance of progress diminished, she would lapse into despair and steel herself for another long night ahead.

So Feo's invitation to "attend" the dinner party had come as a welcome distraction, as her examination of the Admiral's son three days ago had been.

"It's a struggle," Sarina told Feo. "Each day, each hour, each minute."

Feo nodded. "I've been wondering whether the kidnappers might have mistaken your wife for you."

"We *are* pretty similar," Sarina acknowledged, "but why could they possibly want from me that they'd keep her for such a long time?"

Feo shrugged and looked up at the night sky. "Only the stars know."

She followed his glance. Odd how some pull of the stars in the sky still reminded her of God, the Christian God of the Eastern Orthodox Church, whose iconography was festooned with haloes, more ubiquitous than the cross itself. And in spite of the deep roots of Antiochian Christianity, the stars themselves had come to replace the icon as the symbol of His might.

"Well, I wish they'd tell me," Sarina said, the lights of Kiev almost blotting out the stars above. For the first time in days, Sarina felt a moment of peace, of sanctuary, as if somehow she were suspended on this perimeter between two states, neither fully enmeshed in the higher echelons of government nor fully immersed in the bustling populace it governed. And surprisingly aloof from both.

Then the power went out.

"What the hell?" Feo said, his eyes going to the perimeter.

It might have been more frightening had it been sudden, but the transition from brightly lit city to pitch-black night occurred across the count of five, lights dimming as generators failed to compensate, motors winding down, relays kicking off, fuses blowing, and darkness spreading.

Laser fire erupted behind them, beams slashing apart the sky above the Guest Pavilion.

"The Premier!" Feo gasped, his body coiling as though to leap the several hundred yards distance in a single bound.

Sarina put her hand on his arm to stop him.

The laser fire died, leaving a lone fire like a beacon burning on Pavilion Hill.

"Come on," he said, and they broke into a sprint along the path.

Figures leapt in front of them. "Stop right there." A pair of armed commandos in black blocked their way.

Feo blasted one. A third one grabbed Sarina from behind.

Feo ducked a pulse shot with a roll and came up shooting, and the second commando withered, getting off a shot before being splattered.

"Drop the gun or she dies," the third commando ordered, holding Sarina.

In a half-crouch, Feo held the pulse gun out to one side, about to drop it.

Sarina brought her heel up into the groin and batted away the barrel, then spun out of her assailant's grasp. Feo popped him with a shot, and it was over.

Somehow, she'd known he'd find his mark if offered a shot. "You're hurt," Sarina said, stepping to Feo's side.

His left ribcage was blackened and bleeding. "They were after you," he gasped. "You have to get off planet." Somewhere, sirens began to howl.

"You're injured. You'll die without immediate attention."

"No, Sarina, don't worry about me. I'm comming an extraction vehicle. On Salvinus 5, you'll find a sleeper cell. Pass code: insurrection. You'll be safe there. Here comes the hover already. They must have been close. Go with them, Sarina." His gaze went to the Guest Pavilion, where the single flare burned faintly, like hope.

A hum approached, the vehicle without lights, and settled on the grass beside them.

Feo dropped to a knee.

"I'm taking you to get help," Sarina said, the hover door opening only feet away.

He resisted as she tried to pull him that way, and then he fainted. She guided his fall that direction, then grabbed his collar and dragged him into the hover.

His legs still dangling out the door, the hover lifted and banked as it accelerated toward the spaceport.

Sarina pulled him fully inside, and the door snicked shut, cutting off an increasing cacophony of emergency vehicles.

"Driver, a medicoon!"

A panel popped open under the seat right beside Feo's head. In the dim glow of the running lights, his injuries looked far too severe for a medicoon, blood pooling around the wound.

Sarina sprayed the wound with liquid skin, its embedded sterilizer neutralizing any pathogens, the nano-epithelial foam sealing the wound. Then she turned the condicoon inside out and packed the surface to the wounded area and surrounding tissue, then activated it. The condicoon sent its nanostim tendrils into the flesh. While it had some reparative properties, the condicoon was designed primarily to extract toxins and waste tissue, search for and eliminate any genetic instability or precancerous markers. The amount of damaged tissue quickly overwhelmed the condicoon material, and she applied a clean swatch to the wound. A third and a fourth time, the nanostim tendrils extracted suppurated tissues. Sarina kept pushing clean swatches against the wound, and each time the swelling decreased, and the bruising dwindled.

"Approaching the spaceport, miss," the driver's voice came over the intercom. The interior of the cab lighted only by the dim dashboard lights, she saw only his profile.

"Can you help me get him aboard the yacht when we land?"

"Certainly," the driver said. "By the way, Doctor Karinova, her Excellency, the Premier Colima Satsanova has been assassinated."

Sarina's heart sank. Somehow, when laser fire had erupted from the Guest Pavilion, she'd suspected the Premier was the target. "I was afraid of that."

The hover banked and slowed, then settled beside a nondescript hangar, whose door was sliding aside as they settled. A yacht was trundled out, a Fawnorghini Typhoon, already powering up, its lights blinking. Its hatch opened at the same time as the hover doors, and the driver got out to help her. He took the shoulders and she the feet.

Together, they got Feo's unconscious form aboard and into a bunk, where she stuffed a fresh condicoon around the wound.

"Thank you," she told the driver, tempted to ask him along.

"You're welcome. Good luck." And he retreated.

She secured Feo in the bunk, and then strapped herself into the pilot's chaise, his feet visible from the cockpit through the cabin door. "Launch," she said, the yacht's controls appearing on her corn.

"Permission to launch denied by order of Imperial Security. All spaceport traffic is suspended indefinitely," the ship told her.

Sarina frowned. "Override by Imperial Order, pass code 'insurrection.'"

"Imperial pass code verified, override accepted, launch imminent."

She breathed a sigh and sat back.

"Course?" the ship asked.

"Salvinus Five," Sarina said.

The yacht rumbled under her, and the star-filled sky leapt at her, hurtling her into the unknown.

# Chapter 8

"Where are we going, anyway?" Kate asked.

Fred F4RB8C3 looked across at her. "The Capitol, Tantalus," he said, shrugging. They'd abandoned the idea of trying to locate a salvage ship on the garbage planet, Garlivka.

"Why there?"

Why indeed, he asked himself.

Genie-All was based there—the company that had "made" him. And now that he suspected they hadn't made him, that somehow he'd been placed in a uterpod on the asteroid, his memory neutralized, his previous life taken from him, all he could think was that someone somewhere knew who he was, how he'd been removed from that life, and why. And that there was only one place where that person or persons could be, since it couldn't have been done without the tacit consent or active participation from the Genie-All corporate office. That place had to be Tantalus.

He looked over and saw in Kate's face the same concerns that bothered him, that look of preoccupation and smoldering rage, the deep abiding indignation that someone somewhere had so egregiously abused them and had taken their lives in a fashion more foul than murder itself, and placed them where all they might expect was a life of backbreaking labor, their bodies consumed by their freeborn masters in whatever way those masters deemed, whether in salacious abandon or to satisfy some deeper, darker, sado-maso depravity.

He sighed. "Seems Tantalus is the place to start looking."

Kate nodded, extending a hand across the gap between their consoles.

He took her hand, feeling unmoored from his bearings. He'd always wondered as he'd lain in his bunk in the dormicube he'd shared with Greg why he led such a desultory existence, tending to mutaclones in their final stages of uterpod maturation, mindless work requiring no great intellectual or physical effort, a drudge monitoring other drudges, without a chance of some better tomorrow, dreaming of vast worlds beyond the wobbly asteroid circling a faint baby blue-white primary just outside the Pleiades Constellation, the backwater of a scum-covered puddle, too small even to support a fish, and therefore of no interest whatsoever to any big fish in nearby ponds. Not that Fred had ever seen ponds, or fish, or even scum.

He shook his head. "Tantalus seems like a good place to start, but how? Crack the Genie-All database, maybe?"

"Didn't you say I'd been transferred from the escoriant sector?"

He grinned, embarrassed at the conversation he'd had with her when she'd fallen from the uterpod, Kate so beautiful they might have used her genome as the basis for a new line of escoriants. He felt the heat in his face, knew he was bright red.

"You are either the shyest man in the galaxy, or the most moral. My point was, it's records like that which we need to access." Kate shook her head at him, grinning.

"Given the right tools," Fred added.

"So we don't really need to go to Tantalus?"

"Probably not immediately, no. But it'd be a convenient place to hide."

"Why don't we stop at the next borscht shop and think this through. We haven't really had the chance."

Nodding, he pulled up a star map and saw they were nearing Vahotyn, one of ten systems within a parsec of Tantalus. Near the outermost planet of Vahotyn was a tiny moon near the space lanes, near enough to lure weary travelers. Bristling from that tiny moon was a commercial operation called "Unbeetable." The national dish, Fred was thinking, turned into a tourist trap.

Vid feeds of their services swamped the local neuranet channels, the moon sporting innumerable outlets for every imaginable item. He pulled up restaurants on his corn and saw a borscht shop at the end of one isolated docking arm.

Not just any borscht shop, he saw as they approached, but the "Best Borscht" to be found. The sprawl of ships docked around it testified how good it was.

"What do you think?"

"Better than that synthesized mush we've been eating."

His mouth was watering even as they pulled into a docking bay. His magnetized soles kept him from drifting off the deck, the ship's gravinducer shutting off with the power. The walkway threaded its way between sedans, sports-ships, compacts, and space utility vehicles, the latter so fuel inefficient there was talk of taxing them at higher rates. None of the vehicles were quite so beat up as their tug.

Even through the restaurant's glasma ports, Fred could see that the place was packed, families in booths, a long counter where burly, long-haul spacers sat on stools too small for their portly forms, waitclones in bright uniforms pirouetting across a checker-board floor, chrome strips gleaming, vids blaring, and patrons yelling just to be heard over the cacophony.

Then they entered the "Best Borscht."

Fred had seen immersies somewhat like this, nanostim recordings meant to immerse their users in a blare of light, sound, smell, and feel. But the reality was far more overwhelming than any immersie.

"Two please," he mouthed at the waitclone.

The clone nodded and gestured, then sailed toward a booth on the far wall.

Fred and Kate followed on foot, neither accustomed to navigating without gravity.

Their table was a slab of stainless steel, and their chairs were two-foot wide L-shapes of the same. Easier cleaning, Fred thought, sliding in. The menus popped up on their corns, and the waitclone brought water, the cups adhering with suction, the water containing a congealant to keep it in the cup.

Right above their heads was a vid, another just across the aisle. Vids were everywhere.

He ran his head over his face, wondering whether he should have showered. Their allsuits weren't terribly out of place, but neither of them was dressed for a formal state dinner, either.

"What are you getting?"

Fred barely heard her over the noise. He gestured her to lean close. "I suspect the borscht is pretty good," he said in her ear.

"Likewise. Shall we?"

He nodded and pulled back, enjoy the close contact. He traked an order for two bowls of borscht, a side of potatoes, and a small side salad.

"So much for talking," she lipped at him.

He nodded and held up a finger, then requested a second trake-coke connection to her. The channel opened. "There, how's that?"

"Perfect," she said, her face not moving, the sound going directly from her trachea to his cochlea.

"Much better." Although the external noise was still so loud it almost hurt, he could hear her clearly, his coke blotting out other sounds when she spoke.

The hollow gaze returned to her face. "I've been thinking that there's someone in this galaxy living my life right now, enjoying all those things I worked so hard for, and here I am, bewildered, disoriented, and wandering the constellation in a beat up tug with someone I just met, no idea who I am or what I'm supposed to be doing."

"Assuming that someone *is* living that other life," he said. "Maybe someone wanted you out of the way and caused you to disappear."

"Leaving a missing persons and family and friends insisting that police investigate my disappearance?"

Fred nodded thoughtfully. "Probably not, but why? What could be gained by substituting your evil twin for you?"

"Stars know, eh? And what about you—gone five years now? Who's going to notice if they haven't by now?"

"If they have, then there'd be a missing persons report."

She brightened. "Maybe that's the place to start, see if anyone's reported you missing."

"Reported who missing? How can we look if I don't even know who I am? And if we don't find anything, we'd have to assume we've been cloned and replaced."

She nodded, frowning, "If true, why us? To what purpose? What's to be gained?"

"Not to mention the how," he added. "Sophisticated operation, growing a clone to maturity, giving it enough nanostimming to replicate a real person, all that."

"And then there's the other question. How did they wipe out our memories? That type of nanoneural surgery is so unfathomably unconscionable, who would do it?"

"Only the Ruskies are rumored to have developed techniques at Magadan that sophisticated. And that repugnant."

Kate frowned at him. "And if we two have been abducted, then who else has?"

Fred met her gaze, seeing worry on her classic features. Kate had a figure sculpted by the gods, with long supple legs, feisty hips, and a bust line to draw the envy and admiration of men and women alike. In addition to her breathtaking beauty, Kate also had a confidence to her manner that seemed imperturbable. "Think there's a possibility you were targeted for your figure?"

She snorted dismissively. "Far better to use my clone as a sex toy than try to persuade me. No, the motive was to put a clone in my place."

"But why? Why you? Why me? I don't have any sense that I was anyone important." Fred did have the impression that others had looked up to him for leadership. Or was that just a dream, he wondered, like all those dreams I've had of a verdant, fecund jungle world?

"I was..." Kate shook her head. "I don't know. There's some sort of memory block, which raises questions itself. Know any nanostim gengineers? Or neuropsychiatrists?"

Their food arrived, and the borscht was as good as the name suggested. They split the salad and potatoes, the two dishes in the middle between them, each hovering over their borscht.

Fred looked around, aware that something had changed.

The place was quiet, almost pin-drop silent. On screen was a reporter, in the background a burning building. Fred opened his coke.

"...Satsanova assassinated just minutes ago, reports filtering in across Tantalus of continent-wide power outages, rumors of a coup but nothing confirmed. Again, Premier Colima Satsanova assassinated in a vicious attack during a crowded state dinner at the Capitol. Multiple casualties reported, but only the Premier herself confirmed dead, the Cabinet of Ministers convening an emergency session as we speak..."

The reporter went on breathlessly, the vid switching scene to scene, some clips of the palace during the daytime, some of the attack scene itself from above, multiple emergency vehicles hovering around a fire in the process of being doused.

"...Premier's daughter Doctor Tatiana Satsanova in attendance, a still of her from earlier in the evening..."

A comely woman with a V-shaped face in a low-cut evening dress stared right into the camera, a male grinning mischievously beside her, both of them so photogenic they might have graced a fashion spread, both exuding the confidence emanated only by the glitterati, their celebrity as innate as their beauty.

Fred and Kate turned to look at each other.

The face staring at Fred from across the table was the face of the Premier's daughter.

"That man beside her, Fred," Kate said, her voice a whisper. "That's you!"

"And she...her face..." He saw Kate go white, sure his complexion was equally pasty, panic threatening to overwhelm him.

"…The Cabinet of Ministers has announced the emergency appointment of an interim Premier, the Premier's daughter, Doctor Tatiana Satsanova, to lead Ukraine in…"

Kate's face went from white to red. "The bastards!"

\* \* \*

"The bastards!" Livid with rage, Doctor Sarina Karinova knew her face was white. She got up and went to look in on Feo, lying in a bunk. "Did you hear that?"

The newly appointed interim Premier, Tatiana Satsanova, had just issued an alert for the suspected assassins, Chief of Staff Feodor Luzhkov and Doctor Sarina Karinova.

His gaze was dull, but he was awake. And alive. He nodded, motioning her to help him up.

"You can't get up, Feo. You'll probably tear open the wound if you try." Sarina had used the ship's medicoon to do reconstructive surgery, rebuilding the bone and flesh destroyed by the pulse shot to his left side.

He nodded at her, his eyes closing briefly. He'd never be whole again, but at least the wound was healing.

"We can't go to Salvinus Five," she said, "not now, not after that." They were a day away.

"Replay it for me, in here," Feo said.

Sarina traked a request to pipe the announcement to Feo's corn. She watched it on her own corn.

The Interior Minister was speaking: "Preliminary findings indicate that the power outage was triggered from inside the situation room on the palace grounds by Madame Premier's Chief of Staff, Feodor Luzhkov, who was last seen taking off from the Kiev spaceport in the company of Doctor Sarina Karinova." Stills were shown of both. "This pair is considered to be armed and extremely dangerous. If anyone sights them, do not attempt to approach. Contact the authorities immediately."

Feo looked at her, his gaze sad but blunted by the pain. The conditioning cocoon helped to reduce the pain, but that was all it could do. "You disabled the transponders?"

Sarina nodded, feeling lost, angry, hopeless, and helpless.

Not only was the Premier dead, but her daughter had been appointed in her place—she whose examination had precipitated the erasure of Sarina's medical files, the bombing of her clinic, and the kidnapping of her wife. And now Sarina had been accused as a suspect in the Premier's assassination.

Intrigue was not her forte. I'm a doctor, for God's sakes! she thought, biting back tears.

And Feo was in such bad shape, he wasn't able to offer much help. The condicoon wrapping him on the bunk was becoming discolored on the left side, the material absorbing injured cells from the wound site. She'd have to change it soon. She was glad she'd turned off the ship's gravinducers, the weightlessness making Feo more comfortable and making it easier for her to move him around.

What the hell do I do? she wondered. They're sure to take us into custody if we go to Salvinus Five now!

Feo would know what to do, if she could somehow return him to some level of consciousness. The surgery had been necessary to repair his shattered ribcage and rebuild the muscles. If she hadn't, his lungs would have worked their way out through the shattered ribs, and he'd have died from infection. The shot had missed the lungs themselves.

The onboard synthall was programmable, and she'd fed it a schematic for collagen, the basic substrate of cartilage, which she'd molded to the shapes she'd needed, and then had inserted where his ribs had been shot away. He'd need professional reconstructive surgery when they were done with this.

But I need him better now! she thought, wondering how to return him to some semblance of functioning.

"Uzhhorod," Feo whispered.

"Huh?"

"Change course to Uzhhorod," he said, his voice faint.

She leaped into the cockpit and called up the flight controls on her corn.

Uzhhorod was a binary system at the western edge of Ukraine, unremarkable except as the westernmost occupied system in Ukraine. Its main industry was selling "Now Leaving Ukraine" trinkets. It also had a thriving underground market in illicit medical procedures, the kind that provoked horrified indignation among the well-heeled and titillation among the more vicariously inclined, neuromuscular modification to the nether regions among its more sought-after products.

Bod mods are all the rage, Sarina thought, many of her private-practice patients having sought her advice before getting some enhancement, requests for records from the region nearly always signifying that the patient was getting his or her genitals enhanced.

She traked the new destination to the yacht's autonav, then looked at the cockpit around her. The Typhoon's interior was posh and plush. If I could remove one chaise, I might be able to rig a suspensor harness...

Sarina got to work, eager to be doing something, seeking distraction from their completely hopeless situation. By the time they arrived on Uzhhorod, Feo would have a bunk in the cockpit, and even if he were only partly awake...

What she really needed for his injury was a thoracic shell, an exoskeleton to take the pressure off the healing bones and muscles. Absent that, he'd have to remain wrapped in a condicoon and strapped to a bunk in weightlessness.

News reports continued to play in the background while she did reconstructive surgery on the cockpit. When stretched out, the copilot's chaise barely fit in the tiny cabin. Although designed for two people, the Typhoon was as compact as possible, meant for short jaunts. Larger, more elaborate yachts might be had for longer trips. A proctor of hers in medical school had once circumnavigated the galaxy in one such yacht, visiting exotic worlds at the rim, many of them unoccupied.

Finished, she looked at her handiwork.

The copilot's chaise no longer resembled anything of the sort. Its back removed, a stumpy base was all that remained. Sarina then attached antigrav units to Feo's bunk, unscrewed it from the wall, and guided it to the space where the copilot's chaise had been. She secured it, hoping it held during a landing. I'll just have to keep the antigrav units on, she thought, knowing that would minimize but not eliminate any shifts in mass or changes in vector, antigravs able only to cancel any gravitational pull.

"What are you doing?" he said, his eyes coming open just as she finished.

"Making you comfortable. For this to work, I need you up here, in the cockpit."

Feo nodded, giving her a slight smile.

"All right, now what?"

"Now what what?"

Sarina frowned at him. "You're the politician, I'm not. You know this skullduggery better than I do. You had me turn off the transponders and you warned me not to use the neuranet. We've managed to evade the authorities so far, but we can't do it forever. We'll have to refuel soon, so that means stopping at some cross-lanes fuel depot. How are we going to pay for it? I don't have a galacti on me. I don't suppose you're carrying a couple mil, by chance? Why are you smirking? How are we going to pay for your surgery on Uzhhorod?"

He gave her a faint smile, and then winced.

His condicoon needed changing, she saw. After she'd opened it up to remove it, she discovered he'd soiled himself.

"Sorry," he whispered, shedding a tear.

"Happens," she said, shrugging.

He lay still, hovering above the bunk while she cleaned him up. When she was done, a new condicoon now wrapping him, Sarina realized she probably could have wedged him into the sanistall, wound and all, with a fresh syntheskin patch over the wound site, and cleaned him off that way.

In retrospect, she realized she liked tending to him personally, deriving a degree of satisfaction and competency. Her life in disarray, she had little enough to feel competent about.

"Thank you," he whispered, his eyes mere slits, the condicoon leaving only an oval where his face was exposed.

"You're welcome." She cleaned up the last of her materials and then got into the sanistall herself. Afterward, refreshed and wearing a clean allsuit, she got herself a bite from the synthall. Munching and watching muted news on the vidscreen, Sarina wondered what next. As easy as it would be to give into despair, she resisted.

Somewhere, someone knew what was happening and why. Someone had caused all of this to happen. Had conspired to replace two scions with mutaclones. Had engineered the promotion of one mutaclone to the position of Premier. Had destroyed Sarina's life in their efforts to keep that information secret.

To what end? she wondered.

# Chapter 9

"Comrade! It's you! Dobry den, Captain Andropovich! Welcome!"

Fred was just as nonplussed as he'd been at the Best Borscht, seeing his own face on the vid. He dissimulated his discomfiture into surprise. "It's good to see you, Comrade!" He shook hands, hugged the other man, and apologized. "Forgive me, Friend, but I've forgotten your name."

"You don't recognize me?! It's Vasyl Orlyk! How is it you don't recognize me? Those Brygidki guards torture all the memories from your brain? Or perhaps the Ruskies caught you smuggling mutaclones and subjected you to the Magadan method? Wiped your past completely from memory?"

"Vasy, of course, my friend. It's been so long. I can't even remember how long I was in Brygidki. So sorry, Vasy. So old I've gotten."

"Post Graduate needed some shaking up. That place was staid and proper beyond compare. But you and the Dean's wife. Oh, there was a catch! Twenty years your senior. Any of us would have loved to have her cannons grace our battleship decks! Any of us!" The man glanced over Fred's shoulder. "Who's the pretty woman, eh? Someone finally tame those wild ways of yours? Bought the whole hog just to get a little of your magnificent sausage?" He grinned sheepishly at Kate. "Pardon our banter, Mrs. Andropovich, a little spillover from our bachelor days."

"I didn't hear a word, Mr. Orlyk. I was distracted."

Fred was sure she'd heard it all. "What are you doing in this vodka-forsaken part of Ukraine?" He and Kate had changed plans after seeing the still of the new Premier and the Admiral's son, needing to find a quick way to change their appearances. Uzhhorod had suggested itself both for its cosmetic surgery and its quasi-legal activities. Vasyl's instant recognition of Fred—mistaken, but recognition even so—was proof of their need to change their appearances.

"Eh, well, you know," Vasyl said, shrugging, "I couldn't exactly pursue a military career anymore. No, no, don't apologize. I participated with all my heart. It was only what I'd deserved. Scandalized all of my family, but I guess I had to eat a lemon to appreciate what sugar is. Welcome to Vasyl's Bawd Mods, no alteration out of the question."

Fred glanced around, resuming a prurient browsing interrupted by the proprietor's effusive greeting. One side of the shop was given over to female genitalia mods, the other side to male, all of them displayed in explicit, life-size renditions. Drawn inexorably to the female side, Fred glanced at Kate, whose gaze moved around the impressive displays on the male side. He could feel the heat rushing to his face, and Kate looked flush as well.

She grinned at him. "Not quite what we were looking for."

"Couples rarely come together, so perhaps browsing together might help to harmonize the marital relations? Of course, you've no need for augmentation yourself, Fedey." He turned to look at Kate. "You should have seen the princely pestle he sported in those days!"

"Vasy, my friend," Fred said quickly, "I'm afraid genital mods aren't what we're looking for."

"No? What's more important than her satisfaction? Perhaps an augmentation of this style?" He gestured to a dual-pronged structure, the hind penis smaller in girth. "Its emissions are timed to be simultaneous. And in the correct position, the smaller penis can be used solo, too."

He felt he'd just spent a week playing under a hot, tropical sun, his skin aflame.

"What is it you're looking for, Friend?"

Fred pointed at his face. "It's just too famous."

"Ah, I see. Yes, I saw the vid. Tragic, our Premier dying like that. You were there. It must have been horrible. And your wife—" Vasyl stopped. And gawked at Kate. "Aren't you—?"

"No, I'm not," Kate said, interrupting him and laughing lightly. "This isn't the first time I've been mistaken for her. It's so inconvenient to look so much like our new Premier."

Vasyl glanced between them both. Then again.

"Vasyliyich, my friend," Fred said, "it *is* disturbing, isn't it? It's why we both want face mods. And as tempting as it might be to mount a penis on my forehead, I don't need a mod that extreme."

Vasyl threw his head back and laughed.

Fred sighed at being able to distract the other man.

"Sadly, my work isn't quite so good that it withstands the light of day, although it does provide immense satisfaction in the dark of night. I have a friend who might be able to help, Doctor Zoryana Puskinska, on Kinchesh. And come back, Fedey, if you ever find a need for the enhancements on display here."

* * *

"The Magadan method, eh?"

Fred was grateful for the distraction, afraid that his titillation was evident from the front of his allsuit. "Do you think that's possible?"

He and Kate strolled through the bazaar, the yellow-white primary of Uzhhorod a bright pinprick in the sky. The products on display weren't nearly as titillating as those at Vasyl's Bawd Mod, but were certainly bizarre enough.

A young woman stood at the front of a booth, a nimbus of nasal tendrils fanning out in front of her face, revealing the nostril cavity beneath. The tendrils retracted and reassembled the nose to perfect proportion.

At the next booth over, the male proprietor looked at them through a crown of eyes, each mounted on a stalk, each moving independently, each stalk extending from one of the orbital sockets. The muscles around the empty sockets rippled as the stalks flexed.

Across the crowded walkway, a woman held up a handful of hands, each digit ending in another hand. Four of the hands juggled a set of fire balls, while a fifth hand spun a coin between the facile fingers.

Unlike the mods at the mutaclone factory, the mods available on Uzhhorod were primarily surgical. Because of anatomical complexity, surgical mods were less reliable than genetic mods, sometimes requiring follow-up surgery when the modded limb didn't quite function to spec. Gene mods were more reliable for several reasons, despite the difficulty of gengineering a new line of modded mutaclone. With an inviability rate exceeding ninety percent, the few engineered mods that did survive proved far more durable. A mutaclone that grew to maturity with its mods intact adapted much better to the modded appendage.

In his first five years post-uterpod at the Genie-All asteroid factory, Fred had seen mutaclone escoriants with genitalia similar to those on display at Vasyl's Bawd Mod. In late uterpod development, the male specimens like their normavariant counterparts exhibited penile tumescent episodes a quarter to a third of the time, the autonomic engorgement in females similar but not as obvious. Most of the male escoriants had rivaled the enhancements at the Bawd Mod. And the gengineered mods outperformed the surgical mods, Fred was sure.

"So how do we find out about the Magadan method?" Fred asked, trying to distract himself from the five thousand copulation positions attempting to crowd into his mind. Kate, he saw, was grinning at him.

"Well, if anyone knows, they're likely to be here." She took his hand.

At every stop in the past couple of days, just about everyone they'd met had assumed they were a couple, one young woman at a refueling station even remarking how cute they looked together.

The nights were the worst for Fred, his desires articulated in his dreams in ways he wouldn't allow to surface in his waking thoughts. Visiting Vasyl's Bawd Mod today was only going to exacerbate his dreams tonight.

He sighed, enjoying her hand in his even so.

\* \* \*

Just as the attractive couple emerged from Vasyl's Bawd Mod, Sarina's coke and corn flared to life. Feo's vital signs were plummeting. He was going into cardiac arrest.

Sarina loped from the bazaar toward the main boulevard. "Five cc's adrenocortisol!" she traked, hailing a hovertaxi. One pulled to the cub instantly and she was aboard before it had stopped. "Spaceport, stat!"

Doctor Karinova glanced over her shoulder toward the bazaar entrance, catching another glimpse of the comely couple coming out, their enraptured gazes on each other, their mutual attraction obvious.

Sarina swore in her filthiest Rusky.

At first glance, she'd thought for certain it was Premier Tatiana Satsanova and Captain Fadeyka Andropovich.

The woman was generously endowed, wheat-blond hair cascading straight past her shoulders, a V-shaped face, a small, warm, inviting smile below large, wide-set, intelligent eyes. The man sported a marbled Roman face atop a ramrod-straight posture and a sleek, sinuous physique, so trim, regal, disciplined, and stoic. The pair coming out of the bazaar looking just obsessed with each other as they'd looked at the official state dinner on Tantalus minutes before the assassination of Premier Colima Satsanova. The new Premier and the scandalous Captain.

Her second glance as the hovertaxi sped away confirmed what she'd thought.

But they couldn't be here on Uzhhorod! Sarina thought. She swore again as the hovertaxi cleaved through the air above the busy, garish city, trying to reconcile what she'd seen with what she knew.

Feo's heart rate and breathing had picked up at the infusion of adrenocortisol, but his blood pressure was marginal, and from the readings on her corn, Sarina guessed that the condicoon was constricting rhythmically in its efforts to improve the circulation. Slow-moving blood might cause blood clots, risking embolisms or strokes. "Two cc's warfarin," she traked. Thin the blood, help the peripheral circulation. How could Tatiana and Fadeyka be here on Uzhhorod? Sarina wondered. The new Premier was sure to have her hands full on Tantalus, trying to rein in the chaos caused by her mother's assassination. And Fadeyka was on parole, forbidden to leave Tantalus or face being sent back to Brygidki for the remainder of his sentence.

Feo's blood pressure was stabilizing, Sarina saw on her corn. His breathing was still shallow and his pulse weak, his oxy-sat at the ninety-two percent. Any lower and I'll need to give him nano-ox, she thought.

The hovertaxi entered the spaceport. At the gate checkpoint, she had to produce her tarmac pass. With Feo's help, she'd mocked up a passable ID autocard, and with a small bribe, the authorities hadn't scrutinized it too closely. Not that the authorities on Uzhhorod looked too closely at anyone's credentials, no matter what their profession.

She leapt from the hovertaxi, threw a chit at the driver, and rushed into the yacht, just as Feo went into ventricular fibrillation.

"Shock advised, charging," the condicoon said, the sound echoed on her coke. "Delivering shock now, stand clear of patient."

Sarina stepped back.

Feo lurched with the shock and then moaned. "Shock delivered," the condicoon said.

Semi-conscious, she thought, traking the yacht to prepare for launch. "Come on, Feo, you can do it!" Sarina said, hoping the sound of her voice might draw him from semi-consciousness.

"Launch ready," the yacht said. "Please secure all passengers."

She strapped herself in and fed the destination to the autonav.

The yacht leapt from the tarmac and soared toward sub-orbit, their course taking them into the ionosphere, a big arc, a planet hop.

Feo's eyes cracked open, a slight smile on his face, his vitals remaining steady in spite of the acceleration.

She sighed, worried it might have killed him. "Almost lost you for a minute," she said, returning his smile.

"Where?" he croaked, the one word all he could summon.

"Halfway around Uzhhorod," Sarina said. "Surgeon." Sarina had been referred to a surgeon halfway around the planet. Better to take the yacht there than try to get Feo there by ground transportation.

His eyelids half-closed, the closest he could get to a nod.

"Feo?" she said tentatively.

The eyes opened again.

"I think I saw them, Feo. Tatya and Fedey. In the bazaar, coming out of Vasyl's Bawd Mod." She spelled it for him. "I wanted to follow them, but your vitals dropped out of sight. It was them, I swear... or..." She bit her lip, anxiety threatening to overwhelm her.

"Mutaclones," he said, his voice a whisper.

"Mutaclones," she said, staring at him, disbelieving, perplexed, and terrified.

\* \* \*

The antiseptic waiting room was small. No receptaclone sat at the desk. A vid screen with Dr. Boris Todurov's face said in a polite but recorded voice, "I'll be with you momentarily."

Sarina maneuvered the gurney into the waiting room, the antigrav unit humming faintly. On this side of the planet, the towns were small, the spaceports near the towns. She'd walked through town pushing the gurney, drawing a few stares but otherwise not seeming to arouse much consternation.

She didn't know what to infer from seeing Tatiana and Fadeyka at the bazaar. Or their mutaclones, sent among the populace to sew confusion and doubt. Or were they the real individuals, Sarina wondered, somehow loose and free, wandering without identity, their personas at the Tantalus Capitol occupied by mutaclone imposters, one of them attempting to guide the nation through a painful transition with a set of skills clearly inadequate to the task, the other on a course of flaming self-destruction, both incognizant that they were pale shadows of the people they were purported to be?

Dr. Todurov burst into the room, and Sarina jumped to her feet, startled. The gurney drew his attention right away, the condicoon around left rib cage blotched red-brown.

"What kind of injury?"

"Pulse shot."

"Treatment?"

"Mostly condicoon. I synthed some collagen and tried to repair the ribs, but it's not working well."

"Credentials?"

"General practitioner with some experience in gengineering."

"Bring him in. I'll need your assistance."

She pushed the gurney through the door, down the hall and into the operating theater.

"Imaging," Dr. Todurov called to the room.

Two armatures descended from the ceiling and scanned Feo, one along the side, the other from above. A model appeared against the far wall, healthy bone in green, injured bone in red, the image rotating slowly.

"Prep patient," the Surgeon said. "Gloves, masks." He gestured, and Sarina sanitized her hands and put hers on.

Two more armatures descended, each with multiple extensions. The stained condicoon peeled away.

The wound site was red and inflamed.

"Collagen rejection. No anti-rejection regimen?"

"No, none on the yacht."

The Surgeon nodded and plunged into the surgery, occasionally asking a question or prompting her for assistance.

When he was done cleaning the wound, Sarina saw how severe it actually was, something she hadn't been able to see without the proper imaging. Her attempt to repair it had failed not out of ineptitude, but from how deeply serious the wound had been.

Then Dr. Todurov began to repair the wound site, asking for occasional assistance.

Sarina watched fascinated as he worked. She had considered surgery, knew each step as he took it, and admired the deft and methodical way he moved through the procedure.

On the end of each blasted rib, he placed a nanostim enhancer, the nanobots inside facilitating bone growth by supplying the needed chemicals and administering microshocks to the marrow, accelerating its growth, the resulting bone more durable than anything produced on its own, the bone healing in a quarter of the time.

Then he rebuilt the muscles and skin back over the wound site, then stepped back. The Doctor sighed. "With rest, he'll be all right."

Sarina smiled, worried they wouldn't get any. "Do you have a thoracic shell?"

He threw her a glance. "Not expecting to get much rest?"

She shook her head.

"Are you really guilty of all those things they say?"

"Of course not," she said quietly. "Doctor, may I ask your opinion?"

Todurov gave her a small smile. "Of course."

Helping him fit the thoracic shell to Feo's left side, Sarina told him about her examinations of the two scions, leaving aside their names. As they began to sterilize the equipment, she described the results of the genalysis.

The thoracic shell would force Feo to give up nearly all use of his left arm, but at least he'd be ambulatory. And alert. More than anything, I need him alert, Sarina thought. Then she told Dr. Todurov about the mental states of the two scions she'd examined.

By the time Feo was ready, the Doctor was frowning. "Sounds like they're mutaclones, the both of them. But five years? How could they get away with that for five years?"

"His mother is very protective."

"Unless she's politically connected to the highest reaches of the Ukrainian government, he can't have gotten away with all of that."

She grimaced at him.

"Pretty high, huh?"

"Uh huh." Then she told him she thought she'd seen the couple there on Uzhhorod and why she thought that impossible.

"Here? And this after you left Tantalus in a hurry?"

She nodded. "I examined them both. And I was watching them at the dinner, sitting beside each other, moments before the attack."

Doctor Todurov had that preoccupied look of someone accessing information on his or her implants. "This image, that's them? Here, on Uzhhorod?"

She saw on her corn the image he'd accessed. The new Premier, Doctor Tatiana Satsanova, and the Admiral's son, Captain Fadeyka Andropovich. Sarina wasn't surprised he'd guessed, nodding.

"Where were they? Where did you see them?"

"Coming out of Vasyl's Bawd Mod."

Dr. Todurov nodded. "I know the place. Vasyl's a slippery character but honest about his product. Let me send him a trake, see if he remembers them."

While he did that, Sarina checked on Feo, who was just emerging from anesthesia.

Feo smiled up at her, his face looking more alive than he had days. "I heard you talking." The glance lanced Dr. Todurov.

Sarina shrugged. "How are we going to pay for this?"

Feo winked at her. "Madame Satsanova was nothing if not thorough, made sure all her staff had access to resources."

It was the longest sentence she'd heard from him since he'd been shot. Sarina nearly wept with relief.

Feo grasped her hand, her struggle plain on her face.

"He remembers them," Dr. Todurov said. "Sent them to a rhytidectomist. Attractive couple, he said, and clearly enamored of each other."

"A what?" Feo asked.

"A facelift doctor," Sarina said, the term familiar. "Did he say which one?"

"Doctor Zoryana Puskinska, on Kinchesh."

# Chapter 10

Two hours later, after another sub-orbital planet-hop, Sarina and Feo moved from booth to booth through the bizarre bazaar, wearing wigs they'd picked up at the corner drug.

The attachments available to the human body festooning the displays looked like alien proto-tech transmogrifications. On Tantalus, at the center of power, such mods were rare, mutaclones widely available to normavariants, equipped with many such variations in physiognomy. Some on display in the bazaar, Sarina noticed, were designed to collapse into the normal limb or aperture that usually appeared on the human body, leaving the anatomy intact. She'd seen a few of these pseudo mods, meant to give the prosthetics increased utility without detracting from bodily integrity. Close examination could not disguise them however, no matter how craftily they'd been engineered.

Sarina and Feo worked their way toward Vasyl's Bawd Mod, not wanting to reveal their intent to the casual observer, all the while keeping a sharp eye peeled for any surveillance.

Feo had paid Dr. Todurov a princely sum, and the Doctor had protested it was twice his usual fee. Feo had insisted, pointing out the help he'd given in their pursuit of the bawdy doubles.

"Doctor," Sarina had asked, "I have a hypothetical question. If you wanted to remove someone from his or her life and substitute a mutaclone, but not kill the person, how would you go about insuring that that person lost his or her awareness of that previous life?"

Dr. Todurov had stared at her for a full minute. "This couple who came out of Vasyl's Bawd Mod, you think they're the real normavariants?"

"I think so," Sarina exchanged a glance with Feo while the Doctor pondered.

"You're suggesting a highly sophisticated enterprise, using experimental, barbarous, and opprobrious methods."

"I am."

The Doctor shifted uncomfortably. "The Magadan method."

The mere mention sent shivers coursing up Sarina's spine.

During the Rusky upheavals, the oppressive regimes that had replaced one another in rapid succession across nearly a century of infighting had all banished their enemies to the remote gulag outpost at Magadan. Horrific rumors had occasionally emerged of the treatment these prisoners received. Brain soufflé surgery. Neuro nano reprogramming. Gene deconstruction therapy. Multisensory torture. Mnemonic schema erasure.

"Thank you, Doctor," Feo had said, not batting an eye.

The two had taken their leave and had flown back around the planet to ask Vasyl about the couple who'd visited his shop that morning.

The Bawd Mod shop door just a few yards away, Feo browsed a display of digimods, examining one that turned a three-inch finger into a three-foot tentacle. "I'm guessing he'll have some surveillance vid," Feo murmured to her. He moved slowly, with a wooden stiffness that he couldn't disguise, the thoracic shell restricting his left arm at the elbow, limiting its range of motion. Even using his hand caused him to wince.

She knew this much exertion was likely to wear him out, and she wished she'd insisted he rest at least a day before attempting an excursion like this.

He wasn't exactly a young man, in his seventies, but he'd maintained a modicum of the fitness level he'd achieved in training as a member of the Premier's personal guard after she'd first taken office.

Premier Colima Satsanova's political enemies had often smeared her with accusations that the two were lovers.

As if that really mattered, Sarina thought, especially in these times, when sex between individuals might resemble any number of fleshy configurations, depending on their bod mods. The definition of sex had broadened so far beyond its original connotation of the conjunction of two people for mutual pleasure that even clinical sexologists could barely define what sex was and what it wasn't. Holding hands might be sex if both individuals had enhanced the neural sensitivity in their hands. And even the concept of orgasm was as divorced from sex as procreation. The physiological and neurochemical changes needed to induce orgasm were easily replicated without physical contact with another human being, the surge of autoerotic pleasure commonly associated with such lack of contact having long since lost the sobriquet of masturbation. And if a person wanted to procreate, one didn't need to have sex. Nor an ovum and sperm.

While it was still illegal to expose one's genitalia in public, the huge variety of organ configurations gave police and prosecutors conniption fits in their pursuit of offenders. Hence the need for Vasyl to display his wares inside his shop, warnings in twenty different languages adorning the door.

Stepping through the door was like stepping into another world. Sarina's attention was drawn instantly to the right toward the prominently-displayed vulvas, their flowers in full, luscious bloom, dewy and glistening, her own anatomy responding in kind.

"Where's the proprietor?" Feo asked, looking around.

The shop appeared empty.

Somewhere, something groaned.

She and Feo exchanged a glance, and then raced to the counter.

On the floor behind it, a man slowly bled to death. A pulse blast to his stomach had eviscerated him.

The stench hit Sarina, and she nearly vomited. She quelled her nausea and knelt beside him. "Who did this?"

The man peered at her through one half-closed eye, the other bruised shut. Contusions wreathed his face, and one arm was twisted behind him at an angle that the human physiology wasn't capable of. Three fingers on the other hand were bent completely backward. He tried to whisper something, coughed up a gout of blood, and then said in distinct Rusky, "Brothers." He struggled for a moment and blurted, "Zoryana Puskinska."

Then he died.

Sarina looked around for a medicoon, a first-aid kit, or even a condicoon. "Feo, get an ambulance!"

"No, Sari," he said, his voice quiet.

She looked at him, stunned.

"We'll be detained if we try to save him. We can't. Help me search for the surveillance vids." Already, Feo was checking the small area behind the counter, opening cabinets and drawers.

She knew what Feo was saying was sensible. She knew it prudent, advisable, and even appropriate. And yet she had to tear herself away. A man who'd just died cried out to be saved. With the right tools, and in the right circumstance, she could've saved him.

"Whoever did this is working on behalf of our enemies," Feo was saying. "They put a mutaclone in the position of Premier."

She looked him as though from a long way away. Somewhere, in a previous life, she heard herself reciting the Hippocratic Oath. She watched detached, as though from over her own shoulder, as she began searching the cabinet behind the counter. The person standing at the podium reciting an oath sacred to doctors faded ever far away from her, the voice becoming more and more faint, the distance between Sarina in the here-and-now and Dr. Sarina Karinova at the podium growing, a great chasm wrenching open between the two, a cleft so wide and deep that nothing might bridge that gap nor bring back together the two separated selves.

"Here it is," she called, snapping back into her body. She looked upon a blinking machine in a drawer below the counter, a small display showing thumbnails of six different cams.

"Here," Feo said, finding a merchandise bag nearby.

Sarina pulled the entire unit out and put it in the bag. The unit died as it was unplugged.

"Let's go."

She glanced one last time at the still-warm corpse. And prayed for God's forgiveness.

She slipped naturally to Feo's right side as they exited Vasyl's Bawd Mod, the bag in her right hand. They strode through the bazaar, neither looking back, both expecting the alarm to be raised at any moment.

At the curb, Sarina hailed a hovertaxi. "Spaceport," she told the driver, climbing in after Feo.

He looked frail, his eyes half-closed.

He needs to rest, Sarina told herself, wondering how they were going to manage that.

* * *

It's almost time to leave, Dr. Zoryana Puskinska thought, anticipating a stiff shot of vodka on the way home. She looked up from the chart she was reviewing to glance out into the waiting room from behind the tinted reception window.

Only two people left to see. But both of such breathtaking beauty that she stared at them. "Kris, who are *they*?" she whispered.

The receptaclone shook his head. "They wouldn't say," he said in a low voice. "Asked to see you on standby. I told them you had a date at the pub, but they wouldn't take no for an answer."

She didn't know whether to rebuke him for the pub remark or for not telling her about them sooner. "Step this way, please." She retreated far enough into the back room to make sure she wasn't visible from the waiting area, smacked him hard across the cheek, and growled, "Come tell me immediately any time someone like this comes in!"

He cowered, whimpering. "But they told me not to!"

And she cuffed him again. "You work for me, not them! You do what *I* say!" She took one step past him and sank her elbow into his kidney as hard as she could. "And don't *ever* spread my business about town!" He slid down the wall to the floor.

Composing herself, she stepped toward the waiting room. "I'm Doctor Zoryana Puskinska. How about we go into an exam room for confidentiality?" She gestured the magnificent couple to a short hallway opposite the entrance.

Her receptaclone was just crawling back into his chair at the reception window, struggling for breath.

"No more appointments today," she told him.

"Yes, Doctor," Kris whispered, a clear imprint of her hand across his cheek.

I hope I inflicted some kidney damage, too, she thought. She entered behind the couple and pulled the exam door closed. "Names, please?"

The couple exchanged a glance, each so exemplary in face and physique that the Doctor nearly melted.

"Frederick Andropovich," the man said.

"Katarina Satsanova," the woman said.

From the way they sat and how they'd glanced at each other, Zoryana assumed they were married. They were so well matched that they were destined to be lovers. Such a joining could only end in tragedy! she thought. "My apologies for the brevity, but I have an appointment with a shot of vodka. You're not here for cosmetic facial surgery." They're too good-looking for surgery!

Again, that glance between them, more said in a single look than strangers might exchange in a long conversation.

"Well, actually, we are," Katarina said. "My cousin, the new Premier, is so similar to me in appearance that I've been mistaken for her over twenty times since my aunt's assassination. Terribly inconvenient."

Belatedly, Dr. Puskinska recognized her. A still shot of the new Premier and her beau, taken moments before the attack, had been published galaxy-wide, both of them vexatiously handsome, both of them deeply engrossed in each other. Premier Satsanova's husband was rumored to be filing for divorce, citing the now-famous still shot as proof of his wife's infidelity, the new Premier embattled on several fronts, her political enemies capitalizing on her personal travails.

"How different do you want to look?" Zoryana asked, glancing between them. She wondered how Frederick had managed to look so much like the other man, the one whom the new Premier was having the torrid affair with, whose name Zoryana couldn't quite recall. In Dr. Puskinska's business, too many questions—especially questions of the wrong sort—tended to deter customers. And these two, Zoryana thought, they *reek* of wealth!

Again, the couple glanced at each other. "What you can do?" Frederick asked.

Dr. Puskinska looked at him directly, and in that moment recognized him. He looks just like Captain Fadeyka Andropovich, the Admiral's profligate son, the one who'd finally landed at Brygidki Prison after a series of lurid scandals. No wonder he wants to change his face! "I can show you a vid of before-and-after stills, but they won't include my most famous clientele." She smiled. "Those with shyness toward the interstellar authorities."

"Perfect," Katarina said.

"Why don't I leave you with this sample vid, and Kris the receptaclone can make you an appointment for consult, say, next week?"

The couple exchanged yet another glance.

Zoryana was getting annoyed, the two of them sharing an intimacy that made her jealous. How I wished I was intimate with someone on that level! she thought.

"Any sooner than that, please?" Frederick asked.

"For half the time, the price will double."

"And the surgery?" Katarina asked.

Dr. Puskinska shrugged, suppressing a scream. She wanted to run to the pub to drown her loneliness, but this insufferably intimate pair wouldn't let her. "A month out, easy. You want it sooner, you pay more. Ask around. I'm the best and worth the money." Then she smiled.

"Here, I'll start the vid. When you're done, see Kris. Thank you so much for coming in."

Zoryana shook hands with them both, a thrill coursing through her as Frederick stood to see her out, the front of his allsuit taut with the ample sample behind it.

Leaving her clinic, instead of going to the pub, Dr. Puskinska had a gallon of vodka and a young escoriant delivered to her home, needing a fire hose to douse her sorrows.

The male escort variant was the perfect accompaniment to the gallon of vodka, and she reveled the evening away in their company, getting thoroughly lubricated. When the escoriant suggested a rather risqué position, she was happy to let him minister to her. The upended, quarter-full bottle firmly ensconced between her widespread legs, the escoriant lowered his lips to the region and did what she'd paid him to do. Soon afterward, she drifted off to sleep.

When she didn't show up at her clinic the next day, they found her in that position, her body cold.

Making love to a gallon of vodka.

\* \* \*

Doctor Sarina Karinova saw they were too late, yellow police tape across the door. News reports mentioned a prominent local doctor dying by "misadventure" but not citing how. A few discrete inquiries at the local pub where Dr. Puskinska was a known fixture quickly revealed the means. The coroner's report officially ruled it alcohol poisoning.

Sarina supposed alcohol administered through the moderately absorbent tissues of the vagina was a more pleasant way to die than most. Alcohol poisoning was unusual, the vomit reflex often sufficient to ward off too great an intake of ethanol. When administered vaginally, alcohol bypassed the reverse-peristalsis reflex mechanisms. Alcohol administered anally was far more lethal, the tissues lining the colon highly absorbent. Doctor Puskinska's alcohol content upon expiration had been point-nine-five percent, far in excess of the usually lethal threshold of point-five percent. Chronic alcoholics might exceed that point-five threshold and still live, but such levels were nearly always fatal. And Dr. Puskinska's level had been twice that.

Sarina suspected it wasn't misadventure at all.

The receptaclone was being held for questioning, slated for recycling the moment he was no longer needed. The male escoriant who'd left her in that position swore it was the Doctor's idea, revealing he'd pleasured her orally while the bottleneck was inside her. The escoriant was also likely to be recycled by his escort service as a prophylaxis to any liability and to clear its reputation.

Sarina did get lucky. A local cleaning service had sent in a saniclone to clean the office following the police investigation, and in the garbage had been a sheet from the Doctor's appointment book, two names at the bottom noted for consult: Frederick Andropovich and Katarina Satsanova.

The police confiscated the surveillance tapes, so she'd been unable to compare vids, the ones from Vasyl's Bawd Mod having only confirmed her conviction that these two were identical, or nearly identical, to the new Premier and the Admiral's son.

Following the husband's filing for divorce, Dr. Tatiana Satsanova and Captain Fadeyka Andropovich had been seen and photographed together almost daily, frequently wrapped in each other's arms. One lurid vid was purported to show them fornicating on the balcony of the Premier's suite high in the palace, the vid so grainy it was impossible to authenticate.

Instead of feeding the bombast of her opponents, however, their sightings together were garnering the people's support. Comparisons with an Ancient earth tale had begun to emerge. Guinevere and Lancelot, they'd been dubbed. Another comparison closer to home might have been Catherine the Great and Count Grigory Orlov, whose scandalous love affair began while the former was still married to her husband, Peter III. But the Ukraine press shunned all that was Rusky and trumpeted the Camelot legend instead.

"You're going to wear yourself out, reviewing those vids like that," Feo told her, his pallor having abated somewhat, and his gaze clearer than at any time since being shot.

The public vids of Premier Satsanova and Captain Andropovich differed not at all from those of Katarina and Frederick, except for context. The faces were the same.

"What do you make of it?" she asked him.

"Sounds like the plot of a bad science fiction novel."

"I'm serious!"

Feo laughed. "Of course you are. It's difficult to believe this is really happening, mutaclones taking over Ukraine."

"Looks that way to me, too."

"And now, someone's after the real thing."

"Doctor Puskinska's death was *not* 'misadventure.'" Sarina nodded at him. "But now they know it."

"Do they? Or do they think Doctor Puskinska's death was accidental, like everyone else?"

"I think they know it, which is why we haven't seen them again." She and Feo had staked out the neighborhood around the surgeon's office for two days with nary a glimpse of the other couple.

"Whoever's after them wasn't shy about eliminating Vasyl but went to great lengths to conceal their role in Doctor Puskinska's death. Why the change in strategy?"

"They weren't expected to return for a bawdy mod, for one. Maybe they calculated that the story they planted would deter enough suspicion that Kate and Fred wouldn't be alarmed." The Uzhhorod news carried a lurid byline about a jealous wife whose husband's enhancements obtained at Vasyl's Bawd Mod had made him so popular with his female paramours that they'd invaded their home and kicked her out. The wife had then taken her revenge by killing Vasyl at the Bawd Mod.

Unbelievable, Sarina had thought when she'd viewed the story.

Their ship sat on the tarmac at Kinchesh, at the edge of Ukraine's Wild West. Uzhhorod stood at the center of this region infamous for the variety of illicit merchandise that might be obtained. At its edge, Kinchesh at least strode for some claim to legitimacy, attempting to regulate the rampant activity or to stamp out what it couldn't regulate.

Sarina and Feo felt somewhat safe from their own pursuers, of whom they'd seen no sign. Their disguises had helped, and the Premier's personal iniquities had certainly distracted from her mother's assassination and the Ukraine's pursuit of the perpetrators.

Sarina was grateful for the rest, mostly because of Feo. He was looking much better, awake and alert nearly all hours of the day. The nanostim auto enhancers emitted periodic signals on their progress, and the rate of bone growth was over a quarter-inch per day. Given he'd had a four-inch hole blasted in his rib cage, Feo was fortunate he hadn't died from secondary complications. In another day or two, the bone growth would be complete, and in another week, the thoracic shell would come off.

Her one concern was his apparent lack of sleep. Whenever she woke, he was out of bed, staring at the vidscreen. It didn't seem to matter what time of night she awoke, there he sat, absorbed in the pursuit of the normavariant couple who looked identical to the muta-clone Premier and her scandalous beau.

"Where do you suppose they went?" he asked.

Sarina shrugged. "If I were them, I'd go someplace my face wasn't recognized, and I'd try to find out who erased my memory." She met his gaze.

"To Magadan," they both said.

# Chapter 11

On the outer Scutum Arm, dead west of the galactic core, a Siberia of empty space to the nearest Rusky base on the Norman Arm, sat Magadan, lonely and forlorn.

The Magadan base was a precarious foothold at best, so utterly far beyond the edges of the Chin Empire that they regarded its Rusky occupants as ignorant and crazy. Forty-five thousand light years from the galactic core, Magadan possessed the strategic value of absolute Kelvin, or about the IQ of the idiots who'd claimed it for Rusky in the first place. Inward along the broad arc of the Scutum Arm toward the Centaurus interior were the next major population centers belonging to the Chin. Usually the first stop for involuntary vacationers from Moskva, Magadan was infamous for the tight security of its perimeter and for the information it extracted from former Rusky ruling elites. But what came out of Magadan was so wrapped in security that all anyone heard was rampant rumor, facts difficult to come by. What loomed in every Rusky's citizen's mind was that Magadan was inevitably the last stop for former Rusky rulers.

Looking at the impossibly far distances from Urungi to the outpost, mutaclone escoriant Fred F4RB8C3 felt that he and Kate had no choice but to go there, even if rumor turned out to be fantasy. He and Kate had to find out who had wiped their memories and why.

Their ship sitting on the Urungi tarmac, Fred shook his head. When they'd returned to Dr. Puskinska's office on Kinchesh for their consultation appointment, three days later, the office door had been locked and the place had looked shuttered. They'd found out from neighboring businesses how Dr. Puskinska had met her end.

First the Bawd Mod proprietor, at the hands of a jealous wife, then the Rhytidectomist, at the bottom of a vodka bottle.

Fred and Kate had fled, taking their lumbering tug south into Romy before turning west toward Muldovy, crossing into Rusky just south of Crimea, and traveling along the Chin border toward open space.

Toward Magadan.

On the near outer arm, they'd found a Chin chop shop to supply them with a beryl-boro fusion drive, one equipped to travel across the divide between galactic arms to Ukraine, as opposed to taking the slow route they were taking to Magadan.

Fred and Kate had discussed the security at their destination. "You know they have that place sealed off for a reason," she'd said. "I can't even imagine the steps they've taken to keep people out."

"The ninth navy patrolling the Siberian hinter space, blasma emplacements encircling the constellation, stealth neutrino-polonium mines obscured by phase cloaks, micro-massgrav dark matter detectors—" Fred recited a list of security measures, as though he'd been privy to classified information in his previous life.

Simultaneously, they asked each other "How do you know all that?"

They shared a laugh, and Fred had felt his heart grow two sizes larger for her. And then Fred heard Kate's heavy sigh.

"We're way out in the Xinj province of Chin!" she said. "There's nothing between us and Magadan but Mongo."

He was quite sure she was exasperated, but not sure why. She wasn't the only one.

Fred ached from the back of his knees clear up to the middle of his spine. Three days aboard the tug alone with her exacerbated his aching for her with every passing moment. He looked over at her and warmth flooded through him. He sighed, his every concern fleeing, all his fears held at bay, the sureness of purpose possessing him, and only the ache of desire seizing him at the sight of her.

"Oh, Fred," she gasped, folding her arms tightly around her middle. "I turn to jelly when you look at me that way!"

He was in heaven. For an occasional moment or two, he could forget that aboard the ship with him was the most ravishing female in all creation, but those were brief. The tiny cockpit and cabin eliminated any possibility of privacy, the tugboat not meant for extended excursions and the space so small it was crowded with one.

The lack of privacy meant that they both saw more of each other in various stages of undress than most married couples. He'd resigned himself to it by now—her climbing out of the sanistall without a stitch, or her not-so-studiously looking the other way while he attached the excretubes—but she seemed to have no objection whatsoever to walking around without a thread of clothing, and had told him at least twice, point blank, "I'll dress when I'm damn well ready."

Her perfect physique just made the ache worse. But she seemed to know it and tried most of the time not to torment him.

The evenings were tolerable. Typically, they'd eat, Fred fixing the dinner since Kate had no patience for "that domestic crap" as she put it, and then afterwards an immersie or a game or some other diversion. During the immersies, she'd lean against him and lay her head on his shoulder, asking first whether he was comfortable with that.

These were the moments he treasured, the scent of her and the warmth of her wafting across him, the feel of her nearby, her company and companionship setting his entire universe right, as though that was where he belonged, there, beside her.

The nights were torture. Inevitably, as they prepared for bed, they'd have to navigate various states of dishabille in the routines that went along with the transition from evening to night.

Getting into the bunks was the most difficult. For the conditioning cocoons to work most effectively, there needed to be nothing between the nanostim tendrils and the skin. And given the low-gravity environment, they had to use the condicoons.

And Kate didn't warn him before shedding her allsuit, and as much as he tried to anticipate the moment she'd step out of her clothes, so he could turn away, he'd inevitably end up with an eyeful of the most delectable female body this side of the Andromeda Galaxy. And then it would be his turn to undress.

The first day she gave him a long once over before turning toward the wall in her bunk, but it was also the last.

The second day she didn't.

"Hey, I asked you to turn away!" he'd said, his back to her, his allsuit around his knees.

"I'm sorry, I can't!"

"What do you mean you can't?"

"Fred, you have such a wonderful physique that it's impossible for me to look away. It's irresistible."

By that time, his natural biological responses had given him a flagpole of prodigious proportions. "Turn away, and don't look at me like that."

"Fred, I wish I could." And then she made a sound somewhere between the hoarse grunt of a bull in rut and the harsh screech of cat in heat.

Fortunately, he was facing away from her and she wasn't able to see his response. When he felt steady enough, he backed into his bunk slowly, making sure she couldn't see his front, her eyes wild and gaze roving his backside from head to toe, her body wriggling inside the condicoon, her breathing rapid and shallow.

Somehow, he avoided her grasp and secured himself inside his condicoon. He knew what was happening by her thrashing in the bunk above him. He buried his head under his pillow so he didn't have to listen, but of course, how couldn't he hear?

At least it was fast and her thrashing subsided.

When he was sure she was sound asleep, he carefully extracted himself from his bunk and cleaned up the mess he'd made on the far wall, relieved he'd been able to do so before she saw the evidence.

She'd apologized the next day but thereafter wouldn't avert her gaze no matter how much he pleaded, insisting he was so irresistibly beautiful that she couldn't take her eyes off him.

So she wasn't the only one who was exasperated.

The simumems saturating his brain helped not at all, the pre-birth conditioning of all the things expected of him as an escoriant, the five thousand copulation positions crowding into his mind every time he looked at Kate.

The one partner he'd had for a while at the asteroid factory, the Wreck clerk, Jane, had craved his touch to the point of distraction, but out of the bunk, they'd argued much of the time and managed mostly just to annoy each other. In that relationship, his simumems had helped him to keep her satisfied sexually, at least. With Kate, the simumems kept him in a state of near-constant arousal—even when he didn't want to be, exacerbating his exasperation.

So when she folded her arms tightly around her middle and said, "Oh, Fred, I turn to jelly when you look at me that way!" Fred didn't reply, his response quite the opposite of jelly.

So he was ready when they arrived at Urungi to extract himself from the constant saturation. With his decrypting skills, he'd hacked into the galactic communication network—otherwise known as the galaxy-wide web—and had made contact with a broker in counterfeit transponder codes. Without them, the tug wouldn't get past the outer ring of Magadan's defenses.

He stepped to the hatch. "I won't be gone long," he told her.

"I want to come with you," Kate said.

He frowned, considering his options. "Yesterday you said you didn't."

"That was yesterday, and besides, you don't speak a word of Xinja."

He scrunched his face up. "And you do?"

She shrugged at him and spat a mouthful of syllables. "That translates as 'if these codes don't work, I'm coming back for some testicle soup!' "

It'd sounded like legitimate Xinja to him—as if he were some expert. "Where'd you learn that?" He had the sense he'd heard it before. Further, he was guessing she'd used a local idiom. "Get a disguise," he replied, donning his own wig. After the murder of Dr. Puskinska, they hadn't landed anywhere without disguising themselves.

He opened the hatch and waited there for her, looking out over the tarmac at Urungi, the largest city in the province of Xinj. A jumble of vehicles littered the spaceport with no noticeable order, huge freighters towering over tiny yachts, salvagers beside tractors, sleek city-slick ships beside beat-up country clunkers, large ships, small ships, flat ships, and full ships. A veritable nursery rhyme of craft stretched endlessly toward the horizon in all four directions. Their trashy-looking tugboat didn't look out of place at all.

"Oooh, look at that sweet little Fawnorghini," Kate said, pointing at a particularly classy yacht five spaces over. Despite its complete lack of emblems and subdued, almost modest dusk-gray color, the yacht postured with power, its short squat engines looking ready to launch in a blink.

Fred knew the ship just by its profile, a Fawnorghini Typhoon X600S. "The top choice of politicians everywhere," he muttered. "C'mon, let's go." He hoped the agent he was meeting wasn't too startled by Kate's presence. "Just stay in the background and let me do the talking."

The relatively light gravity made walking easy, but the primary, a young blue star, was caught in the death grip of a fast moving pulsar, the two of them whipping around each other some sixty times a second, or about as often as Fred thought about sex with Kate. The pulsing light around the young blue star was almost beyond the ability of the human eye to detect. The ground under their feet vibrated, the pulsar exacerbating the planet's seismic activity.

A tarmac jockey pulled alongside them, driving a hover built for four. "Ride to the gate?" His accent was thick and his Ukraine was so bad that Fred almost hadn't understood him.

Kate said something to the boy.

His face lit up, and he spewed some nonsensical barrage.

"He says for me, he'll charge only half," Kate said, already getting in.

Fred climbed into the back while she rode up front with the driver. He took stock of all the ships they passed while Kate and the tarjockey chatted amiably.

"He says keep a hundred yen in hand at all times as you negotiate rates with the dock master," Kate told him as they got off near the terminal.

Fred thanked the boy with a smile and a chit.

"More," Kate said.

He handed another one over.

Happy, the boy gave him a bow and sped off in search of another customer.

The dock master was a sour old grape, surly toward Fred in spite of the hundred yen he'd just given him. Then Kate stepped from behind Fred and said something in Xinja. A beaming smile spread across the old grape's mouth, and he chattered away with Kate as if she were a long-lost friend.

"Says he'll have the ship fueled and repaired right away."

He glanced askance at her and walked out of the terminal to the curb. Five taxis hovered past him without a glance in spite of his waving and calling.

Kate stepped to the curb and pointed at her foot.

A hover whined to a stop in front of her instantly.

Fred and Kate slid into it, and he rattled off the address.

"Please, driver," Kate added in her perfectly pronounced Xinja, two words that Fred knew.

The hovertaxi wove in and out of traffic, dodging all manner of conveyance—pedal-driven cycle taxis, cargo lorries, pushcarts, steam-belching behemoths, carbon-coughing contraptions, and just about anything people could come up with to avoid having to walk. We spend a million-and-a-half years learning to walk, Fred thought, and the next ten thousand figuring out how to avoid it.

The hover dropped them at the entrance to an alley. "Go up there, no hover go," the driver said in his pidgin Ukraine. Physically, Xinja Chin weren't terribly different from ethnic Rusky, their hair dark and curly, their skin having that same swarthy, sun-soaked coarseness. The eyes did have the characteristic epicanthic fold but without that, Fred might have thought that the people of Xinja were Rusky, the behemoth empire that sat ponderously just across the border.

Standing at the entrance to the alley, Fred and Kate were instantly spotted as foreigners, and every passer-by knew which way to point them.

"Foreigners only come here for one reason, apparently," Kate said. The floppy wig made her look ludicrous, and at Fred's insistence, she'd put invisitape on both cheeks to pull her mouth into a rictus. She thought she looked hideous. Fred had altered his appearance in similar ways. Even so, trepidation ate away at his courage as he stepped into the alley.

Fetid smells mixed with saffron from the street.

"I wonder what died in here."

It was too dark to make out distinct shapes, but the ground appeared smooth. Past the initial stench, the alley widened slightly, curtained doorways lining either side. Fred felt eyes probing them from behind parted curtains.

"You," whispered a voice in clear Ukraine, "step this way." The whine of a blasma pistol emphasized the order, the glowing tip waving in the deep shadow. "Quickly, quietly."

Fred followed obediently, his senses tuned, stepping toward the doorway.

Another pair was approaching down the alley.

"Sst," Kate whispered, "I've seen her somewhere before."

Fred shushed her.

The glowing blasma pistol tip came around toward them at the sound of her voice. "I said quiet!"

The pair passed in the alley. Fred only caught a glimpse of an older, graying man with a stiff walk, and a younger, fortyish woman, hints of Rusky extraction about them.

And afterward, their new guide took them farther along the alley to a doorway more elaborate than others they'd seen. Twin oak pillars capped with dragonheads framed a solid-steel door, its lintel the dragon's body. The door "thunk-thunked" when their guide tapped on it.

A two-inch panel slid aside.

"Two for Mook Sook Chang Wang."

The door opened and they were shown in. Armed guards stood at every doorway, their uniforms looking Chin in style but lacking insignia, decoration, or other ornamentation. Their guide showed them to a pair of double doors, which swung open.

A small man sat Buddha-like at the far end of the room, his slight form draped in heavy silks, a brazier beside him. A saccharine, piquant tang wafted to them when they entered.

The small man stood and came toward them. "Welcome, friends," he said in perfect Ukraine. "Pardon the diversion at the entrance, but confidentiality in these matters—of all my visitors—is of upmost importance. I am Mook Sook Chang Wang." He shook their hands vigorously.

"Frederick." he said.

"Katarina," she said.

"Welcome, Fred and Kate," Mook said. "Please call me Mook. Fred, I'm told your companion is rather fluent in Xinja." He turned to her and uttered a spate of the incomprehensible tongue.

Kate giggled and replied with an equally incomprehensible spate.

"You and Kate," Mook said to Fred, "are well matched and admirably suited for one another, when you're not wearing those silly disguises."

Fred was taken aback.

"Oh, I know you're not wearing them for my benefit. And your travels have brought you through some interesting places. West Ukraine to east, a couple of stops in the Uzhhorod sector, where the mods you sought were, uh, denied your access, and thence north along the Scutum arm into our domains."

"You seem to know much about us, Mook."

"Including the asteroid clone factory." Mook smiled. "But these goings-on in neighboring empires wouldn't be of much interest except for the bear amongst the wolverines—the big bear who sits astride the Chin border for thousands of parsecs—and the adventurous souls who seek to brave the bear's den. Very curious, these adventurous souls."

Fred knew he was being plumbed for information. To refuse outright would be rude and the transponder codes they'd come for would be twice as expensive. Mook profits from information, Fred told himself, and he might be amenable to a little bargaining. "Again, Mook, I'm impressed with how much you know about us already. These codes we seek indicate the dangers we face, given their high classification within the Rusky military." Fred had specifically asked for four sets of codes, one of them for the Bezopasnosti, or security service, the Rusky foreign intelligence arm.

Mook looked slyly at Fred. "Yes, a great curiosity, this desire for these codes."

Fred felt he was having two conversations, one spoken, and the other unspoken. "Allowances must be made for those adventurous souls, since resources are difficult to obtain."

"Allowances are but one item, as it were, on the table."

"Who was that couple who just left here?" Kate asked.

Fred frowned at her, wondering why she felt it so important. That's the second time she's mentioned them.

"Ah, but confidentiality isn't an allowance within humble Mook's ability to breach, so sorry."

"Allowances and information might both be bargained," Fred said, "but info for info is a difficult transaction, since one person's treasure is another person's trash."

"True," Mook said. He glanced at Kate, gave her a smile, and then apologized in Xinja.

Fred knew a few words, greetings and the like, an apology a tremendously useful phrase in any language.

"It is nothing, Mook Lord," Kate replied in Ukraine.

They conducted their barter for the transponder codes and settled on a price. Fred counted out the chits, and Mook handed him a cube.

Fred checked its contents and uploaded the codes through his optimitter, then slipped the cube into an allsuit pocket.

"Tay?" Mook asked.

"Certainly," Fred said, liking the Chin beverage.

Mook snapped his fingers, and a tray floated into the room, a steaming pot and three cups upon it. Mook poured them each a cup and pointedly drank first. "What part of Rusky is your destination, if I may ask?"

Fred sipped contentedly. He glanced at Kate, who shrugged at him through a small shroud of steam. "Magadan."

Mook coughed and sputtered. "Good God, you can't!"

"Oh? Why's that?" Kate asked nonchalantly, as though incognizant of Mook's distress.

Mook shot a glance at the door, and then returned his gaze to her. "Kate is perceptive far beyond the expectations of her mutaclone uterpod. Her nanostim neuralinguist programming must have been extensive."

"What they do at Magadan approaches atrocity," Kate replied.

Again, his eyes glided to the door. "Truer words have never been spoken in this room before. Never!"

Fred and Kate exchanged a glance. Someone else had shown up at Mook Sook Chang Wang's for transponder codes similar to theirs? What was the likelihood someone else was going to Magadan?

"There are many ways to assassinate a character," Fred said.

"The blood from such assassinations saturates many a drawing-room carpet." Mook looked at them inscrutably.

"And sometimes, a dining room carpet." Kate replied.

"A Premier dies. Her Chief of Staff and an unknown doctor are accused in her death." Mook smiled. "But accusation isn't proof."

"And the accused still haven't been captured," Kate said.

Mook hesitated and didn't look toward the doorway. "No."

All the way back to the spaceport, the pulsar pulsating insanely in the sky, Fred was troubled by the conversation. He stopped at the loading ramp, looked four spaces over, and saw another ship where the Fawnorghini Typhoon had been.

\* \* \*

Sarina sighed heavily. "What are we doing way out in Hohhot, somewhere near Inner Mongo?"

She wasn't sure why the Chin had named the province Inner Mongo, when Mongo itself was just next door, nearly all its eastern and northern borders shared with the province. Its name made it sound as if it were inside Mongo, instead of alongside it.

Remote didn't describe the region. Neither did desolate. On a faint, sparsely populated inner spur of the Scutum Arm (or outer spur of the Norman Arm, depending on which astrogator a person consulted), Inner Mongo was among the least populated and least colonized sectors of the Milky Way. Further, with the exception of Kory, very little along the Outer Scutum Arm was colonized; hence, commerce along the Inner Mongo corridor was virtually nil.

Many Inner Mongo peoples lived little differently from their ancestors on Earth. Plains-grazing herds of goats, small subsistence farms, ceramics, and woven textiles with a small market outside its bounds, and no mineral resources to speak of.

Its only marketable characteristic was its isolation.

"It's the perfect place to secure counterfeit identities," Feo told her, which he'd explained were necessary if they were to crack the security at Magadan, where they suspected Fred and Kate might be going.

Sarina's one glimpse of them in the bizarre bazaar outside Vasyl's Bawd Mod had convinced her finally that a conspiracy was afoot to replace Ukraine leadership with mutaclones. Her interviews and genalyses of Tatiana Satsanova and Fadeyka Andropovich had pointed that direction, and Colima Satsanova's assassination had cleared the way for Tatiana to be appointed interim Premier in her mother's place, a fait accompli, as the oligarchy was likely to confirm her to the permanent position any day now.

Tatiana's sexual escapades with Captain Andropovich were being splashed daily across the tabloids, and rather than fueling the fires of her detractors, she was being lionized by the people, her voluptuous form writhing under his sweaty ministrations setting fire to the tinderboxes of men and women alike throughout Ukraine. As though this one human failing of the interim Premier inflamed populist support.

Quite a counterintuitive response, in Sarina's view.

Stills and vids of Tatiana and Fadeyka in various states of dishabille were flooding the neuranet. Her lascivious behavior public, an extortionist wasn't likely to have much advantage in influencing her with the threat of exposure. Premier Satsanova was managing to get quite enough exposure on her own.

"That's not the young woman I reared!" Feo shouted indignantly, after stopping one particularly lurid vid.

"Captain Andropovich seems to have corrupted her."

"Or that escoriant bitch corrupted him!" Feo looked furious.

The woman who was now the Ukraine Premier was clearly an escort variant mutaclone, designed by her gengineers to give sexual pleasure and inculcated by her nanostim neuraplant to behave in lascivious ways. And together, Tatiana and Fadeyka were so personally attractive that they drew the envy of nearly every citizen of Ukraine—and quite a few trillion people beyond Ukraine's borders, drawing desirous glances from individuals of every sex, even those adamantly oriented otherwise.

"Goddamn, they look good together, don't they?"

Feo mumbled begrudging agreement.

Disguised, Sarina stepped to the hatch of the yacht, Feo just completing the touchdown procedures and securing the ship. Pursued by Ukraine authorities for her confabulated part in Premier Colima Satsanova's assassination, Sarina wondered who might have manufactured such accusations. The same faction who had firebombed her clinic in Downtown Kiev? Who had pilfered her confidential medical files and then erased them? Who had kidnapped her wife Anya?

Sarina sincerely hoped so. So she could emasculate the bastards and feed them their own testicles! She sighed, just hoping Anya was safe, fingering her wife's ring on her pinky.

The hatch in front of Sarina opened.

The tarmac before her was as empty and desolate as the last one had been crowded. Four other ships besides theirs were scattered about. The closest one occupied a pad easily a quarter-mile away, an old beat-up tug. It's probably been there for such a long time that it's tacked into the tarmac with cobwebs, she thought.

"Ready?" Feo came up behind her, looking rested. He'd spent much of the trip in his bunk at the advice of his doctor, wrapped in his condi-coon. He hadn't seemed to sleep much, from what Sarina saw, but now the deathly pallor was gone from his complexion, and even under his disguise, he was looking more fit than since he'd been shot.

She looked over at him, his disguise subtle. When they'd landed on Urungi, neither had used a disguise, which they'd decided later had been ill advised. I'll never get used to this spy-thriller mindset, Sarina thought, and I pray I'll never have to! "Let's go."

Feo and Sarina started walking toward the terminal, a quarter mile away, no tarmac jockeys at a place as sparsely populated as this. Sarina didn't mind the walk, the red primary giving everything a sepia glow, a sharp cold wind whistling past her ears. The spaceport sat in a bowl, the skyline of a small city to the west, a ring of wind-worn mountains on the other three sides, dun brown in color as if denuded of tree. Perhaps trees simply haven't been introduced or haven't evolved here, she thought.

Feo handled the port master negotiations. He seemed to know a smattering of every language in the human lexicon, a side benefit of his travel with Premier Colima Satsanova.

The port master seemed particularly impressed with their ship. "Lady like hot ride?" he said to her in garbled Ukraine.

She sighed, supposing that a younger woman with a far older man arriving in a high-class vehicle like the Fawnorghini Typhoon invited speculation as to what she might see in him. Sarina bit her tongue on what she wanted to tell the backwater lout, that she'd much prefer to take his wife to bed than either man present. Rather than offend him and perhaps provoke him to put sugar into their beryl-boro tank, Sarina kept her mouth shut.

The shuttle ride into town was uneventful, across grasslands zigzagged with fence, some plots showing signs of cultivation, most covered with an even stubble of short, brown grasses.

"From Ukraine too, you also?" their driver asked in ungrammatical Ukraine.

Feo raised an eyebrow at Sarina. "Get many visitors from our nation?"

"Second today, reunion having," the driver said, chuckling at her own joke.

"Drop us off here, Driver," Sarina said, their vehicle just entering the outskirts, where "Welcome to Urungi" signs were backed with "Last chance for trinkets" signs.

The corner diner didn't look appetizing. "We'll sit here, at the counter," Sarina told Feo, the main road to the spaceport easily visible. "No coincidence, is it?"

"None at all. Feo, we have to get another ship, something a little less obvious. That dock master practically accused me—"

Feo held up a hand, mirth appearing on his face. Although his gait was still somewhat stiff from the thoracic cage, he exhibited no discomfort.

Last night, she'd inspected the wound and had found it healing satisfactorily. He'd be able to discard the thoracic cage in a day or two.

"You're right about the ship. We need something so nondescript that no one will give it a second glance."

"Like that beat up tug we saw at the spaceport."

Feo snorted. "I wonder if it even runs."

# Chapter 12

"How much did you pay her for those identochips?" Kate asked.

Fred told her, the two of them stepping onto the street, the one real street of modest width through the center of town. The street was a ribbon stretched east and west like a line laid down by a god, burning off everything along that ribbon with a thunderbolt from the heavens so straight and pure that only a god could have crafted such perfection. He wondered where the road west led. East was the spaceport.

They'd just stepped from the counterfeiter's lair, a nondescript two-story building next to an empty culvert whose sides sprouted that same brown stubble that seemed to carpet the entire planet.

"What?" Kate replied, sounding distressed. "I can't believe you paid that much!"

The price for the identochips had been agreed upon beforehand, Fred using encrypted secuchannels, so in spite of Kate's knowing the local Inner Mongo dialect, she hadn't known how much he'd be paying. The language was a variant of Mongo proper and quite dissimilar from Mandar, the principle Chin language. Fred wondered why it was even considered Chin territory. "So, that's a problem?"

"No, it just means we can afford anything we want."

"Not exactly," Fred said, worried that she'd propose they buy a better vessel—like the Fawnorghini Typhoon they'd seen at Urungi. "I had to hack into five accounts to scratch together enough money for the identochips. That's five different ways we might be tracked down. Besides, what more could you want?"

"A better ship!" Kate snorted in exasperation. "I can just see us arriving at Magadan impersonating high-ranking military personnel aboard a pile of shit like that! Come on, Fred! Your head isn't only for putting a hat on."

He'd been wondering about that and hadn't really come up with a solution.

"That Typhoon on the tarmac at Urungi would have been perfect."

Just what Fred was afraid of! He wondered if women were the same throughout the galaxy. Riding their men for the most elaborate model yacht, wanting to impress everyone, more concerned with their hot rides than whom they were with. Fred suspected not, but wasn't about to offend Kate by asking.

He looked over at her. Disguised and all, she was beautiful, and the ache returned to the back of his knees. Knowing it was showing, he distracted himself. "You hungry?"

She nodded, glancing him up and down.

He nearly fell into the culvert, swooning when she undressed him like that. "I saw a diner at the edge of down. Sound good?"

She fell into step beside him, taking his hand.

Fred tingled all over, loving her terribly, wanting her terribly.

\* \* \*

"I just got a trake from the port master," Feo said.

Sarina looked at him sharply. They'd just come out of the counterfeiter's lair, a nondescript two-story building next to an empty culvert whose sides sprouted a brown stubble that seemed to lay like a rug across the whole planet.

"He says the tug is for sale. And bizarrely enough," Feo added, shaking his head, "someone wants to buy the Typhoon."

"Out here in this vodka-forsaken corner of nowhere?"

Feo shrugged at her. "The port master even offered to collect our personal effects from it. The buyer is in a hurry."

"How much?" Sarina asked, and she whistled tonelessly when he told her. "For that price, they can have our personal effects too." She'd been wondering how they were going to approach Magadan disguised as undercover Bezopasnosti in a ship so conspicuously ostentatious that it practically declared they were spies. Typhoons were the choice vehicle of aristocrati throughout the quadrant. A beat-up tug was a far better choice in Sarina's opinion.

"How long until the tug is ready?" she asked.

Sarina waited as Feo stood there, his gaze vacant, his lips moving just perceptibly as he exchanged trakes with the port master.

"Anytime, now."

\* \* \*

Fred walked aboard the Typhoon and instantly smelled the antiseptic.

As though it'd been used as an operating theater.

The port master had told them about the reconfigured cockpit, where the previous owner had rigged a bunk. The walls still showed signs of its hasty removal. The stateroom showed similar signs, the paint around one bunk's fastenings chipped and scarred. Smaller than the tug, the yacht would afford Fred and Kate even less privacy, and he wondered if he would succumb to his urges and give himself up completely to her desires.

He nearly wet himself just thinking about it.

"Even less privacy," Kate said, peering over his shoulder into the stateroom. "I'm all wet just thinking about it."

He pushed past her into the cockpit, barely able to walk, and somehow landed in the pilot's chaise. "Prepare to launch," he told the ship in a hoarse voice as Kate wiggled into the copilot's chair.

She looked over at his lap. "How'd that happen?" she asked, giggling.

The Typhoon catapulted from the tarmac.

\* \* \*

Sarina looked around the cabin of the tugboat. A little more privacy, at least, but still not designed for extended jaunts like theirs. Utilitarian was the only word to describe its accommodations. Where the Typhoon had been sleek, sharp, posh, and plush, the tug was simple, bare, battered, and bruised. It'll do the job, she thought.

"Supposed to have a refurbished beryl-boro drive," Feo said, seeming oblivious to the very pedestrian interior.

"How much did they pay us to take it off their hands?"

He grinned at her, getting comfortable in the pilot's chaise.

She sat in the slab-like copilot's chair and buckled herself in while he stepped through the ignition routines and sought permission to launch from the tower.

"Where to now, Captain Feo?"

"Harbin, Lonja Province," he said.

"Isn't that somewhere near Vladivostok?"

He nodded. "And if you think that's remote, wait 'till we get to Magadan."

"Should have a lively night club scene," she said, snorting.

# Chapter 13

"No, no, no, no, no!"

Fred gaped at the fussy woman in front of him, exasperated.

Sung Chong, proprietor of the fanciest clothier in Harbin, Lonja Province, looked him up and down like a runway judge at a fashion contest. "No, no, no, no, no!" she said again, clucking in discontent.

Outside, a breeze shook the few withered trees, the sky gray with impending rain. Harbin's constant moisture and pervasive cold gave the planet a foreboding feel, a menacing mood. A faint patina of fog half-obscured the view out the window.

Across the room, Kate was admiring herself in her Adjutant Inspector uniform of the Komitet Gosudarstvennoy Bezopasnosti, complete with epaulets, a field of decorations at the left breast broad enough to make a general weep, and a skirt tight enough to make him drool. If she'd been alluring in loose-fitting allsuits, she was now centerfold picturesque. In a military uniform magazine, anyway.

But Sung simply couldn't get Fred's uniform right. It looked perfect to him, but Sung wouldn't have it. "You don't look military!"

Fred wasn't sure how he was supposed to do that. And if he were really the person he suspected he was, it shouldn't have been a problem. Captain Fadeyka Andropovich had been a sterling example of military propriety prior to his five-year slide into dissipation and disillusion.

"It's your brain," Sung finally said. "Your brain is so soaked with testosterone that you can't keep your mind on your posture."

Fred was amazed at her perfect Ukraine and her fastidious observation of detail. How had she known his brain was saturated with thoughts of Kate?

"Here, I have something to distract you from her," Sung said. "That is, if you aren't going to bed her or wife her."

Fred stared at her. The presumption!

"Listen, Mister Fred Orick," she said, a hand on her hip, "You two are so clearly and deeply infatuated with each other that you're going to fail just from the distraction. No one's going to believe that two people who reek with as much andro-estrogens as you two are really from the Bezopasnosti. It won't work." Sung jerked her thumb over her shoulder. "She at least conceals it somewhat, but you, Mister Fred Orick, leave a trail so stinky, a noseless skunk could follow it!" The woman turned and headed for a doorway. "Back in a moment."

Kate across the room was laughing into her hand.

Fred snorted and turned to the mirror, his escoriant simumems feeding him a litany of positions in which to couple with Kate. He sighed, knowing Sung was right. His reflection echoed the sentiment, showing him a handsome man with a bulging crotch. Until he could get his front to flatten, he'd never pass for Bezopasnosti.

Sung came back with an infocube. "Here, upload this."

Fred held the cube in front of his eye, and an optimitter channel opened. At the prompt, he agreed to the EULA. *Twenty-ninth century,* he thought, *and we still haven't rid ourselves of EULAs.*

The recording was that of a drill sergeant, repeating in a sharp, shrill voice the section of the uniform dress code specific to the posture.

"Play that at all times while you're in uniform," Sung said. "Already, you're looking better." Then she glanced between them, first at Kate, then at Fred. For a moment she looked distracted.

*Probably accessing the neuranet on her com,* Fred thought.

"Why do you look so much like the new Ukraine Premier?" Sung asked Kate. "And you, that scandalous Captain she cavorts around with?" she asked Fred in perfect Ukraine.

Fred traded a glance with Kate.

"You're both very sweet and nice," Sung said, "but if I'm going to help you get into Magadan, you've got to be up front with me. Otherwise, no matter how hard you try, the bull will never give milk."

Fred threw his head back and laughed.

Kate came over to stand beside him.

With the drill sergeant in his head remonstrating him on proper posture, Fred felt the part of Lieutenant Investigator of the Bezopasnosti. "We're mutaclones," Fred told Sung. "Or supposed to be. We think we were abducted from our real lives and mutaclones put in our places."

Sung gasped. "Mutaclones running Ukraine? That's terrible!"

"And we don't know why. Further, how they managed to strip our memories—something so unethical, complex, and painstaking—"

"Magadan," Sung said. "That old gulag, heard atrocious stories out of that place. No wonder you're going there. Too bad they haven't caught that Chief of Staff, you know, the one who set up the Premier for assassination. He and some doctor have both evaded the authorities. I'll bet they have some answers for you."

Fred nodded. "I'll bet they do."

"Here, here's the contact information for a friend of mine. Chu Li Fong does stage makeup. If anyone can manufacture a disguise, he can."

"But we already have our identicodes."

"He'll figure that out, too. But you certainly won't get into Magadan looking like the Premier and her buckboy."

\* \* \*

"Am I your buckboy?" Fred asked on their way to get the stage makeup.

Kate burst into laughter, climbing into the hovertaxi after him. "I hope you'll be much more than that, my love!" And she sidled up next to him and leaned into his embrace. "I hope someday you'll be my husband."

"Why would I buy the whole cow just to get a little milk?"

"Yeah? And why would I buy the whole hog just to get a little sausage?"

They collapsed into hysterics in the back of the hovertaxi. He kissed her atop the head and drank in her scent, loving her terribly.

"Hey, none of that back there!" the driver said. "I don't want to have to clean anything up."

Or at least that's what Kate translated. Fred suspected she hadn't translated it all.

"Fortunate that Sung spent some time on Tantalus, wasn't it?" he said. "She spoke Ukraine like a native." She'd told them she'd spent several years in Kiev and had been the mistress of a high-ranking Ukraine official.

"Do you really think we should have told her all the rest?"

Fred shrugged. "We're a long way from Ukraine. It's unlikely it'll be important this far away."

The driver floated them to the entrance of an alley. "Down that way," she said. "Hope you know what you're doing." Kate translated.

Fred exchanged a glance with her as he paid off the driver.

Another alley, he thought. Seems as if they'd lived their lives on tarmacs and in alleys, Fred thought, not liking the look of this one.

Clods of mold and moss hung dark and dreary. A bitter breeze gusted past them, the sky gray. The planet's bleak weather didn't improve the welcoming feel of the alley in front of them. Moisture clung to everything.

Stage makeup, he told himself, knowing the simple disguise he now wore a paltry artifice for the bear's lair, Magadan likely to be wrapped so tightly in security that they'd be lucky to get past the minefields. I can't think about that right now, Fred told himself.

"Stay behind me," he told Kate. He quartered the alley, its deep interior too dark to see.

The buildings on both sides looked to be run-down offices or cheap hotels, nothing permanent. Cracked and peeling paint seemed to be the haute décor, curtains and shades either missing or in disarray behind glasma badly needing a scrub. On the alley sides, both buildings bulged inward above the first floor, occluding much of the sky, the alley façades in worse repair than the fronts, some of it the bare block of construction. Garbage bins sat in a haphazard row along one side, a faint, painted line across the other side with mandarin symbols in fading ideographs warning passersby to keep that side clear, Fred assumed, not able to read it. Metal grate doors on either side broke the solid block walls at intervals, looking like those a prison might have. In between the bins on one side were stacks of random refuse, rejected desks, broken chairs, disassembled partitions, all in multiple stages of moss accretion. The slight slope toward the center drained into a grate clogged with moss, seams in the plascrete bulging with the same, as though the green growth oozed from the very earth itself. Every surface sported either a faint green coat of algae or thick clumps of moss.

Fred advanced into the alley, a faint drip, drip coming from somewhere, the city at their backs preternaturally quiet, as though it held its collective breath while the courageous pair braved the menacing alley. The ground underfoot was a slippery slope. Don't need any continuum fallacies either, he thought idly, eyes probing the way ahead. Fred wished he had a weapon, at least.

Ahead the alley turned, the building above it turning with it.

His inner alarms went off, and he couldn't say why. "It's a trap!" he hissed, and shoved Kate to one side, leaped to the other as an assailant landed.

His foot found the larynx, but even as the Chin collapsed, hands to throat, the metal grate doors all burst open.

Tong, his mind told him, his body bursting into action. He rolled to one side, blocked a kick, spun with leg in hand, bludgeoned the other with the attacker, leaped upon a third, yanked the head back with a snap, dropped to a crouch as a blast blew the head from the broken neck, launched the body at the blaster-wielding fourth, block-blocked a double punch from the fifth and drove a knuckle through the temple, leapt and kicked away the blaster, thrust his knuckles up through the diaphragm to explode the heart, dropped to dodge the beam, swiped the feet from under the sixth and slugged the jaw to drop the Tong into unconsciousness. He finished off the first with a quick twist of the head and looked toward Kate, who cowered between a broken chair and an upright desk. Seven bodies around him, her eyes gaped wide as moons.

"Too bad we don't have time to interrogate this one," he said, indicating the unconscious Chin Tong with his foot.

"Probably wouldn't know who sent them anyway," Kate said.

Her voice sounds steady, Fred thought, her face a blank, white sheet.

"Come on," he said, taking her hand and going deeper into the alley.

"Uh, why not that way?" she said, looking back to the street.

"Backup," he said.

She followed obediently, and he felt her beginning to shake.

They hurried along the deepening alley, the twist taking them into an enclosure, a faint light at the far end. What he'd thought was a turn had actually been the end, with a passageway to one side.

He sensed no danger ahead or at least no human presence. The darkness deepened, but here in the absence of the near-constant drizzle, less moss grew.

The faint light at the end resolved into a courtyard of a type, the ground in the middle cultivated, a lush garden of orderly chaos sprouting between what looked initially to be four vertical block walls.

The growth hid a narrow door, another metal grate so thick with rust it didn't look as if it would move. The grate swung open, silent where it should have screeched in complaint. Beyond stood a girl, beckoning with her finger over lips, a gesture for silence.

He and Kate hurried through, and the girl swung it closed behind them, taking care to close and latch it with nary a sound. She whispered something to Kate.

"Follow, and make no noise," Kate whispered to Fred.

In the near-complete dark, they followed the girl through an underground warren. Fred got the impression of a maze built in far more oppressive times, such as a siege. Harbin had been a bulwark on one of many fronts in the century-long war between Chin and Ruska, a war whose detritus still littered the skies of multiple denuded planets.

A war fought between the Scutum and Norman arms of the Milky Way that had exhausted itself on the prodigious distances between the arms.

A war Ruska had been foolish to pursue, the Chin suffering defeat only once in their twelve-millennia history, and that back on Earth by a ruthless invader known as the Mongo Horde.

The girl seemed to know her way, Fred at first able to track their many turns. At some point, he lost his sense of direction. She brought them into an area whose volume suggested itself only by the nature of its echo. "We are safe here," she said, her voice as soft as a summer rain.

The smell of food reached them, the air pungent with sweet vinegar and salt.

Ventilation, Fred thought, in answer to his question as to why they hadn't smelled it before.

The girl lit a candle, illuminating a twenty-by-twenty room, multiple passages intersecting it. From each passage peered pairs of eyes, three or four pairs from each passage.

"You are safe. The Tong won't come here." The girl spoke further in the Lonja dialect, tones of the Kor language inflecting the speech.

Fred wondered where he'd learned to distinguish languages.

Kate translated. "Her name is Fang Kwon, and this is a mutaclone underground."

Fang tittered rapidly to Kate, who translated: "We occupy these long-abandoned tunnels, ignored by the world above us. Freed from our makers, whom we regard as presumptuous to call themselves that. Our maker is God, who breathed life into us, not these fools who grew us in their asteroid factories. Li Ang, come here."

Fang gestured at one pair of eyes regarding them from a passageway. A boy stepped forward and knelt beside Fang.

She parted the hair on his head. "This is where we removed the neuraplant." A scar two inches long from the crown down the occipital plate flared livid purple even in the dim candlelight.

"And he didn't die?" Kate asked, and repeated Fang's response in Ukraine for Fred's benefit.

"The tamper-prevention secucodes are disabled remotely first, before the surgery. These measures are becoming more invasive and more complex. We haven't been able to decrypt the secucodes in newly-captured mutaclones for the past year. We've lost several brethren in our efforts to free them from their implants. How were you able to free yourselves?"

The question startled Fred, his initial response to deny he had a nanostim neuraplant. Of course, you have an implant, his logical mind told him. No, you don't, his emotions cried in despair. Visions of simumem fornication soaked his brain in androgen.

"Does he always get an erection when he's upset?" he heard Fang say in perfect Ukraine.

"Always," Kate said.

"Then you haven't been freed, have you?"

"No," Kate replied, her voice a hoarse whisper.

Fred realized Fang had been speaking the Lonja dialect for the benefit of the mutaclones listening around them.

His mind reeling, Fred finally put the pieces together. He'd always wondered why mutaclones submitted to the extensive abuse they received at the hands of normavariants, whether it was beatings, rape, or outright murder. He'd always wondered why he struggled to shut off the constant thoughts of sex, the five thousand possible positions churning through his mind all the time, held at bay only by great concentration or by immediate threats to his life.

"Would you like to be freed?"

Fred looked at Kate, she whose amorous advances had seemed like the flirtations of a woman in love, and now he knew them to be motivated in large part by the nanostim neuraplant and its infusions of gonadoestrogens into her system.

"Oh, Fred," she said, looking pained.

"You said you haven't been able to decrypt the secucodes?" He looked at Fang, having revised his estimate of her age by several years.

"No, but you can."

And in those four words, multiple conclusions cascaded through Fred's brain. They knew who he was. They knew what he could do. They'd tracked him since he and Kate had escaped from the asteroid clone factory. This wasn't an isolated enclave.

"How long have you known about me?"

Fang regarded him, her gaze calm. "Since your abduction."

"Then you know I'm not a mutaclone."

"We do."

"And you didn't try to—"

"Fred," Kate said, a hand on his arm.

"And risk exposing ourselves and similar underground enclaves? For a normavariant?" Fang gave him a face full of bemused disgust. "We saved you from the Tong. Consider that our gift. Our letting you leave here with the knowledge that we exist is a bonus we never grant to a normavariant. Consider yourself privileged."

Fred checked himself. It was all too much. Kidnapped following his Summa Cum Laude graduation from the Ukraine Naval Academy with twin degrees in interstellar relations and cryptology, class president and valedictorian, son of Admiral Zenaida Andropova, and destined for a long, glorious military career. He'd ended up with a nanostim neuraplant saturating his brain with androgen, a mutaclone put in his place, his life stolen from him, wrecked by a profligate wastrel escoriant.

Of course, they hadn't helped him. He understood that. But the visceral betrayal, the absolute outright taking of everything he might have been. And they'd known it, here, three quarters of the way out on the Scutum Arm.

Fred raised his gaze to Fang. "Yes, I can crack the encryption." He forced a smile. "I'd be happy to. And thank you for saving us from the Tong."

"There'll be others. You're being pursued. The word has come down to the Triads. We can help you get to Chu Li Fong, but you have to leave Chin as soon as possible afterward. We have some influence, but it's the triads who really control Chin territory."

"What do you want me to do?" Fred asked.

\* \* \*

"What do you want me to do?" Admiral Zenaida Andropova asked, near to tears.

She stood in the Premier's office, in front of the Premier's desk, enduring a drubbing from an un-Premier like young woman who was a complete opposite of the reserved, stately, and well-behaved mother whom the daughter had replaced.

It would have been easy for Zenaida to believe she stood in front of the Premier, a place she'd stood a hundred times before. Cherrywood cabinets and gleaming glasma doors, memorabilia gracing the shelves, behind the Premier a view of the palace lawns, the city of Kiev in the distance past the veil of shielding, thick plush carpet underfoot, leathered chairs made from carmelopardalis-bovine hide, the desk a single chunk of Borealis conifer root. All these furnishings had belonged to her friend and Academy companion Colima Satsanova. Zenaida would have been hard put not to regard the person behind the desk as the Premier, and Zenaida's Commander in Chief.

If she'd behaved with any decency or decorum.

"What do you think I *want* you to do, Admiral?" Tatiana Satsanova said, the whip of scorn lashing across the room.

Zenaida glanced toward the figure behind the Premier, who leered at Tatiana like a strip club patron at a pole dancer. Stills and vids of the pair spreading like a pestilence across the neuranet had mortified Zenaida, and she wished she'd disowned her son immediately at the outset of his profligacy rather than suffer the behavior until its ultimate result manifested in this way.

Suddenly, she was furious. "Whatever it is you want," Zenaida said, "you can thrust your request into whatever orifice he doesn't have his cock crammed into!"

Tatiana shot to her feet. "You salacious bitch!"

"You're the salacious bitch! Fucking him wherever and whenever in full view of any and every camera you can find, disgracing yourself, your office, and the memory of your mother like some she-cat in estrus! The both of you deserve to be flogged in public, but in your sado-maso twisted brains, you'd probably enjoy it! God damn you both to hell!"

And Zenaida turned to leave but stopped.

Soft laughter from the person behind the new Premier stopped her in her tracks.

Fadeyka.

Her son, Captain Fadeyka Andropovich. He whose father had died in battle when the boy was but five years old, who'd never shed a tear for the man they'd both adored, who'd put on his dress uniform for his father's funeral and had marched alongside the coffin as a member of the honor guard, so trim, regal, disciplined and stoic, that Zenaida had wept just seeing him, the picture of propriety.

A picture that had remained intact up to and through his graduation from the Naval Academy, a picture shattered one month shy of his entering the prestigious Post-Graduate school.

Her son, Captain Fadeyka Andropovich, laughing at her.

She whirled on her son. "What do I have to do, pull your cock from her cunt, too?!"

The soft laughter continued as though she hadn't spoken.

"Mother," Fedey said, "you presume too much, and the source of your indignation is wildly conflated. Personally, I'm offended." He smiled at her and stepped around the burl desk, resplendent in uniform, his posture ramrod straight. "How dare you suggest, Mother, that I prefer her cunt over her other orifices. If you were to ask, I daresay she'd probably tell you that any of them is equally enjoyable. She'd even tell you she wished I had two more penises—nay, graft several more cunts to her body and penises to mine, so I can screw her every which way." He stopped in front of the desk. "Isn't that right, Dear?" he said over his shoulder.

Tatiana stepped around the desk and stood beside him, slipping her arm into his. "It certainly is, Dear."

Zenaida stared at them, stunned. Waves of indignation and revulsion washed over her. And she did what she should have done long before.

"Before God, you are no longer my son." Zenaida looked at Premier Tatiana Satsanova, the daughter of the woman she'd served for nearly thirty years. "And, before God, on behalf of my friend and mentor, you are no longer Colima Satsanova's daughter!" She looked at them both, no longer feeling any anger, only pity.

Piteous is all they are, Zenaida thought. Contemptible, piteous animals.

"Well?" Tatiana said.

The expectant look on their faces and their being utterly unfazed by her disowning them disturbed her more deeply than even her son's salacious description. They want something from me, she thought, the sudden realization blossoming across her mind like the rising sun across a primordial landscape.

Now, she knew why they'd called her here. Now, she knew why they'd sought to offend her and goad her.

"You want me to resign, don't you?"

"How you leave is your choice. You could keel over and die, for all I care," Fadeyka said.

Zenaida smiled, her turn to laugh softly. "Go to hell."

\* \* \*

"Sung, this is Dr. Sarina Karinova. Sarina, my old friend Sung Chong."

The small Chinese woman in front of Sarina was the picture of beauty, every bit of makeup accentuating the classic lines. Only a touch of grey in the hair and the beginnings of webs at the eyes indicated the onset of old age. "Very nice to meet you, Dr. Karinova," Sung said in perfect Ukraine.

They shook. "Mutual, Ms. Chong. Feo swears you're the best clothier to be had in Chin."

"He tells the truth when it suits him." She glanced at Feo and raised an eyebrow.

"Our parting might have been more amicable," he said, spreading his hands as if in apology.

"As amicable as our joining was fulfilling?"

Feo threw his head back and laughed. "It was, wasn't it?"

And Sarina knew she'd been forgotten for a moment, the two former lovers deep in memories.

"All these partings and joinings make life far too volatile, eh, Feo? Distressing to hear of Mrs. Satsanova's passing."

"Indeed, Sung. And then to be accused as a conspirator." Feo winced, as though pained. "Which is why we're here."

"A wild tale, if it were to be believed," Sung said.

Sarina glanced between them, sensing that Sung had been filled in on their plight.

"Thank you for attending to that other matter," Feo said. "We'll need livery specific to the civilian commissariat of Ruskva Republic—"

"Good enough to penetrate the security at Magadan?"

Sarina wondered at the level of trust between the two of them, Sung so well informed it seemed an unnecessary risk. Won't Sung be in danger if she knows too much? she wondered.

"Precisely," Feo told Sung. "And in the face of this latest information, our mission is that much more urgent."

"Such a shame, Admiral Andropova's taking her own life like that. And you know who's going to be appointed Admiral in her place, don't you?"

"My greatest fear," Feo said, shaking his head. "Those two will wreck the country faster than any Rusky attack on her borders."

While Sung measured and clucked, trading bluster with Feo, Sarina listened attentively, hers and Feo's fates intertwined no matter what the outcome at Magadan.

And what about the pair of mutaclones who didn't appear to be mutaclones at all, but normavariants, the real Tatiana and Fadeyka, whom she'd glimpsed in the bazaar on Uzhhorod and had followed to the planet of Kinchesh, only to lose them again in the confusion following Dr. Puskinska's death by apparent misadventure, whose blood alcohol content had been twice the lethal level?

And when she and Feo had landed on Harbin, there on the tarmac had sat the Fawnorghini Typhoon, sleek, squat, and powerful, its engines cold as though it had arrived a day or more before they had, the Typhoon's presence an enigma, its owner or owners with whom she and Feo had essentially traded ships on Hohhot beating them to Harbin as though stalking them preemptively, a harbinger of disaster, a portent of change.

It hadn't helped that moments after landing they'd learned of the suicide of Admiral Zenaida Andropova.

And the lack of news about Anya dwelt deep in Sarina's soul like a bitter, pernicious pill, her disbelief and despair still undigested, sticking in her craw all these weeks while Sarina sought somehow to rectify the wreck that someone had made of her life, all because she'd examined Dr. Tatiana Satsanova and had found her to possess the genetic makeup and the disposition of a mutaclone, and all because her discovery imperiled an insidious plan to replace the Ukraine Oligarchy with mutaclones. Sarina wondered idly how many other scions of the Ukraine ruling elite had been abducted and replaced. She shuddered, the thought terrifying.

"Are you cold, Sarina? Sorry to have you stand around in your slip. Here, let me turn the heat up." Sung paused a moment, clearly accessing the environmental controls on her optimitter.

And Harbin was cold. Had the skies been clear and bright, it might have made up for the bone-piercing cold, but on top of the cold, it had rained almost constantly since their arrival that morning. When it wasn't raining, the moisture drifted through the air like some heavy fog, veiling objects farther than a quarter mile with a diaphanous curtain of mist, droplets clinging to everything, causing her nose to run and her clothes to dampen and her mood to sour.

Oh, Anya, Sarina wondered, sighing that she'd ever see her wife again, refusing to cry tears whose source was inexhaustible, the terrifying fate even more terrifying for its being unknown, making Anya's abduction more severe, a circumstance that challenged Sarina's faith in God and fellow man.

Between Anya and Sarina, they'd both regarded Anya as the stronger one. Sarina had remarked as much to Feo in her conversation with him on the night of the Premier's assassination, when he'd speculated that her kidnappers must have mistaken Anya for Dr. Sarina Karinova. Anya must have fed that belief in an effort to protect Sarina. It was something Anya would have done. Sarina fingered her wife's ring on her pinky.

Now, two weeks later, pursued out along the Scutum arm to the northwestern edge of the Chin Empire, their destination even farther out along that galactic arm to an old Rusky gulag called Magadan, infamous for the atrocities perpetuated there by successive Rusky factions seizing power and condemning their toppled enemies to torture at a place so remote it might conceal the heinous deeds perpetrated there.

And that, despite its near impenetrable security and reputation, unsullied by a single heroic act, is our destination, Sarina thought.

Despair threatened to overwhelm her.

No! I won't let it! she thought. For Anya, I'll not give up hope! I'll search for her forever if need be!

And Sarina gathered her strength, set her jaw, and looked at Feo's erstwhile friend and lover.

"Get us in there, Sung, so we can find out who's doing this."

# Chapter 14

The circuits booby-trapping the nanostim neuraplant blinked off. Fred eased back in the chair. A cheer went up behind him as he sighed and closed his eyes.

Along with the secucoded circuits, the implant shut off, its switch accessible now that Fred had disabled the encryption.

The young man, a Chin-genotype mutaclone of the linguist-enhanced line of languaclones, opened his eyes and sat up, looking around the room as if seeing reality for the first time. "I'm…free." He said in the Lonja dialect, and then repeated it in Ukraine. He looked at Fred. "You freed me."

Fred smiled. He'd almost lost him, the security measures built into the neuraplant far more extensive for languaclones than other geno-types. Mostly as a means to insure such clones weren't compromised or co-opted by other governments, such measures frequently resulted in premature recycling, their viable life spans shortened abruptly ei-ther by accident or design.

Fred vaguely recalled a languaclone factory, whose location eluded him, having a uterpod abortirate five to six times higher than similar, less securely implanted genotype mutaclone lines.

I knew they all had nanostim neuraplants, Fred thought, his five years tending to maturing mutaclones on the asteroid factory having given him intimate knowledge of their physiology and circuitry. Why did I think I might be an exception? he wondered, looking across the underground chamber toward Kate.

She stepped to his side. "You did it," she said, her voice full with quiet admiration.

"I did, didn't, I?" Fred accepted her embrace and battled back the surge of gonadotropins and the erection that quickly followed.

He wondered what it would be like to live and love with normal hormonal levels.

"Soon, my love," Kate whispered, as though she knew what he was thinking.

Fang Kwon grinned at them, looking ecstatic at the languaclone's recovery. "Thank you, Fred. Thank you, a thousand times, thank you. We're forever in your debt."

"You said you would get us to Chu Li Fong in spite of the Triads?"

Fang looked at them both. "Yes, but it's become more difficult. Whoever ordered your killing has learned of your escape."

\* \* \*

"What?" Sung said.

Sarina saw her pause in mid-measure, the gaze distracted.

The older woman turned to an external display, and the small vid screen in the corner came to life.

A news report showed a crime scene investigation, lighted hovers surrounding an alley entrance, the caption clear to Sarina, the vid changing the language to Ukraine in response to her optimitter connection. Six bodies of known Tong members found dead in an alley, a seventh one unconscious.

Sarina wondered how it was possible. The Tong were supposed to be martial arts masters. What person or persons would have the ability to defeat seven of them? She looked at Feo, who stared at the screen blankly.

He turned, and his gaze found her face. "A local dispute, unlikely to involve us."

Sung was looking at Feo, a question in her gaze.

"That won't interfere with our leaving, will it, Sung?" Feo asked.

"No!" Sung said, "No, it won't. As you said, some local dispute. They wouldn't close the spaceport because of that." Sung resumed measuring Sarina.

But neither Sung nor Feo, Sarina saw, looked reassured. As the report tittered away in the Lonja dialect, Sarina felt how deeply perturbed the other two were.

"What's going on, Feo?" she asked during the hovertaxi ride back to the spaceport.

Feo was uncharacteristically silent. "My apologies, Sarina," he said finally, as they approached the terminal. "I've been accessing intelligence databases in Ukraine."

She'd seen the telltale twitch of trake in his jaw line. Some people even moved their mouths as they subvocalized over their trakes. The vestigial motions of speech were deeply ingrained and only mindful effort by trake users kept their mouths from moving.

"We're being pursued by a specialized squad within the Ukraine Secret Service called the Directorate of Extraordinary Commissions. The local Tong Lord was alerted to the squad's arrival and sent a welcoming committee."

"Didn't take warmly to the welcome," Sarina said.

"No, but at least we know who's pursing us."

"Are we sure it's us, and not our mutaclone pair?"

"I'm sure. Extraordinary Commissions wouldn't send agents after an ordinary pair of mutaclones."

She snorted. "Not much ordinary about them."

"True, but our capture is their priority at the moment."

She went through customs with him, deep in thought while he navigated the transactions with the dock master, his Chin passable and hers non-existent.

On the tarmac, across the landing space from their own, sitting where it'd been when they'd arrived the day before, was their erstwhile ship, the sleek Typhoon. Their battered tug with its refurbished beryl-boro engine was a sad, sloppy substitute, and Sarina wished for a moment that they'd kept the sport yacht. We can't exactly disguise ourselves in that, she thought, hoping they had enough in materials to get them through Magadan Security.

"It'll be uncomfortable," Feo had warned her. "And there are several risks in our going as mutaclones."

Chief among those he'd emphasized was the probability of abuse. Mutaclones suffered indiscriminate abuse from normavariants daily, usually without consequence. They were property. An owner could kill a mutaclone for the slightest offense or none at all. A normavariant might be sued for killing another normavariant's mutaclone, but rarely more than that. Further, the staff at Magadan—military, civilian, and contract—were under tremendous pressure, isolated from friends and family for two years at a stretch, and this stress frequently found its outlet in violence inflicted on mutaclones, whether in abuse, rape, or death.

Sarina was prepared for anything. Her life wrecked and her wife abducted, she felt she had to find those responsible, and in that, she had Feo's allegiance, he whose life had been torpedoed by the Premier's assassination.

How galling it must feel to be accused of orchestrating it, Sarina thought.

Feo had arranged for a requisition order to be placed in the chain of the Bezopasnosti civilian authority, the agency primarily responsible for facility operations at Magadan. This requisition was for two mutaclones of the saniclone variant line, a requisition that had received approval at both Moskva and Magadan. Forging the secured approvals had been the difficult part, according to Feo. Further, the requisition had been expedited, the Magadan facility having failed its annual maintenance inspection. The expedited order meant that the mutaclones might be ordered from any resource available and be sent to Magadan via the fastest route possible.

Two extra saniclones from the Rusky consulate in Beiji were being appropriated to fill the expedited requisition and would arrive via privately secured vessel along the Scutum Arm, a far faster route than sending them all the way from Moskva on the Norman arm.

The fact he could think of such things amazed Sarina, and that he knew the means for putting them in place astounded her. "We've had the bear sitting on our backs for centuries," he'd told her, grinning. "We've learned how to squirrel in and out of her lair without detection."

As their beat-up tug cleared Harbin's gravity well, Sarina looked deeply at Feo.

She'd removed the thoracic shell when they'd arrived on Harbin, and he seemed to be holding up, evincing only momentary pain on occasion. Her one concern was his apparent lack of sleep. It seemed that every time she awoke, there he was, brooding in the pilot's chaise, as though he'd slept a very short time or hadn't slept at all. "You don't seem to be sleeping much," Sarina said.

Feo turned and blinked at her. "I don't need much at my age."

"Maybe, but you won't heal properly if you don't sleep more. You'll be more susceptible to infection or re-injury. Are you having nightmares?"

He dropped his gaze to the floor. "I let them get to her. I lie awake at night, wondering how I could have let that happen to her." He sighed deeply. "Maybe a sedative would help."

"Let's start off with a mild one and see how that works. I don't want you drowsy the next day."

Feo nodded and smiled at her. "One last step."

"I'm not going to like this, am I?" Sarina could tell by his look.

"No, you're not. The neuraplant."

From her year in residence at the clone production facility, Sarina knew exactly what it was. "You aren't proposing we actually install one in our own brains, are you?"

"No, I'm not, but if we don't have something that simulates its effects, we'll be detected faster than a mutaclone trying to impersonate a normavariant. Subservience is conspicuously absent from our postures, our responses, and our speech. You can spot a mutaclone simply by the way it stands and waits."

Sarina nodded, knowing it. While the two young scions she's examined had masked their mutaclone origins well, they'd not been able to obscure them completely. Both had been missing that core component called conscience. Now, she'd have to subject herself to something intended to obscure her having one. How ironic, she thought. "Will it hurt?"

"No, not at all, and it's reversible, the equivalent of a mind mod."

Sarina recoiled, looking at him skeptically.

"Nothing that severe, believe me," Feo said with a laugh. "What this mod will do is inject subliminal auditory messages through your coke on a constant basis, messages such as, 'I'm a worthless mutaclone,' 'Obey, or they'll beat me,' 'Keep looking at the floor,' and the like. We're subservient, and we'll have to act like it."

"Not like you at all, and I certainly couldn't do it. Not without help."

"I've always been subservient to one person, and only one." Feo looked away, blinking rapidly.

Sarina put her hand on his shoulder, realizing that after the Premier's assassination, Feo hadn't had a chance to mourn the loss of his mentor and proctor, she who had ruled Ukraine for over twenty years. They had all felt Colima Satsanova's loss keenly, but none so keenly as Feo, who had served her for nearly thirty years.

"Sorry," he said, sniffling.

"Take all the time you need." Sarina admired how strong he was, how he poured himself into the pursuit of her assassins.

Just as she did her wife's kidnappers.

"I prepared the mod on the ship's biologic interface. We'll both need to inload the mod. Who's first?"

"I'll go. That way, you can make any adjustments. Is it going to matter that my Rusky has a Ukraine accent?"

"It's barely detectible," Feo said in Rusky, his own pronunciation flawless, having the right touch of the Moskva lift. "You're from the Crimea, according to your profile."

The Crimea was a Rusky-held constellation at the border between the two nations, a region whose governance had switched several times between Rusky and Ukraine across the centuries. For the last fifty years, it had been under Rusky control, but its ethnically-Ukraine citizens were constantly agitating for its return to Ukraine control. The language was a mixture of Ukraine and Rusky, which blended with the smooth consistency of oil and water.

Sarina shook her head at him. "You thought of everything."

"I sure hope so," he said, sighing. "Our lives depend on it."

She met his gaze, having come to admire the wise, fatherly gentleman, the gray at his temple and webbed skin at the corners of eyes giving him the air of a senior diplomat. "Thank you, Feo. Whatever happens, however this turns out, thank you. I speak on my own behalf, but I might as well be speaking for all Ukraines, and most especially for Madame Premier Satsanova. A thousand times, thank you." She leaned over and kissed him on the forehead.

For a second time in just a few minutes, he blinked rapidly and sleeved his face with his arm, eyes glistening. "You're welcome."

She gave him a smile and turned to the console. The vidscreen showed the space ahead. Vladivostok to the west was the only significant occupied system between the Chin border and Magadan, near the end of the Scutum arm.

"Optimitter link on," she said on her trake.

"Tugboat Taty, at your service," said the too-bright female voice, the Pollyannaish tones syrupy with sweetness.

"What's it called?" she asked Feo.

"Mutaclone mod."

"Inload mutaclone mod," she traked.

"Mutaclone mod lacks the sure sign certificates commonly included in vetted trake mods. Proceed?"

"Proceed," she said, wondering whether she'd have to agree to a EULA. Those annoying EULAs! she thought.

A progress bar appeared on her corn. At one hundred percent, a flashing icon indicated installation in progress.

Then it vanished.

Immediately, Sarina felt depressed, anxious, and afraid. She looked up at Feo, and immediately recoiled. "Sorry, Sir, it wasn't my fault." She held up her hands though to ward off an attack, though none was imminent. She couldn't bring herself to look at him directly, unable to overcome her fright of him.

She saw his gaze become distracted. Inloading the mod, she surmised. Even as she deduced these things, she still felt a profound terror of him, the thought of his having the same trake mod no comfort whatsoever.

"Actually, our inloading these mods might prove an advantage," Feo said, jerking away from her as though recoiling from an attack.

"Don't do that," Sarina said, laughing in spite of her terror, unable to imagine that Feo was afraid of anything.

"We certainly won't have to manufacture flight responses, will we?"

He too, she saw, couldn't raise his gaze to her. "Is this what it's like for them?" she asked.

He nodded, his hands leaping to guard his face. "I took the programming from a neuraplant. Depends on the model, but most have this adrenocortico fear coupled with the subliminal auditory underlogue. Some mutaclone models don't have the underlogue, such as escoriants, unless they're masocants. An escoriant with an underlogue of subservience isn't likely to present him or herself as very attractive."

She threw a tentative smile his direction. "Had a little experience with escoriants?" She was instantly afraid she'd offended him, her hands going up again. "Sorry, Sir, I didn't mean to get personal." Even her tone of voice and pitch exuded terror.

"Not offended. Forgive me if I don't answer. You could probably beat the information out of me by batting your eyelashes."

"So what's on their neuraplants?"

Feo shrugged. "I'd imagine it's something to do with sex."

"Instant arousal and readiness, would be my thought. Adrenogonadotropins dumped into the bloodstream at the slightest provocation. But I wonder what the auditory underlogue content is like."

"There's a corn component too, which I didn't include, and usually a simumem library."

"Library? Of what, coupling positions?"

A small smile seeped through the anxiety on Feo's face. "Five thousand of them, I'm told."

Sarina snorted. "Anything would be more pleasant than this."

\* \* \*

Fred paid the dock master what Kate had negotiated, a rate far lower than he expected, and they stepped from the terminal onto the tarmac, his eyes searching among the docked vessels for any that looked out of the ordinary.

No sign of the tug.

He sighed, relieved. His jaw rippled with tension.

The trade they'd made at Hohhot in Inner Mongo with the owner of the Typhoon had been a risky move, particularly since they'd seen the same ship at Urungi, in the Xinja province.

As though they were following us, Fred thought. Since the transaction had been facilitated by the Hohhot dock master and hadn't necessitated face-to-face or even corn-to-corn contact with the owners of the Typhoon, Fred had no idea what they looked like.

His neuraplant now modded to include the attitude of command, he waved down a passing tarmac jockey.

"The Typhoon, please." He gestured vaguely that direction and helped Kate aboard.

Fred looked the picture of command, in both posture and appearance. Chu Li Fong, the stage makeup artist, had crafted him a face to match, adding a goatee, hollowing the checks, putting a peak to each eyebrow, and adding an electrostim microchip to stimulate the mandible muscles. The latter by itself caused his jaw and temple to ripple, giving him the appearance of being constantly angry or stressed.

The new appearance, coupled with the uniform tailored for him by Sung Chong, would go a long way toward convincing the Magadan personnel of his bona fides.

Kate had undergone similar mods.

Fred had already integrated their new physical features into their dossiers on file at Bezopasnosti headquarters in Moskva, the encryption, passwords, firewalls, and other secumeasures easily yielding to Fred's cryptology skills. As though he'd undergone rigorous training in countersecurity and cryptology. Like his hand-to-hand combat skills, the source of his training remained irretrievable.

The tarjockey hovered them out to the Typhoon, Fred scanning continuously for both the tug and suspicious activity.

At the Typhoon, Fred waited while Kate wrangled with the tarjockey over the price, whittling it down to the lowest level he'd ever paid.

He boarded, Kate right behind him, traking a liftoff command to the ship. "We should have gotten the mod first," he told her, "and then went shopping for everything else."

"Quite the negotiating, eh?" Kate replied, throwing him a grin.

The tower granted their ship permission to launch. Buckled and ready, Fred gave the order.

The Typhoon leaped from the tarmac and soon cleared orbit.

Fred programmed a course for Magadan and unbuckled himself, checking the ship transponder codes, their dossier profiles, their neuraplants, and their uniforms, as well as their personal valises that they'd take to their staterooms at the Magadan facility.

Everything had to be precise. Nothing to indicate their origins as anything other than the Moskva Bezopasnosti headquarters.

Kate looked over at him. "You thought of everything, didn't you?"

"I hope so," he told her with a small smile. "Anxious?"

"Of course, but you've got the situation well in hand. Other than one small detail." Kate unbuckled herself and stood, stepping to his side.

"What'd I forget?" he asked, looking up at her. She stood so close he could feel the warmth coming off her, her scent filling him with pleasure. He wasn't sure when he'd come to recognize her scent, but he did, and he warmed at it, the escoriant simumems attempting to intrude.

"Me," Kate said, and her uniform peeled away.

# Chapter 15

Commander Mariya Nikonova whipped her right arm across her body and unleashed a backhand across the saniclone's face, sending him to his knees.

He cowered, his arms over his head to fend off the next blow.

The lights of approaching vessel startled her, stopping her in mid-swing.

A beat-up tug materialized out of the night, the compound lights coming ablaze at the approach.

The Commander frowned. "Who the hell is that?" she said on her trake, watching the battered ship settle precariously to the tarmac.

The civilian director traked her back. "Apologies, Commander Nikonova," Danil Topikovich said, his voice a squeaky whine, "it's the saniclone pair coming in from the Chin Consulate, which I guess we ordered."

"You guess?" These godforsaken civilian bureaucrats never know what they're doing! Mariya thought. "You either did or didn't order new saniclones, Comrade Director. Which is it?"

Topikovich spluttered and stammered. "I guess I did, but I don't remember placing a requisition. Especially not an emergency requisition."

"Did the waste removal system leak into the air ducts again?"

"Huh? When did that—"

"You dolt!" she interrupted. "It was a joke. Well, they're here and since it'll take a year to get more saniclones, we'd better keep them, hadn't we?" *Moskva moves slower than a clogged sewer pipe, I swear!* Mariya thought, a waste system leak into the air ducts not an infrequent event.

*I wonder if either one is any more competent than this lump of meat at my feet,* she thought. It was the third time this week she'd had to beat him for not cleaning her suite adequately. *Not that I demanded absolute perfection, but he could at least clear away all the hair Nadya leaves in my bed!*

Mariya watched the ship settle, not thinking twice about the battered hull, certain it was the best they'd been able to acquire, given the expedited request. And if two saniclones didn't reach their destination due to some in-flight mishap, no loss of any significance, except the time it took to place another order.

"Erik," she said to the saniclone at her feet, "go help them with their things and get that heap of scrap they arrived in off my tarmac! Then show them their quarters."

"Yes, Commander." Erick ducked as if expecting to be cuffed and shambled toward the ship, throwing an occasional glance over his shoulder.

But Commander Nikonova was already headed back into the compound, absently checking the perimeter from long habit, the security at Magadan tighter than a bear's anus. The tug would have been blasted out of the sky at the first perimeter a full parsec away if it hadn't had a set of clearance transponder codes—codes issued by Bezopasnosti Moskva Headquarters. Commander Nikonova didn't have a shred of interest in the beat-up tug except to get it off her tarmac.

She strode into the building, across the foyer, and toward the elevators. On her way up to her office, she received a trake from her receptaclone.

"Be there shortly," she traked back, the elevator just arriving. It whisked her to the fifth floor. "What is it, Liza?" she asked, stepping from between the doors.

Receptaclone Liza L23LZ13 smiled receptively. "Adjutant Inspector Katarina Kupchenko and Lieutenant Investigator Frederick Mosovich from Moskva Headquarters have just passed the outer perimeter, Commander Nikonova."

The blood drained from her face. "Credentials!" she ordered up on her corn, rushing into her office. On her desk vid, the credentials for the approaching pair appeared. Mariya scanned them with a sharp eye, her heart hammering. How dare Moskva send an Adjutant Inspector without warning! Mariya thought, the credentials looking perfect.

She ordered their complete dossiers from Bezopasnosti Central Archives.

Blaring red "classified" warnings blinked on both her corn and desk vid.

She spat an expletive. As Commander of a highly classified operation, Mariya had access to encyclopedic information that remained inaccessible to all but the highest sources in the Kremlin. She was rarely denied access to the information she sought. With a sigh, she put in a request for their dossiers through her supervisor, the Director of State Security himself, Antonin Medvedev, second in power only to the President himself.

"Orders," she said, not realizing she spoke aloud.

On her screen and on her corn, the heavily redacted orders appeared. The redaction wasn't a good sign. That meant this pair was on the hunt for things even Mariya wasn't supposed to know about. Commander Nikonova noted a few references to possible infiltration. Routine review of all security protocols and installations, review of all manifests, status reports for all projects in progress, and a nanostim neuraplant exam of all personnel—civilian, medical, military, and mutaclone.

Mariya nearly messed her breeches. This will disrupt all current operations, she thought, even the one I daren't think about, it's so secret.

"Hold them at the second perimeter," she ordered. "Tell them we're verifying their credentials!"

"Yes, Commander," Liza said.

"Nadya, we've got trouble," Mariya traked.

Medical Director and Gengineer Nadezhda Eltsova came on both corn and coke, a jumble of lab equipment in the background. "Kak dela, Mariya. Trouble? In your paradise? Just do that little thing you did last night, Marushka, and all my troubles go away."

"Not now, Nadya! Inspectors from Moskva, at the perimeter!"

"What? Now? In the middle of—"

"Don't even say it, Nadya! Not a breath! We'll have to isolate that part of the compound immediately."

"But we're almost there. She's about to appoint him Admiral!"

"Hush, I said! They're probably listening. I tried to retrieve their dossiers. Classified! And their orders are redacted!"

"For you? Nothing's classified for you! Nothing! You're right. Real trouble! I'll isolate the lab, even suspend saniclone service. The crew will hate having to clean their own toilets, but we have to. I'll get to it. You'd better warn Danbecile. Out."

Mariya sighed, knowing exactly what to expect from the imbecile, Danil.

"What do you mean, suspend saniclones service?" the civilian commander Danil Topikovich said, his objection legitimate.

More flies with honey than vinegar, she told herself. "Danil, I need your help, at least until we know what they really want. I'd better come to your office. There are implications to this I'd rather not discuss on a trake." She dropped the connection, grabbed a flask of schnapps from her desk drawer, and rushed from her office.

Liza the receptaclone spotted the schnapps. "Persuasion in the works."

"I'd take the electrodes but I need his cooperation."

The two of them shared a giggle, Danil universally despised. Mariya was out the door and taking the stairs. On the way, she checked on the interloper's location.

Held up at the second perimeter, per her order.

Good, she thought, flying past the receptaclone without a glance and bursting into Danil's office.

"Schnapps? Special occasion?"

"Let's just say I'm not averse to proffering bribes. Half their orders are redacted. Do you know what that means?"

"Uh, sorry, my espionage skills are a bit rusty. What's that mean?"

"It means even I don't know half the reason they're here. Listen Danil, a surprise inspection for unknown reasons by a pair of Bezopasnosti whose dossiers aren't accessible to me smacks of political meddling of the worst sort."

Danil pulled out a pair of shot glasses. "Peppermint or peach?"

"Your favorite, of course."

"Peach. You really *do* want my help."

She looked directly at Danil, letting her anxieties show. "I do. Might be a Duma ploy to embarrass the Director and hence the President, or it might be part of a coup. The General Chiefs have been after the President for a full disclosure of our activities here, particularly the clandestine ones. So here's what I need."

"Salud!" The two of them said in time together and tossed back shots.

"Our special project in the basement only has one entrance anyway. I need the entrance relabeled, something innocuous, saniclone closet or the like," Mariya said, refilling their glasses. "No saniclone or other facility services, at all."

"Food, toiletries, messages, nothing?" Danil asked.

"None of it. Complete blackout."

"What about transmissions?"

"All of it will have to be secured electrical. No optimitter, ethernet, radio, subspace, or other signals at all. There are separate circuits for just such an exigency, in case security is ever compromised. Let's use it."

"All right. Salud!"

And they both threw back another shot.

"Now, your staff."

"And mutaclones, too, I presume?"

"Of course."

"Completely mute, all questions about the facility directed back to you and Doctor Nadya. Consider it done."

Mariya was surprised to get such forthright cooperation. "Really? So fast? All right, there's something you want, isn't there?"

"Did you really think I'd agree after a few shots of peach schnapps? I'm daft sometimes by not that daft!"

She shrugged. "Salud!"

And they tossed back another.

"So what do you want?" she asked, the soft fuzz of the aromatic peach drink beginning to seep into her brain. Rarely a drinker, Mariya had little tolerance. Nadya, now there was a woman who could hold her liquor!

"Liza, your receptaclone."

Taken aback, Mariya almost refused outright. The strict lines between civilian and Bezopasnosti personnel were rigorously observed, from top command down to the lowest ranks, even among the mutaclones who served them.

"I've wanted to screw her brains out for the last four years," Danil said. "Don't look so shocked, Commander. As if I can't hear you and your little naughty Nadya going at each other at all hours of the night. The suite walls aren't that thick."

"Naughty Nadya" was her favorite nighttime name for Dr. Eltsova. Mariya wasn't worried about his knowing; in fact, she was certain rumors were rampant throughout the complex. Further, she wasn't worried someone might exploit the knowledge. Both their spouses back in Moskva tacitly acknowledged the relationship, their families close, the modern equivalent of spouse swapping, both at Magadan and in Moskva. But it might not behoove them to engage in the behavior while the Adjutant Inspector and Lieutenant Investigator were here.

"All right," Mariya told Danil, "but on one condition."

"What's that?"

Mariya grinned and poured them each a fourth shot. "That your liaison with Liza wait until we're rid ourselves of this pesky pair from Moskva."

"Prudent. Just as you and Nadya will knock of the bawdy naughties, too, I assume. Salud!"

The two of them clicked their glasses and tossed back a final shot.

Commander Mariya Nikonova returned to her office for a quick infusion of alcohol neutralizer before traking an order to the second perimeter to let the pair from Moskva through, confident now they'd never get wind of that special, ultra-secret project in the basement.

Stupid as he was, Danil was right about her and Nadya.

Mariya sighed, her naughty Nadya nearly irresistible. What's a few nights without her? she asked herself.

The pair of inspectors would want to know about the current projects at Magadan, including the one so secret that Mariya didn't even want to think about it. Antonin Medvedev, Director of State Security, had initiated the Bawdy Double project twenty-five years ago. After five years of initial planning, the first phase had been implemented, but it had gone awry, the mutaclone they'd planted high in the Ukraine bureaucracy going rogue twenty years ago. The project had retrenched after that setback and had poured fifteen more years into refining its techniques. With the project eight years now, Mariya had helped to launch its second phase five years ago, a two-pronged effort whose first aim had been an unqualified success and whose second aim was about to come to fruition.

And I'll stop any meddling from Moskva by any means necessary! she thought.

Then Commander Nikonova descended to the tarmac to greet the pair of visitors.

* * *

"You two don't act like any mutaclones I ever met."

Sarina glanced sharply at Erik, the saniclone who'd greeted them on the tarmac. She'd thought it odd that he'd insisted they move the beat-up tug to a hanger immediately.

"Commander's orders," Erik had replied, a welt on his right cheek.

"Did the Commander do that?" Sari had asked.

Erik nodded.

"He's pretty mean, huh?" Eodo asked.

"Uh, no, Eodo," Erik had replied. "It's a she, and she's knocked me around a few times for missing a single hair on her sheets. You and Sari have a good trip from Beiji?"

Eodo nodded, looking around their meager accommodations. "We each have our own bunks? That's pretty generous. In Beiji, we had to share bunks."

Sarina tried to look excited. Three-tiered bunks occupying three of four walls, two sanistalls on the fourth wall, the door out to a common mess hall beside them. No doors on the sanistalls, even less privacy than the Typhoon had had. The walls were drab, government gray, the floor a textured plascrete. A single glow globe was anchored inside a cage in the center of the ceiling. At the head of each bunk was a small basket for personal effects. Sarina's and Feo's personal effects were too numerous to fit in the paltry baskets.

"The Bezopasnosti mutaclones have it better, but not much," Erik said. "We got the worst of it. We always get the worst of it." He pointed to a bunk. "That's yours, Eodo." Then he pointed to one across the room. "And you can have the one under mine, Sari." Then he smiled. "Pretty name, too, by the way."

Eodo walked over to Erik's bunk and threw his satchel onto it. "Thanks for switching bunks with me, Erik. Sari really appreciates it, too." He eased himself onto it and stretched out.

"Uh, uh," Erik stammered.

"Very nice of you, Erik," Sari said, scooping his few belongings out and taking them across the room. "What a welcome you're giving us, and we were afraid we'd be scorned." The belief was certainly there, encoded into the nanostim neuramod. "When do we report to the facility manager?"

Erik looked nonplussed and said, "You two don't act like any mutaclones I ever met."

Eodo grinned and swung his legs off the bed to sit up. "Come here, Erik."

The saniclone obeyed instantly, a worried look on his face.

"I'm not a young mutaclone, am I?" Eodo said, pointing to his gray temples. "The reason I've lived this long is that I've kept my nose out of other mutaclones' business. Do you want to live a long time, Erik?" Eodo put his hand companionably on the other mutaclone's shoulder. "Do you?"

"Uh, sure, Eodo."

"Well, then, think about what I've said. In fact, tell your friends here about it, would you? Just so you live a little longer. If you do that for me, Erik, I'll forget what you just said about me and my friend, Sari. Thank you, Erik." Eodo clapped him on the shoulder once more. "Wake me when the facility manager gets here."

And Eodo lay down, rolled over, and was instantly asleep.

Sari slipped into the bunk beneath him, watching as Erik backed out the door, his eyes bigger than moons.

* * *

Frederick Mosovich, Lieutenant Investigator, Internal Divisions Branch, Bezopasnosti Moskva, saluted Lieutenant Commander Mariya Nikonova.

Adjutant Inspector Katarina Kupchenko also saluted, mistimed enough to cause Nikonova to hesitate.

"Welcome, Lieutenant," Nikonova said, thrusting a hand at him.

"Thank you for having us, Lieutenant, apologies for the short notice." Fred knew the military protocol wasn't possible to encode on a chip or nanostim through an implant. "Adjutant Kupchenko is just out of basic, having joined after her residencies."

"A rather abrupt change of direction, Doctor Inspector." Nikonova shook hands with Katarina, the look of easy meat in her eyes.

"I'm looking forward to meeting Doctor Eltsova. I've studied her work for years."

"Studied it? I'd assumed it was classified, all of it. Where did you hear about it?"

"Feodosiya Orbital Mutaclone Factory, Crimea, where we developed a mnemonic enhancement regulator based on Doctor Eltsova's work on schematic neural assembly reinforcers. The increased obedience obtained from mutaclones is phenomenal."

"Crimea? I was wondering about your Ukraine accent. One day we'll wipe those agitators' butts off the map. Nice to hear Nadezhda's work has found an audience. She's brilliant, and only our strict security measures here have kept her from the fame she deserves. Come, come on in. We'll get you to your quarters to freshen up. It's lights out already here, our cycles on a thirty-five hour equivalent, which is always disconcerting for new arrivals. Oh, don't worry about your ship, mutaclones will take care of it. Typhoon, isn't it? Lovely craft, always wanted one myself. This way, please."

Fred followed the Commander, Kate close behind.

Nikonova was visibly agitated, her nearly uninterruptible fountain of speech a sure sign. Fred knew she had to be shaking in her combat boots, an unannounced inspection from Bezopasnosti Internal Affairs enough to set off teeth grinding and hair pulling.

For all the nervousness, however, Nikonova was startlingly direct, probably a feature of her Rusky upbringing. Fred didn't wonder at it, accustomed to the brusque Rusky manner from experiences he had no memory of in that dream-like déjà vu of his, his memory a blur.

Memory extirpation that Magadan was infamous for. Dr. Eltsova was renowned for her work on schematic neural assembly reinforcers—and deinforcers.

Fred had also noted Commander Nikonova's references to the Doctor by first name. The two had been colleagues for eight or more years. Why wouldn't they be on a first name basis? It was, however, enough of a breach of protocol that Fred noted it. Such familiar references were rarely made, especially in front of strangers.

They were shown to a suite on the third floor, one clearly assembled in just the hour that it had taken their ship to clear the perimeters. A center office with two private rooms on either side occupied that end of the third floor, the view beyond the window of a mountainside, just visible in the wan moonlight.

Portable sanistalls had been hastily installed in both private rooms, bare pipes protruding from new, still-drying plascrete.

"A saniclone will be assigned in the morning," Commander Nikonova was saying. "Might as well have one who can attend to all your needs. I have the perfect one in mind. Just trake the environmental staff if you need anything, and remember to beat them roundly at the slightest infraction, lest they get lazy and intractable. Good night." And she was gone.

Fred suppressed a smile at her departure and took his bag into his room.

Back in the center office, Kate was frowning and watching him.

Holding her bag, he saw. "Sorry, wouldn't be a good idea," he said, immediately aroused, memories of the last few nights indelibly etched into his soul. They hadn't slept much.

She whimpered, slumping.

"The saniclones are sure to talk."

"I know," Kate replied. "Good night, Fred. I love you."

"Love you, too. Good night, Kate."

# Chapter 16

The saniclone uniform tight across her bodice, Sari knocked on the third-floor door, the personal suites housed at the west end of the complex. All the other quarters were on the first and second floors, she'd noticed.

"Whatever you do," Eodo had told her, "don't shut off or resist the nanostim neuramod. You're a saniclone."

A tall, sharp-looking man wearing a goatee whipped open the door.

Sari recoiled, the man's jaws rippling in obvious agitation. "Pardon, Sir, saniclone Sari, at your service. I didn't mean to disturb you." She couldn't look at his face, compelled to keep her gaze on the floor. "I can come back."

The man retreated. "No, uh, not necessary. Come in." Marching across the room to the floor-to-ceiling window opposite the entrance, he reminded her of someone.

Sari entered and closed the door behind her. Just inside the door was a makeshift kitchen. "I'm assigned to you and Adjutant Inspector Kupchenko, Sir. May I fix you breakfast?"

"Uh, certainly."

She quailed when he glanced her direction, but the glance was momentary, and she turned to the kitchen.

No food. Not a scrap.

She traked Eodo, panicking. The adrenocortico flight response didn't help.

"Calm down. There's a cafeteria on the first floor. Simply excuse yourself and get two meals from the cafeteria. These are new arrivals you've been assigned to. They won't know any different."

Sari approached the man at the window. "Sir?"

"Yes, Sari?"

She quailed at his glance again. "Not a scrap of food. I'll go downstairs to the cafeteria to get you something. Any requests?"

"Do you know what they have?"

She burst into tears. "I'm sorry, Sir, I don't. I'm new here. Please don't beat me."

"It's all right, Sari. No one's going to beat you. Just get us each a tray. It'll be fine." He guided her gently toward the door.

I can't believe I'm such a wreck, Sari thought, wiping the tears off her face with her sleeve. Eodo's got to adjust this neuramod. It's way too strong.

She found the cafeteria, the kitchen clones having already prepared trays for the new arrivals, to Sari's immense relief.

On her way back up, Sari tried to recall whom it was the man reminded her of. That first impression, him standing in the doorway, looking as startled as she felt, a handsome man with a sleek, sinuous physique, redolent of strict military training, with muscles that bulged moderately, as with rigorous strength training, a fluidity to his stance that bespoke instant readiness.

Carrying the two trays, one atop the other, Sari simply couldn't place where or in what circumstance she might have met him—or someone very like him. The rippling jaw, the sharp, nearly pointed brows, the tight cheeks and the almost-gaunt hollows beneath the cheekbones were incongruent with her impression of having met him before.

"Thank you," he said, when she brought him a tray.

"And Ms. Adjutant? Do you know if she's ready for breakfast?"

The man shrugged. "Just take it in. She's probably hungry." He turned to the window, his tray on the low table in front of him, his back to the Adjutant's door.

Sari eased the door open with one hand, the tray in the other. The sanistall was going full force. Sari stepped into the room and pulled the door closed behind her.

The woman beyond the clear sanistall door had the most magnificent body Sari had ever seen.

Fortunately, the neuramod dumped a load of adrenocortisol into her bloodstream. "Breakfast," she called, taking the tray to the bed, where she saw a uniform already laid out. "Would the lady like help getting dressed?" Sari kept her gaze averted, the sanistall shutting off.

"Breakfast? Oh, thank you, I'm famished." The woman stepped out of the sanistall to the bed, dug immediately into the kasha, took a quick bite of the butter brot, quaffed some coffee, and had a spoonful of tuorog. "Oh, my, look at me, and not a stitch of clothing!" She looked at Sari, chewing quickly and trying not to grin. "Sorry."

Sari spun away to try to conceal her responses, apologizing profusely. Her breasts were missiles and her vagina an overflowing canal. She doesn't look a bit sorry, Sari thought, her gaze on the floor. Oriented to females, Sari couldn't help attribute her arousal to the naked goddess in front of her. Fight-or-flight response being a state of autonomic arousal, what a person attributed the arousal to depended to a great degree on the circumstance.

"I'd better get dressed on my own, hadn't I?" the woman said.

Sari nodded stiffly, apologizing again. Keeping her gaze averted, she slipped out the door. "I'll clean your room while you're eating, Sir." She hurried across the suite before he could answer and set about tidying the bed. It was a welcome distraction from desires coursing through her.

Feo had said it'd be difficult, but Sarina hadn't an inkling it would be this difficult.

Further, the woman reminded Sari of someone. Tall, stately, buxom, heart-shaped hips and supple legs. The V-shaped face and hair weren't as familiar, the long straight nose and the eyebrows somehow incongruent. Why do I think I've met both of them before? Sari wondered.

Dr. Sarina Karinova had met thousands of people in her years of practicing medicine, so it was inevitable she'd meet people so similar in characteristics and appearance that she'd be instantly reminded of others. The statistical chances of doing so were relatively high.

But two in one place? Sari wondered. Not such high chances. At a facility near the end of the Scutum Arm? Highly diminished chances.

A coincidence? Couldn't be.

By the time she finished with the Lieutenant's room, setting out a uniform for him, the Adjutant had emerged from hers. "I'll clean your room now, Miss," she muttered quickly, crossing the suite with her gaze averted.

Deeply engrossed in a conversation, neither the Lieutenant nor the Adjutant seemed to notice.

\* \* \*

"I have a special assignment for you."

Sari glanced up quickly at the man before returning her gaze to the floor. "Yes, Sir?"

"I'm Danil Topikovich, by the way."

The Director of Civilian Services at Magadan, she knew. "Sari S832A57, Sir. What are your instructions?" She was surprised he was supervising saniclones directly.

"Commander Nikonova requests that her room be cleaned. She's rather, uh, demanding. If she comes in while you're there, you're to leave immediately."

"Yes, Sir. Hers in the corner suite at the west end, fifth floor, yes?"

"Indeed. And avoidance works best with her."

"Thank you, Sir." Sari nodded, gaze on the floor, and turned to attend to it.

"Oh, uh, Eodo tells me he supervised the environmental services mutaclones at the Rusky Consulate on Beiji. Clearly an older model whose implant has weakened somewhat. Why did they send him? He seems competent enough."

Sari repeated the story she and Eodo had agreed upon. "The Consul's daughter was taking a bit of a liking to him." Then Sari tried not to smile. "Well, more than a bit." Liaisons between female normavariants and their male mutaclone servants had been the subject of satirical romances and tragedies for centuries.

"I see. Thank you, Sari."

Seems affable enough, she thought, heading for the sanicloset on the fifth floor. It was just after midday on her first day, and she'd survived the first challenge—cleaning the new arrivals' suite. She wondered how Eodo had worked himself already into the confidences of Director Topikovich.

Eodo continued to surprise her, resourceful in ways she wouldn't have expected. Privacy that morning as she and five other saniclones had dressed for the day had been nonexistent, and Sari had steeled herself for it, the other two males assigned to the room taking long admiring glances at her.

"Don't let those pricks bother you." One of the fem saniclones, Rula, had taken Sari under her wing and had volunteered to show her all the closets.

Sari got the cart from the fifth floor closet and checked its stock, and then wheeled it down the corridor, all the personal suites empty this time of day.

She let herself into Commander Nikonova's corner suite, leaving the cart at the door to prop it open, as per protocol. "You don't want a closed door while you're in anyone's personal suite, unless you want to be alone with them," Rula had told her.

The view was as magnificent as views could be on Magadan, a watery world with archipelagos strewn randomly across its surface under a gray-blue sky, its red dwarf primary always encircled with a purplish ring. Below, the landscape tumbled toward the sea down a wind-and-water-worn escarpment speckled with lichen and grasses, but devoid of other life. A young world in evolutionary terms, the local flora and fauna had barely begun to develop.

She turned from the view and started immediately on the bedroom. As she whipped through the room, dusting and wiping all surfaces, arranging toiletries, replacing towels, sheets, bedding, resupplying the lotions, soaps, shampoos, she noticed several strands of long, auburn hair throughout the suite. *I thought Dr. Eltsova was the one with red hair, not Commander Nikonova*, Sari thought. Even the bed was strewn with multiple strands alongside several brunette ones. Sari held up two strands right beside each other. Not only were they different colors, but they were different in consistency, the brown one having a slight curl, and the auburn one thick and straight.

She and Eodo reconnoitered in a sanicloset on the third floor at the west end, just outside the suite of the new arrivals. It was their only opportunity to talk privately. "I don't know what it means," he said, his gray temples and webbed corners looking old in this bastion of youth, no one at Magadan seeming older than forty. "Maybe she's got a lover." Eodo looked bothered by something. "There's an area it appears they want us to stay away from," he said when she asked. "East end ground floor, there's a door marked sanicloset, but my key codes don't work. And it has a retina-lock."

"A retina-lock on a sanicloset?" Sari snorted.

"Exactly. Director tells me it leads to the basement, which he says hasn't been used in years. The other saniclones won't even discuss it, no matter how much I threaten them."

Sari asked about the Director.

Eodo nodded. "Seems he's looking for someone to supervise the crew here. He hasn't been able to recruit a normavariant for the job, apparently. Two years straight without a furlough, a place as isolated as this, supervising mutaclones. Not surprising he can't find a normavariant. So I guess I'll be taking that on."

She'd seen that morning how the other saniclones avoided him.

"He's a dangerous one, isn't he?" Rula had whispered to her.

Sari hadn't contradicted her, an element of safety for Sari if the other saniclones were wary of Eodo.

"One small benefit is that I get my own room," Eodo said, grinning.

And privacy, Sari thought. "Do you think it's wise for you and me to room together?"

"The rumors are already rampant. Do you mind?"

"The rumors? Not at all. Do *you* mind?" she asked.

"Us sharing? Not a bit. I'm too old to worry about my three chins or sagging gut."

"What about that male brain of yours?"

"And its preprogrammed predilection for female anatomy, such as yours? Not to worry. I've lived in this testosterone-saturated environment for a long time. I'm pretty good at shutting it off."

They'd agreed to reconnoiter again just before dinner, and Sari had gone to clean an office on the second floor at the west end, two floors above the "sanicloset" basement.

On the west end of the second floor, emptying trash throughout a rat's maze of cubes, where some twenty to thirty communications personnel were so absorbed in their trakes, corns, cokes, and desksets that they barely noticed her coming and going, Sari reached a corner cube near an emergency stairwell, the door clearly marked, "Alarm will sound."

A woman in a cube grinned at her and crooked a finger. "I'm Uliana, I've got a favor to ask." She spoke in a low voice, peered out her cube to see if anyone were listening, put her finger over her lips, and leaned close. "You're Sari, the new saniclone, right?"

Sari nodded, resisting the urge to flinch away.

"No, no, don't be afraid. Just come with me." And Uliana peered again around the corner of the cube and stepped to the stairwell to the door clearly marked, "Alarm will sound."

She opened the door silently and gestured Sari to follow. The alarm didn't sound.

She backed into the stairwell while Uliana quietly closed the door.

Again the finger to the lips, and she descended gingerly, her shoes soundless on the metal-grate stairs. Sari followed, careful to make no sound.

They passed the first floor exit, this door also marked, "Alarm will sound."

The basement door was similarly marked but also didn't sound when Uliana led her through it, again taking extreme care to be perfectly silent.

In the basement beyond was a laboratory, and prominent at the other end, a single green light glared above a door, a clean room, free of contaminants.

"Oh, don't worry about that. You won't be asked to clean in there," Uliana said. "We just need the basics—trash, washrooms, quarters. These chauvinist pigs think I'm going to do all the cleaning. I have research to do. Those slobs wouldn't clean their own damn sanistalls if they were filled with shit. Don't cringe, none of us will harm you. What's your name?"

"I'm...Sari S832A57."

"I'll leave you to it, Sari. Come get me when you're ready to leave. I'm the only one who can disable the door alarms. I'll be right over there at my desk."

As Sari moved through the basement emptying trashes, the other two researchers, both men, blithely ignored her, one smirking, "I wondered who'd be doing that," before returning to his work.

Inside the glass-walled clean room, a mutaclone in a uterpod twitched under nanostim simumem infusion. Sarina's year of residency at the mutaclone factory had exposed her to their production in the hundreds of thousands.

Why a clean room? she wondered, not daring to stare and only able to steal occasional glances. Clean rooms weren't used in standard mutaclone production.

Sari came across a side office with two cots and a sanistall, the room strewn with the implements of personal care, its haphazard conversion from office to bedroom evidenced by the two desks stacked one atop the other just outside its door.

"I wouldn't if I were you," Uliana said, appearing at her shoulder. "What a pigsty! 'Let 'em wallow,' I say. No matter how hard you try, you can't get milk from a bull, eh?"

Sari smiled, the Ukraine homily amusing to hear from a Rusky. She left the room the way it was.

When Sari was finished, Uliana took her back up to the second floor, asking Sari to meet her at the same time near the second-floor stairwell the next day.

"Oh, and uh, don't worry about vid surveillance. I disabled the cam above the door."

"A mutaclone in a uterpod?" Eodo said, when she told him about the basement. "I guess I'll adjust your schedule to accommodate those duties."

Then Sari, told him what Uliana had said.

" 'Milk from a bull'?" Eodo snorted. "Certainly not a Rusky phrase, eh?"

Sarina and Feo smiled at each other.

"I think we may have found our operatives."

\* \* \*

Fred parted ways finally with Commander Nikonova.

The ramrod stiff, black-haired woman had given him a guided tour of the entire facility, showing him every last security feature, including a quick tour of the multiple perimeters, the randomized mine fields, the blasma-beam emplacements, the redundant watch points, and the beryl-boro particles detection systems. It was, he knew, an exhaustive effort to keep his attention off his actual goal, his fake redacted orders clearly iterating his investigation of security breaches. Nikonova had managed to consume the bulk of his day. *As I'm sure she intended,* Fred thought.

He met Kate in the cafeteria, the room mostly empty, only one or two staff on break or having knocked off nearly. Fred had arrived first, famished, and had already supped, the thirty-two hour days on Magadan throwing off his circadian rhythms. He'd gone twelve hours without eating, Nikonova dragging him throughout the facility without pause the entire time.

That morning, after the saniclone Sari had brought them breakfast, Kate had told him a subdued whisper, "I know her from someplace."

"Ridiculous," Fred had whispered back. "You're a month old. How could you have met anyone and see them again here, someplace this remote?"

Kate had shrugged in frustration. "I know I've seen her some place before. I know it!"

Now, meeting with Kate in the afternoon—after an entire day under the yammering barrage of the over-anxious Commander Nikonova—Fred was just happy to see her. "I hope your day was better than mine."

All four of them had met briefly that morning, Lieutenant Commander Mariya Nikonova and Medical Director Nadezhda Eltsova with Fred and Kate, before parting ways.

Eltsova, a flaming redhead, had introduced herself as "Nadya, please."

Fred had settled on "Doctor Nadya," while Kate and Nadya had struck up an immediate friendship, lapsing into the jargon of mutaclone biogenesis and development within minutes of shaking hands.

Fred and Commander Nikonova had soon found themselves exchanging the uncomfortable glances of mutual exclusion, the other two so wrapped in their exchange they'd forgotten anyone else was present.

He didn't think they'd noticed when he and Nikonova excused themselves.

Doctor Eltsova had then given Kate an analogous tour of the facilities' medical operations, all housed on the lower three floors of the building's east end, the top two floors administrative.

"She's brilliant," Kate said, a tray of food in front of her, a forkful already in her mouth. "The heart of the operation here. Nikonova just gives her the envelope. This really is the cutting edge of mutaclone innovation. They've developed a self-assembling nanostim neuraplant, introducible through water, food, or sub-q injection—"

"Sub-q?" More jargon beyond Fred's expertise. He'd heard enough jargon to fill a small lexicon in just the few minutes of the exchange between the doctors.

"Sorry, subcutaneous, under the skin."

"Self-assembling? What's that mean?"

"The carbo-nanobots migrate to the brain and invade the necessary cortical and subcortical regions to install a nanostim neuraplant—obviating the need for surgical interventions. Imagine the implications!"

A shiver shook Fred.

Kate frowned, as if expecting more enthusiasm. "What's the matter?"

He made sure no one was nearby. "So *that* was how they did it." He'd been wondering how they'd installed a nanostim neuraplant into his brain.

Her face fell. "Oh." She pushed the food around on her plate. "Oh."

He saw she now realized the implications.

"Oh, I guess I didn't really think it through."

"It's all right. You're a mutaclone researcher. You're not supposed to consider the other side of the equation." He glanced around again, no one nearby but an older saniclone clearing tables. "How would you know that's how they did it?" He pushed his empty tray toward the saniclone.

"Thank you, Sir," the gray-templed saniclone said.

Fred gave a brief nod, not really looking at him. "They could have introduced the neuraplant in a number of ways, couldn't they?"

"I suppose." Kate's gaze was fixed to his, her body stiff and still. She blinked at him rapidly, shot a glance at the mutaclone, and then returned her riveting gaze to his face.

"Probably immaterial, though," he said nonchalantly, Kate obviously alarmed. We're probably being monitored at all times, he thought. Although he'd swept their suite for monitoring devices that morning—finding three mikes and four cams—he was sure they'd planted new ones in the meantime. And it wouldn't have surprised him it they'd rigged their saniclones with monitoring equipment as well.

It's what I'd do, Fred thought.

He waited until the saniclone moved on. Unusual to see one that advanced in age, Fred was thinking, guessing the saniclone was sixty or better, the webbed corners of the eyes and graying temples just the most obvious signs. Given the unusual environment, one that subjected its inhabitants to far more stress than average urban life, it was even more remarkable someone hadn't recycled the saniclone long ago. Unless the saniclone were new to the complex.

Fred made a mental note to request nanostim neuraplant checks on all the mutaclones at the facility. It would be a glaring omission if he didn't, a routine part of any investigation.

"I know him from someplace!" she whispered through a tight grimace.

Fred looked around for eavesdroppers. "Who, the saniclone? Ridiculous," he said, also in a whisper. Déjà vu, he thought, recalling their conversation that morning.

"And don't tell me I'm a month old," she shot back in disgust.

Take aback by the vehemence in her voice, Fred held up his hands. "Fool me once, shame on you. Fool me twice, shame on me. Or something like that. I believe you, all right? Where from?" Twice in one day couldn't be coincidental. She knew them, he was convinced of that.

"I don't know." Suddenly, she yawned.

Uh oh, Fred thought. The daylight streaming in the windows was disconcerting. Sixteen hours since we last woke.

"Come on." He led the way back to their third-floor suite, getting glances from the Bezopasnosti military staff they passed. He was sure the rumors were already starting.

Once there, Fred swept the interior for passive sensors. Finding none, he looked at Kate. "Two is too many. Let's assume it's no coincidence, and that they're following us."

"And not out to kill us," Kate said.

He nodded. "Or can't do so blatantly."

"Fred, this makes no sense."

"Huh?"

"It can't be the same faction as the ones who wiped out our memories and installed neuraplants in us. If it were, they'd just take us prisoner now and re-wipe our memories."

"Or they'd kill us outright," Fred said. "Doesn't seem like they're pursuing us, does it?"

"And if they aren't, what *are* they doing? And why?"

Fred frowned. "I don't know. And we have to find out."

# Chapter 17

Sari flopped onto her bunk, exhausted.

Eodo had become supervisor of the saniclone crew, Danil having just left the sanicrew quarters after making the pronouncement. Eodo had rearranged their accommodations, putting them in a two-bunk room with its own sanistall.

The twenty-four hour workday had sapped her, and all she could think about was sleep.

The other saniclones appeared to be accustomed to the long days, none of them evincing the sheer exhaustion that seemed to weigh Sari down. The only reprieve was that the Magadan gravity was eight-tenths normal.

Here in the saniclone dorms, in the windowless basement at the west end, she couldn't see the surf far below, but when she listened closely, she could almost feel the rumble as waves battered the cliffs below them, the sound articulating through rock as a slight vibration.

Eodo came in, looking anxious. "These two inspectors from Bezopasnosti Moskva Headquarters are asking too many questions."

Sari could barely keep her head up, doubting she had enough energy even to throw herself into the sanistall. "It's not coincidental that they both look familiar to me, is it?" She kept her voice low.

"No, it isn't." Feo looked at her, his eyes older, his hair grayer. "I shouldn't have brought you here. It's too dangerous."

"We didn't know they'd show up. How could we have known?"

"You're right, we couldn't. Listen, there's a request to clean the inside of their ship. Right after you clean the basement tomorrow, I want you to do that." Eodo pulled a device from his pocket, a green cube one inch to each side. "It's a data crawler. Place it on the control console when you start, pick it up when you're finished. It'll copy the contents of the on-board autonav."

Sari tucked it into a pocket, yawning.

"Go to bed, Sari. I have a few things to do." He stepped toward the door. "You did well today. Hopefully, we'll find out what we need soon."

\* \* \*

The Bezopasnosti pair from Moskva let Sari into their suite the next morning, barely giving her a glance.

Both had their attention riveted to a vid screen, which showed the new Premier of Ukraine, Tatiana Satsanova. The mutaclone Premier.

Beside the Premier at the podium was Captain Fadeyka Andropovich, looking resplendent in full-dress uniform.

Lieutenant Investigator Frederick Mosovich turned to his colleague, also in uniform.

Terror clutched at Sari's heart. Wide-eyed, she stared at him.

"What's the matter?" the woman said, turning.

The new Premier on screen introduced the Captain, turning.

Sari gaped at them both. "It's you!"

The other two exchanged a glance and leapt upon her.

"No, no, don't hurt me, you don't understand. I'm here to help, please don't beat me. I know what happened. I didn't mean it, you're them, I'm just a saniclone, they're escoriants, please don't recycle me, mmff, hmmph, phmmm—"

They pinned her to the floor and covered her mouth.

Their weight on her and someone's hand over her mouth, Sari struggled to breathe, the barrel of a blaster hot against her temple.

"Calm down, just calm down," the woman was saying to her.

On screen, the same voice stated, "It's with great honor and anticipation that I announce the appointment of Captain Fadeyka Andropovich to the position of Admiral and Commander in Chief of the Ukraine Navy—"

The man cursed and spat.

On screen, in the same voice, the Admiral accepted the appointment and thanked the new Premier.

"Now they've done it," the woman said. She turned her attention on Sari. "All right, who are you?"

Despite the adrenocorticotropins inciting terror inside her, Sari stopped struggling. "I'm Doctor Sarina Karinova, and I'm here to stop them."

On screen, the Premier and the Admiral stood side by side, their hands linked and held high in the air in triumph, a crowd roaring in the background.

The man lowered the blaster barrel. "How do you know about any of this?"

"I examined both of them, first Tatiana and then Fadeyka. I also did a genalysis. They're both clones, *both* of them! And you two, you don't belong here. You belong there."

The two of them met gazes, and then let her up. "How did you end up here?"

"They kidnapped my wife, bombed my clinic, and destroyed my patient files. And Feo—Eodo—he helped me escape. He was injured in the assassination and we traced the plot here, to Magadan, probably the same way you did."

"Vasyl's Bawd Mod?"

"And Doctor Puskinska," Sari said. "They killed them both."

"I thought Doctor Puskinska died of alcohol poisoning," the woman said.

"That's what they wanted you to think."

"Of course. That much alcohol couldn't possibly be introduced through the vaginal tissues," the woman said. "Only the digestive and rectal tissues are that osmotic."

"What about the Tong attack on Harbin?" the man asked.

"That was you?" Sarina looked at them wide-eyed. "Feo said it was meant for us. Look, what do I call you? What are your names?"

They exchanged a glance. "I'm Kate," the woman said.

"I'm Fred," the man said.

Sarina looked from them to the screen. "How'd you find out that that's where you belong?"

"We knew too much," Kate said. "I'm a doctor of something or other. And I speak ten languages."

"And I can crack any kind of encryption."

"You should see him fight. Seven Tong in that one fight."

"We didn't learn those skills in uterpod."

"And then we saw our faces—"

"Among other anatomical features—"

"—on the vids coming from Tantalus. Our faces." The woman bit off a sob. "Our lives, lived by others."

Sari put her hand on Kate's shoulder. "They took my life, too. Let me get Feo in here. He can—"

"Who?"

"Feodor Luzhkov, otherwise known as Eodo E610557, the gray-templed saniclone."

"No, we can't," Fred said. "Anything out of the ordinary is sure to alert Commander Nikonova. We have to proceed cautiously. You'll just have to wait until you see him. You mustn't do anything different. Whoever's doing this, the orders are sure to have come from the highest Rusky authority, possibly the Kremlin itself. They'll think that they've achieved their goal with Fadeyka's appointment to Admiral. Now is when they're most vulnerable. The difficulty is, we're not ready. We don't know how they expunged our memories."

"But we know where," Sari said. "In the basement, east end. Everyone's been told not to tell you about it. But they've got a mutaclone down there now."

"How did *you* find out about it?" Kate asked.

"One of the researchers came and got me, said the place wouldn't get cleaned otherwise. She has some way of disabling the alarms on the emergency stairwell. She's taking me down there again today, just after lunch."

"Let me guess—the door on the first floor marked as a sanicloset."

Sari nodded. "But you're right. We still don't know how they're expunging memories. Let me see what I can find out today."

Fred and Kate traded a glance. "You have to be careful," Kate said. "There doesn't appear to be any record of this operation anywhere. Must be authorized by the Director of State Security himself, Antonin Medvedev."

"But to what end?" Sarina asked.

"That, too, we have to find out."

\* \* \*

Promptly at one pm, Uliana had retrieved Sari from the second floor emergency stairwell, had taken her to the basement, and then had said, "Come to get me when you're finished."

The basement was large enough to support a crew of thirty, its workstations partitioned off from each other by six-foot panels. Sari worked in isolation, Uliana and the other two researchers blithely ignoring her, their desks some distance from the glasma-walled chamber at one end.

She'd been able to enter the uterpod chamber without being seen. Sari saw a door in the back wall of the mutaclone gestation chamber, partially hidden by the mutaclone hanging from the harness.

The mutaclone inside the uterpod looked near-term. Sari picked out clear anatomical features indicating maturity. The breasts were well developed and the labia bloomed like a flower. The fetal position obscured the face from Sari, but the hair was similar in color to her own, a chestnut brown. A bundle of nanostim tendrils bound the mutaclone's head and neck, and thicker feedtubes and wastetubes snaked around the abdomen.

Then the mutaclone shifted, the hands coming away from the face. Anya!

Sarina's heart leaped into her throat. Pounding rang in her ears, and sweat broke out on her forehead.

Frantically, she looked for a sign that this was Anya, and not a mutaclone copy. Think! she told herself.

A month before Sarina had examined Captain Fadeyka Andropovich, Anya had slipped and fallen at work and had split open her knee, an injury Sarina had treated at home. Although no permanent scarring was likely, by the time of Anya's kidnapping, the wound had still exhibited the smooth, shiny epidermis of recently-healed skin.

Which knee? Sarina asked herself.

The figure in the uterpod sported two intact, unscarred knees.

Sari sighed in relief. She looked at the door just behind and to the left of the uterpod. Without thinking, she stepped through it.

Mutaclone harnesses along one wall hung empty. The wall itself was a tapestry of multicolored tubes, among them nanostim tendrils, feedtubes, and wastetubes. All that was missing were the uterpods. In front of each harness was a control panel, all the vidscreens dark.

All but one, the very last. At the far end, in the last harness, hung a mutaclone.

Sari stepped gingerly toward the figure hanging suspended in the harness, terror and hope and disbelief at war within her, wanting it to be Anya and hoping it was Anya and dreading it would be Anya and wishing to God it weren't Anya so she could deny that this whole nightmare had never happened.

The body hung limp and lifeless, and only the soft rise and fall of the chest and the bleeping pulse on the monitor indicated there was any life left in the body.

At the right knee was a strip of new, pink flesh.

Oh, Anya! Sari strangled a sob.

She stopped herself from weeping on the spot, knowing she had to get Anya out of here.

Sarina opened a secuchannel to Kate.

"You found her? That's wonderful. Of course, we'll get her out, Sari. Have Uliana return you to the second floor, all right? See you there."

Sari made her way out, her posture wooden, grief and disbelief ready to burst forth from her fragile shell.

"You're done early," Uliana said, heading her back up stairs. "You look upset. Did either of my colleagues take advantage of you? Jakov can't keep it in his pants, I swear. It wasn't that? Well, I hope you feel better tomorrow."

Uliana paused at the second floor landing and peered out the door. "All clear," she said, and pushed the door open.

A blasma pistol was shoved in her face, Fred on the other end, Kate right behind him. "Take us downstairs," he hissed at Uliana.

Kate guided Sari back down to the basement. "We'll have to get her aboard the Typhoon, somehow."

Sari shot a glance at her. "Which you bought on Hohhot."

Kate gave her a bewildered look. They reached the basement landing.

"How many people down here?" Fred asked Uliana, pressing the barrel to her face, her arms pinned to her back.

Uliana glanced at Sari. "Just two."

"Here, I'll go first." Sari stepped through the door and looked over the top of the cubes. "All clear," she whispered and led the way.

Neither of the other two researchers was seated near the mutaclone chamber, and Sari led them quietly through it into the second room.

Anya hung limp and lifeless from the last mutaclone harness.

"Get a condicoon," Fred said to Kate. He asked Uliana, "How are you doing this?" He shoved her hands upward, and she gasped in pain.

Sari helped Kate lower Anya from the harness, the nanostim tendrils withdrawing automatically at the first pull. They bundled the frail, unconscious woman into the conditioning cocoon.

"We need a gravgurney."

Uliana pointed to a closet. "In there."

The "gurney" was a pole connecting two antigrav units. Sari unfolded it, and she and Kate slipped it under Anya's limp form.

"How do we get to the Typhoon without being seen?"

"There's a passage at the other end, opposite the emergency exit," Uliana said. "I don't have the codes to disable the alarms."

Fred smiled. "I'll take care of that. Sari, lead the way, please."

She peered out from the inner chamber. "All clear, but the route to the underground parking garage will take us past the other two researchers."

"I have an idea," Fred said. "Thank you, Uliana, and my apologies." He struck her across the jaw, and Uliana slid to the ground. "Here. Help me tie her up."

Within minutes, they'd bound and gagged Uliana, and then for safety, Sari tucked a condicoon around the unconscious woman.

"Good idea," Kate said, "in case she asphyxiates or goes into cardiac arrest."

While Kate waited in the mutaclone harness chamber with Anya on the gravgurney, Fred secreted himself in the room where the two male scientists were bunking.

Then Sari lured them, one by one, into the room.

They each fell unconscious at Fred's first blow.

"I've disabled their optimitters, trakes, cokes, and corns," he said as Sari helped him tie them up.

She retrieved their condicoons from their beds and tucked them around the two limp forms. Kate joined them, pushing the gravgurney. Together, they headed to the exit.

At the door to the underground tarmac, Fred paused, a distracted look on his face. "Alarm disabled," he said.

They pushed through the door. Beyond, five ships sat in the underground, each on an antigrav jack, the Typhoon beside a beat-up tugboat.

"That *was* you on Urungi," Sari said.

Kate nodded, helping her navigate the limp form on the gravgurney through the narrow doorway.

Sari and Kate got Anya into a bunk, the conditioning cocoon wrapping all but the face. "Oh, Anya," Sarina said, choking back a sob. "I'll be back just a few minutes, my love." Sarina pulled herself away, knowing they hadn't escaped yet. "We have to get Feo," she told Fred, who was watching at the stateroom doorway.

"I'll go," Fred said. "You stay here with your wife."

And he was gone before Sarina could object.

\* \* \*

Fred arranged the green beans on his plate and pushed his nearly empty tray toward the gray-haired saniclone.

The man froze, his stare riveted to the green beans.

"Anya," they spelled.

"Where?" the saniclone asked, his voice low.

Fred pointed downward.

"Safe?" the saniclone muttered, gaze carefully averted.

"Yes," Fred murmured. "Meet me on the second floor at the emergency stairwell on the east end in five minutes." Fred got up to leave and strode from the cafeteria.

Nikonova, Topikovich, and Eltsova were just stepping off the elevator.

Lieutenant Investigator Frederick Mosovich saluted Commander Nikonova. Although nominally her superior, Fred was still under her command, all Bezopasnosti at the facility subject to her orders.

"Lieutenant Investigator, glad we found you," Nikonova said. "Listen, there's some concern about your ordering neuraplant exams for all base personnel."

Eltsova and Topikovich watched from over her shoulder.

"And Comrade Topikovich may not see the need," Fred said. "Am I mistaken, Comrade?" He grinned at Topikovich, wondering how to extract himself quickly. "Particularly for the mutaclone staff, if I'm correct?"

"Uh, well, yes, but—" Danil started.

Fred interrupted. "Given their proven reliability and the deep encryption on their neuraplants, Comrade Topikovich, it would seem an unnecessary step for the four hundred mutaclone here at Magadan, an inordinate investment of time and staff. Unfortunately, Comrade, cells of freed mutaclone have been discovered in ghettos across Rusky, their neuraplants decrypted and disabled. Further, it appears that the knowledge of how to disable them has spread rapidly among mutaclones. Didn't Magadan just receive two new saniclones from the embassy in Beiji? Who knows what knowledge they brought with them, eh, Comrade?" Fred smiled in a placating way.

"Er, well, yes, but, all four hundred?"

"My orders were explicit on that point, Comrade."

"But that'll take weeks," Dr. Eltsova said, a hand on her hip, throwing a glance at Commander Nikonova.

"If Doctor Kupchenko and I had some help," Fred said, frowning to himself. "A nanometrium simubilicus would be essential." He looked up suddenly at Dr. Eltsova. "Didn't I see an inventory entry for ten of them? Ones your staff are using for mutaclone experiments?"

Dr. Eltsova took a step backward. "Well, uh, we're not using them currently."

"I didn't think so, since you don't have any mutaclone experiments underway. Where are they?"

The red-haired Doctor shrugged elaborately. "Probably in some sanicloset somewhere. I'll see if my staff can locate a few for you."

"That would save us a tremendous amount of time. Doctor Kupchenko and I will also need to examine the civilian, military, and medical personnel."

The three base administrators all interjected at once. "You can't do that!" "Have you any idea what that'll do to morale!?" "How dare you march in here like some criminal investigator!?"

"Read my orders, people," Fred said. "Handed down by the Director of State Security himself, Antonin Medvedev." Now that I've rattled them sufficiently, I'll just excuse myself, Fred thought. "You'll have plenty of time to register your objections with the Director's office while we're examining the mutaclones. Until then, I'll need to requisition some cafeteria space and a few partitions for those exams. Thanks for your help, Comrade Danil, for setting up the exam cubes. Just inside the door will be fine." He clapped Topikovich on the shoulder, tipped his hat to Dr. Eltsova, and saluted Commander Nikonova. Then he stepped to the elevator.

Fred took it to the third floor, made sure the corridor was clear, and opened an optimitter channel into the base control system. Disabling its encryption, he opened the emergency stairwell to the basement, substituted blank vid feeds to the cameras, and entered the stairwell.

At the second floor, he opened the door from the inside.

Just outside stood Feo, who slipped into the stairwell.

Fred eased the door closed, finger to his lips. Gesturing the older man to follow, Fred descended to the basement and navigated his way through the cubes to the garage.

Kate was peering from the Typhoon hatch as he entered. "Here he comes with Feo," she said over her shoulder to the other woman.

The cabin was so crowded, Fred could barely breathe, five people aboard a ship that felt cramped with two. *We'll have to sleep in shifts,* he thought.

"Feodor Luzhkov, former Chief of Staff to Madame Premier Colima Satsanova," the gray-templed man said, no trace of subservience to his manner. He shook hands with Fred and Kate.

"Captain Fadeyka Andropovich, the original," Fred said.

"Doctor Tatiana Satsanova, the original," Kate said.

"Doctor Sarina Karinova," Sarina said, grinning. And then she frowned. "And this is my wife, Physicist Anya Karinova." She gestured at the limp form on the bunk.

"Any improvement?" Fred asked her.

A tear slipped down Sari's cheek as she shook her head. "Just get us out of here, Captain."

Fred nodded and squirmed into the cockpit, the controls coming alight to his touch. "Feo, you can pilot the ship, right?"

Feo nodded. "Flew her from Tantalus to Hohhot, Captain Andropovich. You'll disable Magadan's defenses while I pilot. Secure yourselves, everyone. We're in for a rough ride."

"All we have are two bunks and two chaises. That's not enough for five people."

"I can secure myself in the antigrav units from the gurney," Kate said. "There are holes in the cockpit wall already."

"My fault," Sari admitted. "I had to install a bunk up here after Feo was injured."

"Took great care of me, too," Feo said, grinning at Sari. Then he looked at Kate. "Sorry about your mother, Tatya. I wish there was something I could've done to stop them. Everything that's been taken from you and Captain Andropovich—" Feo bit off what he was going to say. The older man looked small and vulnerable, his years visibly weighing him down.

Fred patted him on the shoulder. "Thanks, Feo. Problem is, we have to get of here first."

* * *

Sarina watched on vid piped from the cockpit as Feodor and Fred—Fadeyka—plotted a path through Magadan's battery emplacements, minefields, beryl-boro detectors, and plasma disruptors.

"How about a few diversions?" Feo asked.

Sarina gave the vid only half her attention, her bunk right beside that of Anya. Her wife lay there, her face inanimate, her breathing smooth and regular, her vitals, chem levels, and blood counts all within normal limits.

Gazing upon the slack face of her wife, Sarina felt overwhelmed by the torturing inflicted upon Anya and her partial conversion from lively, autonomous human being to the shell of her former self, bereft of memory and locked into a neuraplant-induced hell, as Fred and Kate had been.

And the perpetrators had sought to replace Anya with a mutaclone, too? To what end? Sarina wondered. A physicist studying the galactic core, Anya wasn't anyone important! Why had they targeted her? Because her wife had inadvertently stumbled upon a plot of replace the Ukraine Oligarchy with mutaclones?

Or had Anya convinced them she was me, their plan to replace me with a senseless mutaclone? Sarina wondered.

"I'm sorry, my love," she whispered, not knowing whether Anya could hear her. "I'm so very sorry I dragged you into this," she whispered, no longer able to hold back her grief. Sobbing, she reached across the bunk frames and pulled herself toward her wife, her cheek to Anya's cheek.

And Sarina wept.

The Typhoon slewed wildly in its gyrations to avoid something-or-other, but Sarina paid it scant attention, trusting that Feo and Fred would somehow maneuver through the multiple layers of security at Magadan. Each alone had gotten in, and together they couldn't fail to get out.

And all the while Sarina wept, holding her wife's limp body, not knowing what atrocities they'd performed on Anya's mind in the basement of the most notorious gulag this side of the galactic core, not knowing how much of Anya's memory they'd destroyed, not knowing what level of cognition or even recognition Anya might have upon waking, not knowing whether Anya would ever wake again.

And while Sarina wept out her guilt for her part in bringing this terrible fate upon the person she cared more about than anyone else in the galaxy, a cheer went up in the cockpit, but the Typhoon still swerved and slewed in wild evasion, the changes in acceleration hurling Sarina against her restraints with bruising force.

But the pain in being tossed about couldn't compare to the agony that Sarina had held at bay for weeks and the tragic condition in which they'd finally found Anya, unconscious and half-mummified, a shell of the person she'd been.

There was a lurch, and the other three cheered in jubilation, talking excitedly amongst themselves.

Kate poked her head in. "Everyone all right in here?"

Sarina nodded, looking at her wife's empty face. "We escaped?"

"Yes," Kate said, stepping to the bunk.

Sari looked up at her. "I'm glad we're safe."

And she gave herself over to her grief.

# Chapter 18

"It's a neuraplant-induced coma," Dr. Boris Todurov said, looking amongst his readouts and then at the four somber faces staring at him.

Fred wondered what they looked like, the four of them now in plain allsuits, only Feo's age really distinguishing him from the rest. Four conscious mutaclones with a fifth unconscious one in a conditioning cocoon.

"What can you do?" Sarina asked, looking down at the inert form on the gravgurney.

Fred knew she hadn't slept well for the last five days, waking at night nearly every hour to check Anya's condition in spite of the constant watch the others had kept. The five days it'd taken them to follow the Scutum Arm back toward the galactic core had been exhausting for them all, their quarters cramped, their nerves frayed, and privacy non-existent.

The two doctors, Sarina and Kate, had done all they could to make Anya comfortable. Given their limited equipment, the unconscious woman's condition had grown gradually worse throughout the five-day flight across the Rusky border through Harbin, Hohhot, and Urungi, and then across the Stani Republics to Ukraine. They'd changed the conditioning cocoon wrapping Anya on the gravgurney several times, but without a mutaclone harness and a full array of nanostim tendril feedtubes and wastetubes, Anya had grown thin.

Dr. Todurov had seen them coming in and had instantly taken the patient back to the examination room, the room large enough for them all.

"This was where I brought Feo for surgery," Sarina had said. "Very discreet."

"Help me off with this condicoon," Todurov instructed.

Sarina and Kate quickly stripped it away from Anya.

"How long off the mutaclone harness?" the Doctor asked.

"Five days," Fred said. "No way to feed her aboard the Typhoon."

"Five people aboard a Typhoon for five days?" The Doctor whistled softly. "Best you could do, I guess. Look, while it would be helpful for me to know where you brought her from, maybe it's better that I don't know. They were giving her the infamous Magadan treatment, I'm assuming. Given that and her condition—" he gestured at the ribs showing through the nearly translucent skin, Anya's frailty evident—"we don't know what will happen if I bring her out of a coma. She needs an intensive care unit, an ICU, and the nearest is halfway around Kinchesh. But to get her into the hospital, you'll need a false identofile for her." Dr. Todurov looked at Feo. "You're still a wanted man, Comrade Luzhkov."

"Sarina and I, both," Feo said. "If she goes in as Anya Karinova, the place will be swarming with Ukraine security forces. Fred, can you adapt one of the indentofiles we picked up on Harbin?"

"In a heartbeat," Fred told him.

"I'll get an ambulance," Dr. Todurov said.

Fred withdrew to concentrate on altering the identofile while activity exploded around him.

The suborbital gravamb was there in a few minutes, and the altered identofile was ready, Anya's and Sarina's physical characteristics so similar that the alterations had been minimal.

Sarina boarded the suborbital gravamb with the patient, and the vehicle rocketed into the ionosphere.

Fred, Kate, and Feo left Dr. Todurov's office for a short walk back through the small town to the spaceport, where the Typhoon awaited them, its engines rumbling already.

At its hatch, Feo stopped him, Kate having already entered the ship. "Listen, Fred, there's something I want to tell you."

Fred stopped, the older man leaning close as if to say something in confidence.

Feo put his left hand on Fred's right shoulder.

The right fist caught Fred's chin. Stars exploded across his eyesight, and unconsciousness swallowed him like a black hole.

\* \* \*

Pain and dizziness intruded first, and then the awareness that he was bound to a bunk aboard the Typhoon, the figure beside him similarly bound.

Kate's terrified eyes stared into Fred's. "Why are you doing this, you motherless turd!?"

Feodor cackled, his face on the vid an open gloat. "Shut the hell up, bitch, or I'll gag you, too. Ah, I see Fedey's awake. Good. Listen up, you sniveling, spoiled spawns of privilege. You and all your tripe stripe deserve the debasing fate that both of you are going to suffer. Snotnose scions across the galaxy should all be relieved of their miserably-acquired wealth and status. Death to the ignorant!" Feo threw his head back and laughed.

Fred tested his bonds, but they cinched even tighter.

"That's shrinkrope I've tied you up with," Feo said. "The more you struggle, the tighter it gets, until your limbs fall off!" He laughed again.

Fred tried to use his optimitter but was met with silence. His trake wouldn't respond either, his corn blank and his coke silent.

"Oh, of course I disabled all your implanted neuratronics—all but your nanostim neuraplant," Feo said, his corrosive cackle coming from both the vid and the cockpit.

"We're on our way to Tantalus, where even now the new Premier and her beau the Admiral will be announcing my capture of a pair of mutaclones made from their DNA, mutaclones manufactured at Magadan whom the Ruskies intended to substitute for Tatiana and Fadeyka in a plot to take over Ukraine. You two will exhibit all the usual indications of cloning—DNA smoothing and the nanostim neuraplants with escoriant simumems—and you'll be recycled accordingly. The Ruskies will suffer enough interstellar embarrassment that they'll cede the Crimea back to Ukraine and shut down Magadan for good, force Medvedev from office and possibly even Sputin himself.

"And of course, I'll be exonerated of all charges and restored to my position as Chief of Staff. And then Premier Tatiana Satsanova and Admiral Fadeyka Andropovich will do exactly as I tell them, something that bitch Colima never would, and I'll rule Ukraine with an iron fist through their velvet gloves!" Again Feo threw his head back and laughed.

He's lost his mind, Fred thought, the man so unutterably sure of his course and his success that he can't see the one flaw that's glaringly obvious to me.

"Oh, and don't worry about Sarina and her wife. I only needed her long enough to track you down and help me embarrass the Ruskies. She won't know the difference. She'll never be given another opportunity to interact with your Bawdy Doubles.

"And beyond that, all that's left is the genalyses she did. Easy enough to substitute those results as yours, isn't it, Fred Fadeyka Andropovich? Son of Admiral Zenaida Andropova, who finally took her own life after the shame and degradation of your public profligacy, cavorting and carousing with Premier Tatiana Satsanova across vidscreens galaxy-wide, like a pair of gonadotropin-fueled escoriants.

"Oh, and don't you two worry—I see you exchanging glances like forlorn lovers denied the pleasures of each other's bodies—you'll get one last episode of languorous lascivious lecherous lewd libidinous licentious lubricious lustful and luxuriant sex. Did I neglect one or two lurid adjectives? Have I said enough or nothing at all?"

"What you two will do is demonstrate for the universe exactly the escoriants you are. Your neuraplants will be set to extreme and you'll be videoed in your prison cell with each other while you fornicate until you drop from exhaustion. Such a carnal carnival will be remarked upon for centuries to come!

"And then you'll be recycled, and only the vid will remain, your actual origins veiled from history."

\* \* \*

Sarina watched the trepidation as the medical staff reversed the coma.

Anya's hand in hers twitched, and Sarina knelt close. Anya's eyelids fluttered and then opened. The gaze focused and the mouth smiled. "I knew you'd find me."

Sarina wept with joy, having been terrified that Anya wouldn't recognize her. "Anya, oh, my love, I thought I'd lost you!" She pulled her wife close and the two of them cried together for what seemed hours, overwhelmed with relief.

"I held them off as long as I could," Anya said. "They thought I was you for at least a week, until they accused you of helping that Chief of Staff." Anya looked at her. "How'd you get mixed up with all this?"

"It's a long story, and you should rest."

"Probably. I feel so weak, as though I've been starved. You didn't have anything to do with the Premier's assassination, did you?"

"No, no, of course not," Sarina replied. "Wrong place, wrong time. I helped the Chief of Staff escape. You'll see. I'm not sure how yet, but Feo will expose it all."

"All what?" Anya struggled to sit up, too weak to do even that for herself.

Sarina helped her, and then caressed her cheek, fresh tears coursing down her own cheeks, grateful to have her wife back and cognizant that that was all she could have asked for. She gave thanks to a merciful God for her wife's return. "Here, I have something for you," Sarina said. She pulled her wife's ring from her pinky, took Anya's hand, and slipped it onto the finger where it belonged.

The spouses held each other, looking their left hands, two rings glittering on two ring fingers, both women weeping.

When she was able, Sarina began telling Anya about her examinations of Tatiana and Fadeyka, how she'd discovered the bawdy doubles, how the perpetrators had attempted to kidnap her and abducted Anya instead, and how Chief of Staff Feodor Luzhkov had helped her throughout, accused of conspiring to assassinate Premier Colima Satsanova despite being injured in the attack, Sarina's flight from Tantalus and somehow picking up the trail of the real scions, the Premier's daughter and the Admiral's son, their memories expunged, but their skills intact.

At some point during Sarina's narrative, Anya fell asleep, but Sarina kept talking, as much for the relief it gave her as to lend Anya that simple reassurance that even in sleep, she wasn't far away.

And when visiting hours were over, she asked that they bring in a chair for her so she could stay by her wife. Instead, they brought another hospital bed and pushed it against Anya's, and that was how Sarina woke the next morning, in the bed beside her wife's.

Not her own bed, which would have restored everything to the way it should have been, but at least beside her wife, the person she'd committed to be with, whom she'd vowed to love and to hold, in sickness and health, till death do they part.

And Sarina shuddered in horror at the monstrosity she'd seen in the mutaclone uterpod in the Magadan basement, a mutaclone grown from Anya's genome, being given simumems through its nanostim neuraplant, enough programming that the clone might be reintroduced into Sarina's life as her wife's substitute, an Anya bawdy double.

"You're awake," Anya said.

Sarina smiled through sleep-saturated eyes, blinking away the terrors of what might have been, grateful to have Anya back.

Anya pushed aside the bundle of nanotubing attached to her abdomen and leaned toward Sarina. They kissed. A sense of deep satisfaction and relief reached past the injured places in Sarina's heart.

"When can I get out of here?" Anya asked.

Sarina smiled and shook her head. "At least a week. You were in a harness for almost a month, and then we had no way to feed you for five days. We kept you in a conditioning cocoon, but you still didn't get enough nutrients. It's going to take at least a week."

"Yes, Doctor," Anya said.

Sarina laughed, overjoyed to have Anya back. "And there's still a small matter we'll have to wait upon, so you'd have to stay anyway."

"What matter is that?"

"You're married to an interstellar fugitive, and you're officially listed as missing, presumed abducted."

"How's that going to be resolved?"

"I'm not sure exactly, but Feo, Kate, and Fred will figure it out. They're really resourceful."

"Can we go home to Tantalus after that?"

"Yes, my love, we can go home after that."

"They cloned Tatiana Satsanova and Fadeyka Andropovich, eh? And a mutaclone is now Premier of Ukraine?" Anya shook her head as if in disbelief.

"All of it a Rusky plot to take over Ukraine completely."

# Chapter 19

Fred rolled away from Kate, his bulbospongiosus muscle spasms declining, his ejaculate nearly nonexistent.

They'd been at it for days, it seemed, the epidermis at penis and vagina now wearing thin, their lubricious fluids blood-laced, and the sting of superficial lacerations having set in hours ago. Kate was lying on her side, hands over her genitals, weeping softly. On the cell bunk where they'd been copulating was a large splotch of blood.

Amidst the constant copulation across the last forty-eight hours, Fred had examined the cell thoroughly, both in an attempt to find some weakness in the cell walls and to try to distract himself. But the gonadotropins saturating his system and his constant bombardment to explicit neuraplant images had only yielded briefly.

The first eight hours had been a blissful hell, the two of them trying at least a hundred of the five thousand copulation positions hard-wired into their brains through their escoriant implants.

Along with the thickened epidermal tissues, Fred also had a hormonal shunt between the corpora cavernosa and saphenous veins to prevent low-flow priapism and help induce engorgement. The infusion of an alpha agonist exerted smooth muscle constriction and induced venous outflow to keep the penile tissues aspirating. A beta-Z agonist increased the permeability of the erectile cavernosa tissue. These nanosurgically-installed modifications enabled him to maintain an erection permanently without the risks of discoloration, clotting, or necrosis, resulting in a tumescence of truly stupendous proportions.

To which Kate had been immediately receptive, her own hormonal and physiological systems similarly enhanced.

It hadn't been possible during that first eight hours for Fred to give more than a moment of his attention to anything except fornication. Further, no matter what position they tried, no how vigorously they lavished their pleasures upon each other, neither could reach orgasm. The muscles clenched as though to spasm and their pleasure kept building but the crest couldn't be reached as they climbed inexorably toward a peak always just beyond their grasp.

Their explosion was mutual and glorious as he held her above him and thrust from below, their mixed moistures dribbling down him, dripping onto his stomach, and pooling around his hips, their cries wrenched from them as spasms tore through their bodies, her constrictions seeming to suction the ejaculate from him, his hips slamming into hers splashing their fluids in all directions.

Now, forty-eight hours—and a lifetime—later, her muscles trembling with exhaustion, his heart hammering to keep him erect, his desire nonexistent but his hormones declaring otherwise, Fred bit off a sob at the sight of Kate on the bunk. He'd ravaged her quite against her will, a rape so savage and so antithetical to the person he was that he didn't know how she could ever forgive him, nor how he could forgive himself, never mind that it'd been against his own will as well.

And it didn't matter that he'd apologized to her every few hours, or she to him after leaping upon him and ravaging him in a salacious abandon with every orifice at her disposal, her three apertures to his one extension, this last episode so painful that he'd gasped in agony at her every thrust.

But to see her, weeping forlornly and holding herself as though she too were lacerated within, so worn she was bleeding, all Fred could think in his remorseful mind was how he might die and end this mutual torture.

If only I could take Luzhkov with me, Fred thought, trying to keep his emotions checked, any type of arousal likely to amplify his sexual arousal.

His corn, coke, trake, and optimitter were all disabled, and the only implanted device Fred still had working inside him was the nanostim neuraplant. All it was doing was causing his hypothalamus to excrete adrenogonadotropins in buckets and infusing his sensorimotor cortex with escoriant simumems.

Now, on hands and knees in the middle of the cell, Fred looked down at himself, his princely pestle nearly reaching the floor. A single drop of blood gathered at the tip, threatening to drop into the palm-size puddle of blood already congealing under his penis. Fred cast glances to the corners of the room, each holding a camera, a vent above the door. The single glasma window was too small for anyone to wriggle through. The one bunk was wide enough for two people, its industrial mattress too thin to keep cold from seeping through, the walls merely painted cinderblock. These bare surroundings were all that graced this final place of debauchery.

Lacking corn, trake or coke, he had no way to call for help.

The cameras recorded his every move.

I'll either bleed to death or die from exhaustion, Fred thought, convinced that Luzhkov had a very nasty public recycling in store for them.

The pattern of stimulation induced by his neuraplant was far too familiar. Set to imitate the average male sexual responses, the implant took his body through each stage right up to ejaculation, where it stopped just short and started again at the beginning. Fred found he could push his autoerotic responses but could not stop the constant repetition.

I have to disable it somehow, he thought, his mind now so sensitized to the images that they now played unheeded in his mind's eye.

In them too he saw a pattern.

Patterns were what he did. Patterns gave him the key to unlock any encryption. Patterns indicated both repetition and vulnerability.

Pattern is predictability, he thought, a lesson from early cryptology, the basis of all efforts to decode any cipher.

Of course, he thought. He'd known it all along. The nanostim neuraplant was a machine, and machines were programmable. The underground community of escaped mutaclones on Harbin had reprogrammed or removed the neuraplants of all their members. Similar mutaclone enclaves had done the same throughout the galaxy.

Brought into the cell unconscious, Fred wasn't sure where they were confined. He suspected it was Brygidki, where his bawdy double had spent two years in solitary confinement.

Now if I can just disable the neuraplant, he thought.

Like any biologic nanostim device, the neuraplant monitored his metabolism and made adjustments depending on the result of the monitoring. Set to high stimulation, it pumped out adrenogonadotropins along all its tendrils to the mesodiencephalic transition zone, and the midbrain's subsidiary structures, the lateral central tegmental field, the subparafascicular nucleus, and the zona incerta.

For this to work, he had to tunnel into the implant itself and turn it down.

"Here it comes again," Kate said hoarsely, her eyes wild under a head of hair that might have come off a lion. "Can't you make it stop?!"

He too felt the increasing stimulation to his adrenocortex, and he wondered how Luzhkov had synchronized his and Kate's neuraplants.

It occurred to Fred that they were self-synchronizing.

Thalamic optimitter! he thought. "Kate, don't look at me. Our implants are synchronized through our optimitters."

"It that why I melt whenever I see you?"

He melted inside at her saying so, his penis growing harder.

Her voice!

And probably her touch and her smell, too. And why not complete it with taste!

"Do exactly as I say, Kate. Go to the opposite corner, face away, and don't speak to me or even think of me." He stood and stepped to the corner opposite from her, and the neuraplant stimulation reduced.

Got it! he thought, and he knew now how Luzhkov had altered their implants.

How can I alter it back? Fred wondered. Without an interface, some external programming device, there wasn't a way for him to co-opt the optimitter and reprogram his implant.

He looked up.

The camera up in the corner, just out of reach behind a triangular sheet of glasma. If I can just remove the backing and rewire the charged couplers to emit rather than absorb!

The flat stone walls couldn't be climbed, so he leapt to try to grab the edge where glasma met ceiling, and on his second leap he got enough of a grip to pull it away.

The camera came out easily, its power and signal conducted wirelessly.

He changed the polarity of the charged coupler and held the camera to his eye. The optimitter pattern yielded its secrets, the encryption a simple 128-bit phase-shift cipher, ludicrously simple. Fred reprogrammed the camera to emit the disable signal and held it to his eye.

His nanostim neuraplant shut off.

As the adrenalin and gonadotropin wore off, pain and fatigue set in. The lacerations to his penis felt like fire. Flames of pain tore into his urethra and bladder. He probably had a urethral infection, a natural consequence of hyper-fornication, semen the body's usual means of cleansing the urethra.

He turned toward Kate, who stood in the opposite corner, masturbating wildly.

"Fred, make me stop!" she wept, blood-laced runnels of moisture seeping down her thighs.

He spun her toward him and put the camera to her eye.

Immediately, she collapsed against him, sobbing.

"It wasn't you. It was the implant," he whispered, his own helplessness threatening to overwhelm him. We've been frogs in boiling water for forty-eight hours, he told himself. Of course, we feel helpless. Rendering an enemy helpless and maintaining one's own locus of control were standard combat tactics. Fred re-exerted his mastery of self without a second thought, his training at the academy coming back to him, even if his memory of that training was gone. Something not so easy for Kate, who lacked such training.

"We have to get out of here." Fred stepped to the door, pulling Kate with him. He had no idea how long it would be before someone noticed they weren't fornicating vigorously. Nor if sensors on the camera had alerted someone to its removal.

He inspected the door.

Hinged on the outside, windowed with a single sheet of glasma, framed with solid metal plate on three sides, and an additional metal lip across the threshold, the door looked impenetrable.

Before he'd even touched it, the bolt mechanism unlocked and the door opened outward. In the corridor stood a mutaclone, grinning.

"Fang Kwon sends her greetings. Here, put these one." In her hand were two condicoon allsuits, the clothing made of conditioning cocoon material.

The pain subsided upon his donning the suit, its nanostim tendrils finding his lacerations first. Blotches spread at his crotch, the discoloration indicating the wastes, injured tissues, and pathogens being drawn off by the material.

Kate's suit also blossomed at her crotch, front and back.

He hoped his multiple penetrations of her didn't result in any permanent damage. Shame and helplessness suffused him briefly. *I can't think about that!* he told himself, admonishing himself to stay focused, and he turned to follow the mutaclone down the corridor.

"This way," the mutaclone said, running full tilt down the corridor, her feet flying.

Fred and Kate followed with stiff-limbed waddles, their muscles cramping from lack of nutrients, both of them looking gaunt from forty-eight hours without sustenance or fluids or even pause in their carnal activities.

His head now clearer, Fred shuddered at some of the things they'd done, his heart aching for the innocent time aboard the battered tug when he'd declined to be intimate with her despite her blandishments and advances.

The mutaclone turned a corner and skidded to a halt.

A portcullis slid from the ceiling and slammed into the floor, separating the mutaclone from them.

Another slammed into place behind Fred and Kate.

Soldiers flooded the corridor on either side, the mutaclone struggling as she was hauled away. The thunk of a blow silenced her struggles.

Luzhkov stepped up to the metal grid on one side, a wide grin on his face. "Excellent show, my lascivious mutaclones, a performance far beyond any a porn star might give." He turned his head to the side. "Prepare them for recycling per my instructions."

Fred hurled the camera.

It shattered against the metal grid, and Feodor recoiled. When he turned back them, one socket bled profusely, a fragment of camera housing protruding from the empty orbital socket.

A lieutenant pulled a blaster.

"No!" Luzhkov barked, his arms relaxed at his sides, a stream of blood down his cheek.

Icicles sank into Fred's bowels at the realization, Feodor's lack of reaction telling.

"No, don't kill them," the mutaclone Luzhkov said. "I'll not be deprived of their public recycling."

\* \* \*

Mutaclone secuguards in black-on-black uniforms escorted Sarina through a tangle of props to the stage, their uniforms marking them as members of the Premier's personal security force. Thousands of them appeared to be on duty. Given the scale and the importance of the event, Sarina wasn't surprised by the high level of security.

In her clutch was the genalyzer she'd been asked to bring. None of the mutaclone secuguards had questioned its presence on her person.

The last five days since Anya had been brought out of the implant-induced coma had been a tornado of activity. The day after she came out of the coma, a squad of black-clad mutaclone secuguards—the Premier's personal guard—had descended upon the Kinchesh hospital and had escorted Sarina and Anya in an ambuship to Tantalus, directly to the Premier's suite on the top floor of Kiev Principle Hospital, not five blocks from the boarded-up ground-floor office where Dr. Sarina Karinova had maintained an outpatient practice.

Feo had come to visit them within an hour of their arrival, dressed to the nines as though he'd just arrived from the palace. "On behalf of her Ladyship, the Premier Tatiana Satsanova," he'd said, extending a gilt-edged portfolio, "a pardon and full exoneration of any and all accusations."

Sarina had wept with relief. "How'd you manage that so quickly?"

Feodor Luzhkov had shrugged. "Within the administration were those as concerned as we were about the Premier's and Admiral's behavior. Once I'd explained what was going on, they were happy to help." Then Feo had given her an invitation to the event.

Sarina was greeted briefly by a chaperone who guided her toward her seat. A long set of chairs lined one side of the stage, among them an elevated one, the chair more elaborate than its neighbors, Sarina's place right beside the Premier's.

Cabinet members and top administration officials filed in, greeting her by turns and introducing themselves, expressing their gratitude, and taking their seats. Across the stage sat a funneled chute, its open maw facing toward the stage front, three-foot blades of gleaming alloy lining the mouth like shark's teeth.

Sarina kept looking for Fred and Kate to appear, bedecked in their royal sequins, their names Tatiana and Fadeyka now, having been restored to their respective positions, their bawdy doubles imprisoned.

*Why was I asked to bring the hand-held genalyzer?* Sarina wondered.

Yesterday, hovering over Anya in her hospital bed in the palatial Premier's suite atop Kiev Principle Hospital, Sarina had looked up to find a package in a secuguard's hand.

"Chief of Staff Luzhkov asked me to give this to you," the secuguard had said.

The small, three-by-three-by-three box looked innocuous enough, wrapped neatly in plain brown film. Attached was a note, and inside was a brand-new, handheld genalyzer.

"Bring this with you to the ceremony tomorrow," the handwritten note had said, signed "Feo."

Assuming she'd need to use it, Sarina had tested it on herself. When pressed to the skin, the genalyzer took a sample with its nanostim tendrils. The small machine then analyzed the sample and projected the results to a person's corn through the optimitter. Sarina looked at her own results, the genalyzer flashing a green "Normavariant" at her, her genes exhibiting all the variations that would normally accrete to a four-million-year old evolution, its complexity a fraction of the loblolly pine, a tree species over three hundred million years old.

"May I try this on you?" Sarina had asked her wife.

Anya was growing stronger by the day, but gaps in her memory were becoming more and more apparent. She could remember more distant events, such as her upbringing on Lutsk, and her education in astrophysics on Alchersk. And she knew Sarina and knew they were married, but Anya wasn't able to remember the specifics of their marriage, the when, where, and other circumstance, nor that they'd honeymooned in the Eur Constellation, on the Mediterranean world of Malt.

"A genalyzer? Well, all right," Anya had said.

The results had been similar to Sarina's, the convoluted sequencing having none of the smoothing that a mutaclone's would. The readout flashed "Normavariant" in green letters.

Though outwardly calm, Sarina had been inwardly relieved.

Seated as the guest of honor beside the empty, elevated chair of Premier Tatiana Satsanova—Tatya, as Sarina had come to know her—Dr. Karinova waited patiently for the ceremony to begin. The curtains were still closed, the noise from the crowded stadium sub-dued but irrepressible, the broadcast media piping live video from the event throughout the galaxy.

The Kremlin in neighboring Rusky had already began issuing ve-hement, if vague, denials of any interference in its neighbor's politics, and Magadan was abuzz with activity, its history and current opera-tions being featured prominently in the Kremlin mediocracy, its usual venue of misinformation and indoctrination, the vids looking nothing like Magadan itself.

Sarina self-consciously checked the shoulder straps of her evening gown, her plunging neckline de rigueur but unlikely to attract much attention to her modest bodice, and not nearly the amount likely to be given to the Premier's bust line, Kate amply endowed. Her Bawdy Double had exhibited how amply on numerous occasions, usually in some state of flagrant dishabille with her paramour, the mutaclone Admiral Fadeyka Andropovich.

Neither had been seen in public in five days, however. This cere-mony was their first public appearance since Feo's return from Ma-gadan. Rumors of a deep disturbance at the center of power had be-gun to spread. The Chief of Staff Feodor Luzhkov's and Doctor Sarina Karinova's exonerations in the former Premier's assassination had un-leashed a slew of speculation about a coup.

Suddenly, in rapid succession, the curtain opened, and the Emcee announced, "Assembled Citizens of Ukraine, her Ladyship, Madame Premier Tatiana Satsanova, and his Lordship, Admiral Fadeyka An-dropovich."

The Premier and Admiral walked on stage arm-in-arm. Chief of Staff Feodor Luzhkov was right behind them.

A roar went up, and bouquets of flowers flew toward the stage, none of them able to reach past the wide perimeter enforced by the muta-clone secuguard. Tatiana and Fadeyka strode to the front of the stage while Feo retreated to the seat beside Sarina's, all of the guests on stage now standing and applauding.

Premier Satsanova wore a modest tiara. Her evening gown covered her shoulders and showed nothing of her cleavage. Little could disguise the proud breast. Her hair styled fashionably and her V-shaped face having all the characteristics of classic beauty, the Premier cut an admirable figure. Admiral Andropovich in full dress uniform beside her completed the picture fabulously.

The pair stood at the front of the stage for a full twenty minutes, the applause deafening and unremitting, holding hands, bowing occasionally, and waving at the crowd, Tatiana throwing a kiss or two, inciting crescendos of cheering from the adoring audience.

Sarina watched them from behind and to one side. Feo had greeted her with kiss and an embrace, his face aglow and his gratitude plain. A battle-scarred veteran of a thousand political fights, Feodor Luzhkov applauded alongside Sarina, weeping at the restoration of the Ukraine leader to her rightful position.

Watching Kate and Fred, Sarina felt her gratitude and relief spilling down her face, throwing a glance to two at Feo as she stood shoulder-to-shoulder with the older man, feeling close to Feo for their shared vicissitudes, respecting and admiring his fortitude and resourcefulness.

The pair at the front of the stage was the epitome of legend, the ancient tale of Camelot often repeated in the press, Tatiana and Fadeyka eminently admirable, rumors of the recent events at Magadan having inevitably leaked, many of them far in excess of the actual events.

"Ladies and gentleman," Tatiana said, stepping forward to the podium. "Thank you, thank you." Her voice became clearer as the wild cheering began to dwindle. "It is such an honor and privilege to stand before you tonight. Admiral Fadeyka Andropovich and I—" she paused while the roar crescendoed and subsided—"The Admiral and I have a strange and awkward tale to tell, one terrifying for its implications for all Ukraine and for people throughout the galaxy."

Tatiana stopped to look around. "My nightmare began about a month ago, when I woke inside a uterpod on an asteroid mutaclone factory, without a memory of how I got there. My travails had just started. The first person I saw was the man who stands beside me now."

Fadeyka stepped forward to the podium, his uniform resplendent, a field of medals at the left breast. "My nightmare began five years ago when I woke inside a uterpod on that asteroid mutaclone factory, without a memory of how I got there. For five years, I worked the incubation sectors in that factory, unaware that someone was living my life in my place."

Tatiana looked around. "My life as Doctor Tatiana Satsanova, daughter of her Ladyship, Madame Premier Colima Satsanova, was being lived out by a mutaclone."

Fadeyka looked around. "My life as Captain Fadeyka Andropovich, son of Admiral Zenaida Andropova, was lived out across five years by a mutaclone." He threw his arm toward the recycling chute to one side of the stage.

Beside it, two cages rose through the floor, inside each a forlorn figure. On the huge screen behind Tatiana and Fadeyka, the mutaclones' faces were projected.

"This mutaclone proceeded to wreck my life," Fadeyka continued, "engaging in licentious behavior that violated all honor and decency, finally incurring a two-year sentence in solitary at Brygidki Prison. Alas, for five years, I toiled away aboard an asteroid factory, unaware that my life was being ruined by this escoriant."

Tatiana stepped forward as Fadeyka stepped back. "As I too awoke in a uterpod on that asteroid, this mutaclone proceeded to live my life in my place without anyone the wiser.

"Except for one person." Tatiana paused dramatically. "My late mother. She noticed the change, and she asked Chief of Staff Feodor Luzhkov to have me examined. Comrade Luzhkov took this bawdy double to Dr. Sarina Karinova, who ran a genalysis. And when those results indicated that a mutaclone had been substituted for me, Doctor Karinova's medical files were destroyed, her clinic was bombed, and her wife was kidnapped."

Fadeyka stepped forward as Tatiana stepped back. "I escaped the asteroid factory with Doctor Satsanova just before her mother the Premier was assassinated. We made our way to Magadan in Siberia, where we discovered evidence of a clandestine Rusky operation whose purpose was to replace Ukraine leaders with mutaclones. We were followed there by Chief of Staff Luzhkov and Doctor Karinova, and it was they who found Doctor Karinova's wife, undergoing the same memory erasure procedure that had been used on us."

Tatiana waved to Feo and Sarina to join them at the front of the stage. Feo in his formal tuxedo escorted Sarina to their side.

"It was Doctor Karinova and Chief of Staff Luzhkov," Tatiana said, "who extracted us all from Magadan safely and restored me and Admiral Andropovich to our places. For his courage in the face of adversity," Tatiana continued, her voice rising, "it is my honor, duty, and privilege to award to Comrade Feodor Luzhkov the Ukraine Medal of Valor." A page ran out from the side of the stage carrying two boxes.

Tatiana took one box and extracted a ribbon. From it dangled a shiny, silver disk. She placed the medal over Feo's head and hung it around his neck, then kissed each of his cheeks.

Admiral Andropovich shook Feo's hand with both of his and planted a kiss on each of his cheeks.

As the cheering subsided, Tatiana stepped to Sarina. "And for her courage in the face of adversity, and for dedication far beyond the call of duty, it is my honor, duty, and humble privilege to present to comrade Doctor Sarina Karinova the Ukraine Medal of Valor, and to elevate Doctor Karinova to the position of Knight of the Realm with all the responsibilities and privileges associated thereto." Tatiana took the second box and extracted two ribbons, one dangling a gold disk, the other a silver disk.

She placed the medals around Sarina's neck and kissed each of her cheeks. Admiral Fadeyka shook Sarina's hands in both of his and planted a kiss on each of her cheeks.

"And now, good folk of Ukraine," Admiral Andropovich said as the cheering settled down. "Now, it is time that we rid ourselves of the trash who had the temerity to masquerade themselves as your leaders, to conduct themselves in unseemly and lascivious ways, and to bring down calumny and disapprobation upon the highest offices in our fair domains."

Premier Satsanova picked up where he left off. "In the last four days, since being removed from the lives that Premier Satsanova and I should have been living, these two libidinous mutaclones have been imprisoned together, and unbeknownst to them, their activates recorded. Here is what they did for two days straight."

A clip began to play on screen, albeit so fast that their exact motions couldn't be distinguished. They were a blur, but it was clear they were fornicating.

Vigorously. Constantly. Continually.

Admiral Fadeyka Andropovich waved his hand, and the vid was replaced with a live feed of the two prisoners.

"No!" the caged male mutaclone yelled, "They're the mutaclones, not us!"

The Admiral threw his hack and laughed. "Even now, they protest at the injustice. Of course, they believe they're the real thing. What mutaclone wouldn't?" Fadeyka turned to face the mutaclone in the cage.

On the display above them, the two men's faces were juxtaposed. Sarina couldn't tell the difference, except that the male mutaclone's face was drawn and desperate, and Fadeyka's was calm and composed.

"Sarina, it's me, Tatya," the caged mutaclone fem pleaded from inside her cage, stretching an arm out toward her. "Please, tell them who we are! Don't let them do this!"

"Even now," Tatiana said, her voice booming across the audience, "they declare themselves to be the real Tatiana and Fadeyka, as if they hadn't fornicated to their hearts' content for the last two days, as if they hadn't set out to debauch themselves across the last month in front of every camera they could find." Tatiana turned to face the mutaclone in the cage.

On the display above them, the two women's faces were juxtaposed. Sarina couldn't tell the difference, except that the fem mutaclone's face was haggard and frantic, and Tatiana's was somber and stern.

Sarina looked closely at the prisoners. Oddly, she felt pity for their plight. Their lives had never been their own. Grown to viability in a mutaclone harness, infused with nanostim neuraprogramming, inculcated into the escoriant lifestyle with nanostim neuraplants, and placed as pale substitutes into the lives of real people, these two mutaclones had never experienced a moment of freedom.

"For your crimes," Tatiana said, "both of you will now be recycled."

As if on signal, a squad of black-suited mutaclone secuguards converged on the two cages. The fem mutaclone was extracted without problem, but the male mutaclone struggled briefly, and extra secuguards were needed to subdue him.

They hauled the fem mutaclone toward the recycler. The three-foot blades gleaming inside the maw began to spin, scintillating in the bright stage lights.

Then the recycler shut off and shuddered to a halt.

"What's going on?" Feo muttered beside Sarina.

A man wearing a simple allsuit walked calmly onto the stage, his temples graying and webbed skin at the corners of his eyes.

Feo? Sarina wondered.

"Eodo E610557," said the allsuit-clad Feo, "It's over."

Terror seized Sarina. She turned to look at Feo beside her.

"It's another mutaclone!" the tuxedo-clad Feo yelled. "Guards! Seize him!"

None of the secuguards moved to obey. Instead, the black-suited mutaclone secuguards all turned their backs on the audience and marched inward to surround the quartet.

"Now!" Feo repeated, "I said, 'Seize him!' Immediately!"

Tatiana and Fadeyka appeared bewildered, both of them glancing worriedly at Feo in his formal tuxedo.

What's the matter with them? Sarina wondered, neither of them acting like the Kate and Fred she'd come to know. Her feet numb and her heart pounding, the roar in her ears grew louder.

Two secuguards escorted Sarina away from Tatiana, Fadeyka and Feodor. Sarina blanched, her gaze on Feo in his tux.

"Where are *you* going?!" the tuxedoed Feo roared. He lunged toward her but a phalanx of mutaclone secuguards intercepted him and held him suspended. Two other groups surrounded Tatiana and Fadeyka.

"Ladies and Gentleman," the allsuit Feo said, his voice calm, commanding, and sonorous. "I am the real Feodor Luzhkov, and my nightmare began twenty years ago, when this mutaclone scum was put in my place." He pointed to the tuxedoed man with graying temples.

"Prove it, you slime bucket dregs of protoplasmic abortivariant! You're the mutaclone and you know it!"

"My pleasure," Feo in the allsuit said. "Doctor Karinova?"

She groped for her clutch. From it, she drew the portable genalyzer. Somehow, Sarina found her voice. "I can prove who's a mutaclone and who's not!" She held the genalyzer above her head.

The tuxedoed Feo froze, his eyes wide, his face pale. "You salacious bitch!" he sneered, attempting to break free, the guards holding him fast.

"Doctor Sarina Karinova will now test us all," the allsuited Feo said. "Starting with these supposed mutaclones over here."

He stepped to her side and murmured, "The secuguards are freed mutaclones from the underground network." Feo escorted her to the male in his disheveled allsuit.

The eyes that gazed upon Sarina were Fred's eyes, and Sarina choked back a sob at the near-injustice that had been but moments away. Sarina pressed the genalyzer to Fred's arm and diverted the results to the screen behind them. On the screen over their heads flashed a single word in green: "Normavariant."

"Now Kate," Feo said, his voice calm.

Sarina looked into the woman's eyes and knew already what the results would be, Kate's gaze was too full of awareness for the results to be otherwise.

On the screen again flashed the same single word in green: "Normavariant."

"Now me, Doctor Karinova," Feo said.

She pressed the genalyzer to his arm, and a third time, the green word flashed on the screen overhead.

Feo turned to the crowd. "Now it is time that *they* be tested!"

Fadeyka struggled against the restraints that bound his ankles and wrists but could not free himself.

Sarina looked in his eyes and saw only a wild, desperate animal. Ten mutaclone secuguards had to hold him to the ground for her to obtain the sample she needed. On the screen above their heads flashed the results in red: "Mutavariant."

A rumble rippled through the crowd.

"Wait!" Feo in the allsuit said. "We have two more tests. Doctor Karinova?" He gestured toward Premier Tatiana Satsanova.

The woman looked at Sarina with a dull bewilderment. She didn't struggle at all as Sarina obtained her sample. The word "Mutavariant" flashed in red upon the screen above them.

Now, the noise of the crowd was menacing.

"Yes, good people of Ukraine, you were very nearly duped into recycling your own Premier. Just one more test to run, Doctor Karinova."

Sarina stepped toward the Feodor Luzhkov who wore the tailored tuxedo.

He struggled against his secuguards as she approached. In his eyes was the full spark of life. He spat epithets at her as she drew closer, two secuguards on each of his limbs.

"I almost fooled you all," he said, his struggle ceasing abruptly. He bit down with his incisor, and gas seeped from his mouth. He drew in a sharp breath, his face grew pale, and he slumped into the arms of the secuguards holding him. They lowered him to the stage.

Sarina knelt beside him and felt for a pulse. There was none.

She pressed her genalyzer to his skin anyway. On the screen flashed a word in red: "Mutavariant."

# Epilogue

Fred looked over at Feo, who stood resplendent in his tuxedo, the real Feodor Luzhkov, looking eerily like the mutaclone who, on stage one week ago with an entire galaxy watching, had tacitly admitted to engineering the replacement of Ukraine's top leaders with bawdy doubles.

Feo certainly deserves to be awarded the Medal of Valor, Fred told himself.

This time, though, the ceremony was private, held in the Entertainment Pavilion on the palace grounds, where Premier Colima Satsanova had been assassinated, where she was now interred, Pavilion Hill now her crypt.

Along one wall, the Premier's life was depicted in mural, and at its center was a simple sconce where her ashes were interred, beside it a life-size statue in bronze.

Earlier, Kate had stood before the statue of her mother in silent reflection while Fred had stood back in reverence.

When she'd come away, all she'd said was, "I wish I'd known her."

The day before, Fred had visited his mother's gravesite and had felt similar. Admiral Zenaida Andropova had lived an exemplary life, and Fadeyka Andropovich, her one and only son, had no memory of her, just the visceral sense that somewhere deep inside, he might have once known her.

For Kate, there was a small hope that her memories might be recovered, given how recently she'd been subjected to the inhumane expungement techniques at Magadan.

But for Fred, who'd had his memory expunged five years ago, the neurologists held out a little hope.

And Feo, the first of them to be subjected to the memory expungement nearly twenty years ago, was beyond hope of any memory retrieval whatsoever.

Fred looked over at Sarina, she who by virtue of a simple examination had had her life destroyed. Not that they hadn't all been devastated by the Bawdy Double plot. But Dr. Sarina Karinova and her wife hadn't lived out their lives as leaders, as part of the Ukraine Oligarchy, and therefore, as possible targets of foreign interference.

Dr. Karinova stood in the colonnaded hall beside her wife, Anya, a cool morning breeze blowing in through the arches, the pair in their formal evening gowns rapt in conversation and clearly happy in each other's company.

The incomplete erasure of Anya's memory had turned out to be mostly reversible, and the astrophysicist was set to return to work in about a week, fully recovered from her ordeal—or as fully as possible.

Fred looked over at his wife, Kate.

As much as he tried, Fred wasn't able to think of her as Premier Tatiana Satsanova, nor of himself as Admiral Fadeyka Andropovich. It was still disconcerting to him that the duties of his position seemed as natural to him as breathing air. While he had no memory of graduating Summa Cum Laude from the Naval Academy, top of his class, valedictorian and class president, and captain of the football, hand-to-hand combat, and fencing teams, Fred knew he'd done these things, leadership fitting him like a glove.

Kate struggled somewhat with the innuendoes of her position, but having been reared to interstellar politics at her mother's knee, she too seemed to be adjusting well to the Premier's duties. Her highest priority was holding the perpetrators accountable for her mother's assassination and securing interstellar sanctions against the Bawdy Double masterminds.

In his mind, he'd always be Fred and she'd always be Kate.

It was Feodor Luzhkov who struggled the most. Consigned to a brothel on Antibes for nearly twenty years, where the services provided were primarily of the bondage-domination-sado-masochistic variety, Feo had been blithely unaware that his life was being lived out on Tantalus by a mutaclone, the first bawdy double having gone rogue.

Until the underground network of freed mutaclones had contacted him and had alerted him to the events transpiring on Tantalus. A full thirty years in the service of Colima Satsanova had not gone to waste, buried beneath twenty years of inflicting pleasurable pain on paying customers.

" 'Chief of Staff?' " Feo had quipped when Kate had asked him to take the position, "I should be able to do that. Politics isn't so different from BDSM."

\* \* \*

Dear reader,

We hope you enjoyed reading *Bawdy Double*. Please take a moment to leave a review, even if it's a short one. Your opinion is important to us.

Discover more books by Scott Michael Decker at https://www.nextchapter.pub/authors/scott-michael-decker-novelist-sacramento-us.

Want to know when one of our books is free or discounted? Join the newsletter at http://eepurl.com/bqqB3H.

Best regards,
Scott Michael Decker and the Next Chapter Team

You might also like:
The Gael Gates by Scott Michael Decker

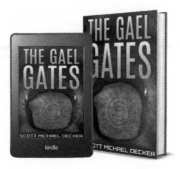

To read the first chapter for free, please head to:
https://www.nextchapter.pub/books/the-gael-gates

# About the Author

Scott Michael Decker, MSW, is an author by avocation and a social worker by trade. He is the author of twenty-plus novels in the Science Fiction and Fantasy genres, dabbling among the sub-genres of space opera, biopunk, spy-fi, and sword and sorcery. His biggest fantasy is wishing he were published. Asked about the MSW after his name, the author is adamant it stands for Masters in Social Work, and not "Municipal Solid Waste," which he spreads pretty thick as well. His favorite quote goes, "Scott is a social work novelist, who never had time for a life" (apologies to Billy Joel). He lives and dreams happily with his wife near Sacramento, California.

**Where to Find/How to Contact the Author**

Websites:
http://ScottMichaelDecker.com/
https://twitter.com/smdmsw
https://www.facebook.com/AuthorSmdMsw

Bawdy Double
ISBN: 978-4-86747-729-8

Published by
Next Chapter
1-60-20 Minami-Otsuka
170-0005 Toshima-Ku, Tokyo
+818035793528
24th May 2021

Lightning Source UK Ltd.
Milton Keynes UK
UKHW012059030621
384904UK00001B/187